The right side of the law . . .

"Do you have children, Mr. Winters?"

He hesitated slightly and his broad shoulders tightened beneath his sweatshirt. "No."

"Then you can't understand the torture I've been living with." She raised her chin and swallowed back her tears. "Usually I'm a proud woman, a woman who wouldn't beg a man for anything, but these aren't usual circumstances and I'm at the end of my rope. I *need* your help."

He understood more than he would like to admit. Zachary Winters had felt the black abyss of personal loss more than once in his thirty-five years.

"I was told by people I trust that you might be able to help me. I love my children, Mr. Winters, more than anything in this life, and I'll do anything, *anything* to get them back!"

Dear Reader:

Romance offers us all so much. It makes us "walk on sunshine." It gives us hope. It takes us out of our own lives, encouraging us to reach out to others. Janet Dailey is fond of saying that romance is a state of mind, that it could happen anywhere. Yet nowhere does romance seem to be as good as when it happens *here*.

Starting in February 1986, Silhouette Special Edition is featuring the AMERICAN TRIBUTE—a tribute to America, where romance has never been so wonderful. For six consecutive months, one out of every six Special Editions will be an episode in the AMERICAN TRIBUTE, a portrait of the lives of six women, all from Oklahoma. Look for the first book, *Love's Haunting Refrain* by Ada Steward, as well as stories by other favorites—Jeanne Stephens, Gena Dalton, Elaine Camp and Renee Roszel. You'll know the AMERICAN TRIBUTE by its patriotic stripe under the Silhouette Special Edition border.

AMERICAN TRIBUTE—six women, six stories, starting in February.

AMERICAN TRIBUTE—one of the reasons Silhouette Special Edition is just that—Special.

The Editors at Silhouette Books

LISA JACKSON
Zachary's Law

Silhouette Special Edition

Published by Silhouette Books New York

America's Publisher of Contemporary Romance

SILHOUETTE BOOKS
300 E. 42nd St., New York, N.Y. 10017

Copyright © 1986 by Lisa Jackson

ISBN: 0-373-09296-2

First Silhouette Books printing March 1986

America's Publisher of Contemporary Romance

Printed in the U.S.A.

Books by Lisa Jackson

Silhouette Intimate Moments

Dark Side of the Moon #39
Gypsy Wind #79

Silhouette Special Edition

A Twist of Fate #118
The Shadow of Time #180
Tears of Pride #194
Pirate's Gold #215
A Dangerous Precedent #233
Innocent by Association #244
Midnight Sun #264
Devil's Gambit #282
Zachary's Law #296

LISA JACKSON

was raised in Molalla, Oregon, and now lives with her husband, Mark, and her two sons in a suburb of Portland, Oregon. Lisa and her sister, Natalie Bishop, who is also a Silhouette author, live within an earshot of each other and do all of their work in Natalie's basement. Lisa and Natalie are both represented in the Silhouette Special Edition list this month.

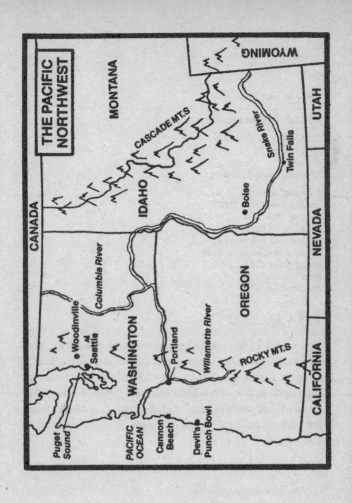

Chapter One

The realization that Zachary Winters was Lauren's last hope, perhaps her only chance of ever seeing her children again, was a grim but undeniable conclusion. And Lauren was stuck with it.

Swallowing hard, she withdrew her keys from the ignition of the car and closed her eyes, fighting a growing sense of desperation. The tears threatening her green eyes were as hot and fresh as they'd been for nearly a year, but she refused to give in to the overwhelming desire to cry.

How many tears had she already wasted? How many times had her hopes of finding her children soared only to be dashed against the cold, cruel stones of reality?

This time, she silently vowed to herself, she wouldn't fail. And if Zachary Winters was her only hope of finding Alicia and Ryan, then Lauren would have to plead her case to him and ignore the rumors and mystery surrounding the roguish lawyer.

As she stepped out of the car, Lauren realized just how little she knew about the man who held her destiny in his hands. What she had pieced together in the last two weeks was sketchy. Rumor had it that at one time, long before she had moved back to Portland, Seattle-born Zachary Winters had been one of the finest attorneys in the Pacific Northwest. However, because of some scandal revolving around his dead wife, Winters's practice, as well as his name, had suffered.

The tarnish on Zachary Winters's reputation didn't deter Lauren, however. Her only concern was for the welfare of her children. Nothing else mattered. If there was a way to reach Winters and interest him in her case, she would find it. She had no choice; her options had run out.

Lauren walked the short distance from her car to the Elliott Building, where the offices of Winters and Tate were housed. It began to rain, and though it was only mid-October, the chilling promise of winter lingered in the wind blowing across the murky Willamette River. Gray clouds shrouded the city of Portland, and water collected in clear pools on the uneven concrete sidewalk.

Lauren didn't notice. She gathered her raincoat more closely around her and took in a long breath as she approached the brick building located in the heart of Old Town on the western shores of the river.

Old Town was slowly being renovated and older, once decrepit buildings were being revamped into their original grandeur. The clean lines of contemporary concrete and steel skyscrapers towered over their older, Victorian counterparts and gave the city an eclectic blend of modern sophistication and turn-of-the-century charm.

The oak and glass doors of the once elegant Elliott Building groaned as Lauren shouldered her way into the office building. Without glancing around the interior of the lobby, she strode into a waiting elevator car and pushed the button for the eighth floor. As the elevator ascended, she leaned against the paneled walls and steeled herself against the possibility of rejection by the one man who could help her. What if Winters refused the case? Despite her determination, there was a chance that the unpredictable attorney would close the door in her face...and destroy the little remaining hope she had of seeing Alicia and Ryan again. New fear, ice cold and desperate, clutched at her heart. She closed her eyes for a second and tried to pick up the shattered pieces of her life.

It had been a little over a year and the pain was as fresh as if it had been only yesterday when she had opened the door of the house and found that everything was gone...including her beloved children.

The elevator stopped with a jolt and Lauren was forced back to reality. The soft line of her jaw hardened, and her fingers whitened as she clutched her purse. Resolutely, she walked down a short hallway before hesitating slightly at the glass door. *Please be here, Zachary Winters. I need you,* she thought before leaning heavily on the door and pushing her way inside the sparse suite of offices.

A red-haired woman whose unlined face indicated that she was no older than twenty-five looked up from the scattered paperwork on her desk and smiled pleasantly. "May I help you?"

Lauren returned the smile uneasily. "I'd like an appointment with Mr. Winters. My name is Lauren Regis."

Recognition flashed in the secretary's gray eyes at the mention of Lauren's name. Her brows pulled into an anxious frown. "Ms. Regis. You've called the office, haven't you?"

"Several times," Lauren replied. "Is Mr. Winters in?"

The redhead, whose brass name plate indicated that she was Amanda Nelson, shook her head, and her smile faded slightly. "I'm sorry, but I don't expect Mr. Winters this morning."

Lauren's piercing green eyes never wavered from the woman's concerned face. Amanda Nelson seemed more than slightly perturbed.

"And he wasn't in yesterday or the day before or the day before that. Is he out of town?" Lauren asked.

There was a hint of defiance in Ms. Nelson's even features. "No. What Mr. Winters is—is busy."

Lauren's dark eyebrows arched at the pointed remark. "I don't mean to be pushy, Ms. Nelson, but it's very important that I speak with Mr. Winters," she explained, glancing at the empty reception area before returning to the secretary's face. "Is it possible to make an appointment with him?"

Amanda tapped her pencil on the desk. "As I said, he's very busy. Let me give Mr. Winters your number, and he'll arrange an appointment with you at a time convenient for you both."

"Can't *you* do that?" Lauren asked, wondering at the odd procedure. Her voice was tiredly impatient. She was weary of playing cat-and-mouse games with the man.

Amanda Nelson managed a stiff smile, and her composure slipped a bit. "Usually I can. But right now Mr. Winters is unavailable. Let me take your name and number."

"No."

"Pardon me?" The secretary's eyes hardened.

"I phoned last week and left my number; Mr. Winters didn't bother to call. I phoned again two days ago...."

The secretary didn't seem surprised. "And Mr. Winters didn't bother to contact you?" she asked, already surmising the answer.

"No."

Amanda's lips pursed in frustration, and Lauren had a premonition that there was something intangibly but undeniably wrong in the law offices of Winters and Tate.

"I suppose you hear this all the time," Lauren said, her voice and eyes softening a little, "but I really do have to see Mr. Winters as soon as possible. He's been referred to me by my attorney, Patrick Evans."

At the mention of the prestigious lawyer's name, the corners of Amanda's mouth tightened.

"Do you mind if I wait?" Lauren asked.

Amanda eyed Lauren skeptically and then lifted her shoulders in a dismissive gesture. "I don't think he plans to come into the office," she replied.

"I've got a little time," Lauren responded firmly. "I may as well spend it here." Thank God for Bob Harding—the rotund co-worker had agreed to see all of her clients this morning.

Lauren dropped into a side chair and picked up a glossy-covered business magazine, casually tossing her thick auburn curls over her shoulder. Her nerves were stretched to the breaking point, but she carefully hid that fact behind a facade of poise. Her gaze swept over the top of the magazine, and she noted that there were no other clients in the reception area. The plush gray carpet was slightly worn near Amanda's desk, and the modern tweed chairs and couch looked as if they had seen better days. Spiky-leaved plants seemed lifeless and out of place on the eighth floor of the elegant old building.

The once revered firm of Winters and Tate looked as if it were slowly dying from neglect. Again Lauren experienced the uneasy feeling that something wasn't right in the hushed law offices.

If Lauren hadn't been so desperate, and if two other lawyers in town hadn't failed her, she would never have crossed the threshold of Winters and Tate. As it was, she had no other choice.

Bob Harding, the man now holding down the fort at the bank, had been the first to mention Winters's name. Bob had insisted that Zachary Winters was the one man in Portland who could help her.

"I don't care what other people seem to think," Bob had stated emphatically, frowning and shaking his balding head. "If anyone can find those kids, Winters can. His methods might not be..."

"Ethical?" Lauren had asked, eyeing her friend as he tugged at the knot of his tie and adjusted his glasses.

Bob had pursed his thin lips and scowled at the ledgers on the desk. "I was going to say 'conventional.' In my experience with Zachary Winters, everything he did was aboveboard." Bob had looked through thick lenses, and his myopic eyes had pierced the doubt in Lauren's gaze. "And even if his methods were 'unethical,' as you suggested, would it make any difference to you?"

"No," Lauren had replied in a rough whisper. She'd been through a lot in her twenty-nine years. Even if Winters turned out to be slightly unscrupulous, she was sure she could handle him. Past experience had taught her well. Her first attorney, Tyrone Robbins, had proved to be nothing more than a self-serving, second-rate lawyer whose interest in her case was limited to his fascination with her as a woman. As bad as the experience had been, Lauren had learned a lesson and was still undaunted in her quest for locating her children. She'd been able to handle Tyrone—Zachary Winters could certainly be no worse.

"Then take my advice—talk to the man," Bob had insisted.

Perhaps she should have asked Bob Harding about the scandal that had nearly ruined Zachary Winters. But she hadn't inquired, because she hadn't cared. Her only thought was of finding her children.

Lauren had already decided to follow Bob's well-intentioned advice when the second attorney she had employed, Patrick Evans, had haltingly mentioned Winters's name less than a week later.

"Five years ago, I would have recommended Zachary Winters for the job," the sharp-minded lawyer had thought aloud, pensively rubbing his chin while studying his client.

"And now?" Lauren had asked.

Patrick Evans had wavered only slightly. "It depends on how serious you are about this, Lauren."

"Dead serious," she had returned, green eyes glinting with righteous indignation and defiance. "We're talking about my children, for God's sake."

Patrick had shrugged defeatedly, settling into his comfortable desk chair in his well-appointed office. "Then you might look him up."

Patrick had withdrawn a yellowed business card from his wallet and handed it to Lauren. "Just remember—things have changed for Zack. He might not accept the case," Evans had cautioned.

Lauren had left the opulent offices of Evans, Peters, Willis and Kennedy, Zachary Winters's card clutched tightly in her fist, with renewed determination....

From somewhere down the hall a clock softly chimed, bringing Lauren back to the present. She checked her watch and realized that she had waited forty minutes already for the elusive attorney. As she shifted uncomfortably in the chair, Lauren straightened the hem of her skirt. The door from the outer hall swung forcefully inward, and the man she had been trying to track down for the better part of two weeks entered the reception area.

Zachary Winters's windblown sable-brown hair looked nearly black from the mixture of rain and sweat clinging to the dark strands. It had begun to curl slightly at the nape of his neck and near his ears. Moisture was trickling down his ruggedly handsome face and neck to collect in a dark triangle on his worn gray sweatshirt. He was breathing heavily from the exertion of his run along the waterfront. With only a fleeting glance and polite smile in Lauren's direction, he wiped the sweat from his forehead with his hand and approached the secretary's desk.

Amanda Nelson, who had seemed to lose more than a little of her composure at the sight of her employer, quickly managed a patient smile for him, while her worried eyes darted to Lauren and then returned to Winters.

She covers for him, Lauren thought in angry amazement. *Amanda Nelson is trying to hold this office together, and one of the partners in the firm doesn't give a damn.*

"Mr. Winters," Amanda was saying, loud enough so that Lauren could overhear the conversation. "I didn't expect you in today."

"I'm not." The tall attorney with the piercing dark eyes and rough-hewn features reached into a nearby closet, withdrew a towel, looped it behind his neck and wiped his face with the edge of the terry fabric. "I just thought I'd pick up the McClosky deposition—is it ready?''

"On your desk.''

"Good.''

Without further comment, Zachary Winters started down the corridor behind Amanda's desk. Lauren, whom the lawyer had barely noticed, realized that the man she had been waiting for was about to make a quick exit. As his long strides took him around a corner, Lauren grabbed her purse and stood.

"Is it possible to see him now?'' she asked the nervous Amanda, who was staring after her boss and chewing on her lower lip in frustration.

"Oh . . . no, he's just in to pick up something.''

"He's been avoiding me.''

"I don't think so. . . .'' But the expression on the young woman's face belied her words.

"It's important,'' Lauren stated, her nerves beginning to fray. She couldn't let him slip out a back stairway. Too much was at stake.

"Let me talk to him—''

"I think it would be best if I handled it myself,'' Lauren decided, and without waiting for the secretary's approval, she strode down the short hall in the direction of the retreating attorney.

"Wait a minute—''

Lauren ignored Amanda's command and rounded the corner, only to stop abruptly. Zachary Winters filled the hallway. He was leaning against the windowsill, stretching tired leg muscles. His hands were braced against the painted sill, and his head was lowered between broad, muscular shoulders.

His faded navy-blue running shorts were wet and clung to his buttocks. Lean, well-muscled thighs strained as the cramps from the long run slowly eased out of his calves.

Lauren's eyes fastened on the straining features of his face. "Mr. Winters?"

He lifted his head, turned his near black eyes on her and managed a slightly embarrassed smile as he straightened. Though he was more interested in relieving the tension from the back of his neck with his fingers, he cocked a dark, inquisitive brow in her direction. "Yes?" he replied in a clipped voice.

It was apparent she was disturbing him, but Lauren extended her hand and met his slightly inquisitive stare. "I'm Lauren Regis." Winters's rugged features didn't indicate that he had ever heard of her before—or that he cared. "I've been trying to reach you for over two weeks."

His dark, knowing eyes were rimmed with ebony-colored lashes and guarded by thick, slightly arched brows. They glimmered with respect when he took her small palm in his strong fingers and gave it a cursory shake.

The man staring at her was a far cry from what she had expected. He smelled faintly of fresh rain mingled with the earthy scent of musk, and he wore an inquisitive, slightly cynical smile on his handsome face.

In Lauren's mind Zachary Winters had worn an expensively tailored three-piece suit and polished leather shoes; he'd radiated a formidable self-assurance, wielded a deadly charm . . . Or so she'd hoped.

"I told her you were busy," the secretary explained nervously as she approached, obviously trying to protect her boss and provide him with an easy excuse to avoid

Lauren if he wanted to. Amanda's lips were compressed in a thin, worried line.

Winters's interested grin widened to a dazzling smile, and he held up a silencing palm in the redhead's direction. "It's all right, Mandy," he said, his quiet brown eyes never leaving the elegant contours of Lauren's face. "I've got a few minutes—I can talk to Ms. Regis. We'll be in my office."

Amanda started to protest but thought better of it when she caught her employer's warning glance.

Zachary's gaze returned to Lauren. "Right down the hall, first door on the left...." He nodded in the direction of his office and smiled at Lauren. "We can talk now, if it's convenient."

Relief swept over Lauren. Maybe now, after a long, agonizing year of running in circles, she would, with the help of this man, find the path leading to Alicia and Ryan.

Zachary Winters felt an uneasy stirring at the sight of the proud woman standing before him. There was an intriguing sadness in her soft green eyes that suggested she'd been through more than her share of pain. The defiant tilt of her finely sculpted chin and the cautious arch of her dark brows lent a quiet vulnerability to her air of sophistication.

Though he knew instinctively that he should dismiss Lauren Regis and whatever business she'd her mind set on, Zachary found it difficult. Her eyes were the most intriguing shade of green he had ever seen. Round and softened by the gentle sweep of dark lashes, they were darkened by an intelligence and pride that he didn't often find in the opposite sex. It was a rare quality in a woman, and it touched a very dark and primitive part of him. A seductive mystique was evidenced by the pout on her lips, and her auburn hair fell around her face in somewhat tousled, layered curls that added the right amount of sophistication to the soft allure of her eyes.

You're a fool, he thought inwardly, *a damned fool who's intrigued by a beautiful face. Didn't you learn your lesson five years ago—with Rosemary?*

Zachary led her to an inauspicious office near the back of the building. Though it had a window view of the Broadway Bridge spanning the dark Willamette River, the office itself was a small, confining room littered with documents and worn law books.

Despite the austere suite of offices and Winters's attempts to brush her off, Lauren began to feel hopeful. Maybe, at last, she'd found someone who could help her. She tried to temper that hope with reality. *Don't expect miracles,* she silently cautioned herself. *You've been this far before, and where did it lead? Only to a dead end.* She couldn't begin to count the times in the last year that all her hopes had been scattered like dry leaves in the wind. Each time she'd had to start the agonizing search for her children all over again.

"Have a seat," the lawyer suggested as he scooped up a stack of law journals haphazardly occupying one of the leather side chairs near his desk. He opened the window a crack, letting the brisk autumn breeze filter into the airless room, then placed the journals on the floor near a crowded bookcase. When he settled into the desk chair, it groaned as if unaccustomed to his weight. Zachary rotated his head to wipe a fresh accumulation of sweat from his brow with the towel still draped around his neck, then once again faced Lauren.

She looked at the disorganization in the office and felt an uncomfortable knot forming in her stomach. It was becoming clear that Zachary Winters practiced very little law these days. All the mysterious rumors surrounding the man came hauntingly to mind, and she frowned at the papers strewn on his desk. The untidiness of the office and the studious gaze of the attorney made her uncomfortable.

The lawyer must have read her thoughts. "Maid's day off," he explained with a charming, slightly rueful smile. After straightening a few papers on the desk, he looked around his office as if noticing the clutter for the first time.

Lauren sat on the edge of her chair and dropped her hands into her lap. She wondered if she had made a mistake in forcing herself upon the lawyer...jogger... whatever he was.

"What can I do for you?" Winters asked as he pushed up the sleeves of his sweatshirt to expose tanned, rock-hard forearms. He leaned back in the desk chair.

Lauren drew a long breath. "Mr. Winters—"

"Zachary." When she didn't immediately respond, he grinned. It was a killer grin—slightly off-center, but devastating nevertheless—and it did strange things to her insides. When he used it in court, it probably coaxed witnesses into divulging secrets better left unsaid. "It just makes things simpler."

She nodded, slightly taken aback by his lack of formality. She needed a lawyer—a strong, decisive attorney who would be ruthless in his quest for the truth and single-minded in his search for her children. The man sitting before her, wearing jogging shorts and a sweatshirt, didn't fit the image she had in mind.

"So—you need an attorney. Right?" His interest appeared genuine as his brown eyes met hers.

"Yes. Patrick Evans recommended you." At the mention of the other attorney's name, Zachary flinched. "He gave me your card." She handed the yellowed business card to Zachary, who extracted a pair of glasses from his top desk drawer, studied the embossed card and set it aside.

"You're a client of Pat's?"

"I was."

Zachary's fingers drummed nervously on the arm of his chair, but his eyes never left Lauren's face. "And he couldn't help you?"

"No," she whispered, avoiding his probing stare. The lump in her throat made speech difficult. "And . . . your name came up in another conversation."

"Go on."

"I work with Bob Harding. He told me that you were the one man in Portland who might be able to help me."

Zachary nodded curtly, removed his reading glasses and set them on a stack of legal documents on the corner of his desk. "That was several years ago."

"He insists you're the best in Portland."

A humbling grin spread across the attorney's bold features. "Like I said, a lot of time has passed since I worked on Bob's case—water under the bridge."

"I need help," Lauren stated, suddenly fearing that he was about to turn down her request. Her heart thudded painfully in her chest at the thought of another dead end. This man was about to close the door again on her chances of finding the children, unless she could convince him of the desperation of her plight.

Zachary inclined his head, encouraging her to continue.

"You see...my husband...my ex-husband, kid-napped my children." She tried in vain to keep her voice from shaking, and her hands trembled in her lap.

Her green eyes turned cold as the bitterness she felt at the injustice of her situation deepened. It was still diffi-cult to talk about the circumstances that had left her feeling bereft and empty.

Zachary's eyes glittered with concern, and his square jaw tightened a fraction. "How long ago was this?"

"A little over a year—about thirteen months," she whispered, tears gathering in the corners of her eyes.

He expelled a long whistle. "And so why did you wait this long to start looking for them?"

"I didn't! I've spent every waking moment of the last year searching for them. I hired a private investigator and two other attorneys." *All who failed miserably,* she added silently.

"One being Pat Evans."

"Yes."

"And the other?"

Lauren swallowed the sickening feeling rising in her throat at the thought of the first man she had enlisted to help her. "Tyrone Robbins," she replied.

Zachary's lips twisted downward at the familiar name. "Robbins? How did you end up with him?"

"I didn't. I started with him.... It...our profes-sional relationship, that is, didn't work out." *Not by a long shot.*

"I'll bet," Zachary mumbled as if to himself, and his dark eyes flashed with scorn.

He waited for a further explanation, but Lauren didn't elaborate. She wasn't about to let what had transpired between herself and Tyrone Robbins cloud the current issue—the *only* issue that mattered. She wanted Zachary

Winters to help her find Alicia and Ryan, nothing more. The problem with Tyrone Robbins she could handle herself.

A muscle worked convulsively in the corner of Zachary's jaw as he tried to push aside his personal feelings for Tyrone Robbins. "I assume, because you're here, that both your previous attorneys came up empty-handed," Zachary surmised. He swiveled in the desk chair and stared out the window as he pondered the problem at hand. Lauren's case wasn't the first of this type to cross his desk. But they never got any easier. And they only served to remind him of his own tragic past.

"Doug didn't leave any clues."

"Doug is—was your husband?"

"Yes."

Zachary turned to face her again. "Do you keep in contact with any of your husband's family—his parents...a brother, sister, cousin, anyone?"

Lauren shook her head and her auburn curls fell forward. The feeling of utter hopelessness she had learned to live with overtook her. "Doug had no brothers or sisters, and his parents were killed when he was young. The only family he has is the children."

Zachary tapped his fingers thoughtfully over his lips. "What about close friends?"

Again Lauren shook her head. "We hadn't lived in Portland long enough to make any really close friends. I called all the people we knew, everyone I could think of— even people I hadn't met, people who had sent Christmas cards to Doug—but no one knew where he was, or at least they wouldn't tell me."

"How long had you been divorced?" Zachary asked, his eyes glinting fiercely.

"About six months... but we had been separated for nearly a year." She didn't understand his sudden wariness but was thankful that he was interested. If only he would help her find Alicia and Ryan.

"And you had custody of the kids—right?"

"Yes. He came and took them, supposedly for a weekend at the coast and...and...he never came back."

"What about a forwarding address?"

"General delivery, here in Portland." She stood and looked out the window. Her shoulders sagged with the weight of the memory. "A private investigator, a man hired by Patrick Evans, tried to track him down, and couldn't."

Zachary frowned and rubbed his chin. "But school records—"

"Alicia was just about to enter kindergarten and Ryan was just two...." Lauren's lips quivered slightly, and tears welled in the corners of her eyes. "He took my babies," she whispered, swallowing hard. Her fingers curled into fists of frustration and helplessness. "He took them, and he had no intention of ever bringing them back!"

Zachary rubbed his chin, and a muscle began to work in the corner of his jaw. "What about work records? Your husband's employer must have had to send him withholding statements, in order that he prepare his taxes."

"He worked for Evergreen Industries. They haven't heard from him. And I didn't get any further with the IRS or the Social Security Administration." She shrugged her shoulders. "Either he hasn't yet filed a tax return...or the IRS hasn't processed it...or they're not telling me where he is." Her lips trembled slightly, and she ran her fingers through her hair. "For all I know, he could have changed his name, used an alias or left the country...."

Zachary took a long, steadying breath. His dark gaze held hers, and the look on his face was serious but filled with compassion. He phrased the next question carefully. "Lauren," he said softly, aware that she was near tears and damning himself for feeling compelled to explore every angle to her story, "have you considered the possibility that your children might not be alive?"

"No!" She let out a shuddering sigh and lowered her eyes. "Oh, dear God," she murmured. "I ... I just can't believe that." She shook her head in physical denial of her blackest fears. For a moment she thought she might break down completely.

Zachary cursed himself silently and felt an overwhelming urge to comfort her. When she lifted her flushed face, he saw that she was fighting a losing battle with tears.

"I have to find them, Mr. Winters," she said hoarsely, determination burning in her sea-green eyes. "Will you help me?"

Rubbing the tension from the back of his neck, he wondered why he couldn't just say no to this woman. His narrowed gaze held hers. "I don't know if I can," he admitted with obvious reluctance. "It sounds as if you've exhausted all your resources."

"Bob Harding swears by you," she whispered, desperation creeping into her voice.

"Harding's case was a simple matter of locating a lost relative, one that *wanted* to be found."

"Don't you think my children want me to find them?"

Zachary studied the anguished lines of her face and noticed the trembling of her lower lip. How easy it would be to lie to her, to accept her case, make a good fee, and then come up dry... just as the others had done. But he couldn't. Basically, despite public sentiment and a few skeletons in his closet, he was an honest man. And the thought that she'd sought help from scum like Tyrone Robbins stuck in his craw. To top it off, Pat Evans had had the nerve to recommend him; the wily s.o.b. had thrown a challenge in his face, daring him to accept the case. The entire situation didn't sit well with Zachary, not at all. "I don't know, Lauren. Your children were very young when they were taken away from you, and it's been—"

"A year. A little more. It happened in early September."

"So now your daughter is... what? Seven?"

"Six."

"And your son is three?"

"Yes," she whispered while remembering Ryan's cherubic face. How he must have grown in the past year....

"They might not even remember you," Zachary said gently.

Lauren forced a sound of protest past the constriction in her throat. "They have to, Mr. Winters. I'm... I'm their mother, for God's sake." Her fist opened and closed as she tried to control the indignation and rage enveloping her. How could he sit there, across the desk, and slowly destroy all her hopes of finding her children?

Zachary felt as if a knife were being slowly twisted in his stomach. Old wounds were reopening. His eyes were soft but direct. "Look, I'm not trying to be cruel, but you have to understand what you're up against. For all we know your husband could have remarried and another woman is raising your kids."

Lauren's face drained of all color. Everything this man was saying brought out her worst fears. She wrapped her arms over her waist. "I can handle that," she said breathlessly.

"Can you? Can you come face-to-face with the fact that they might not want to return? That they might call another woman 'Mommy' and cling to her when you show up on their doorstep?"

Lauren was trembling. Fear, rage, hatred and jealousy roiled within her. Two large tears slid down her face. "I can handle just about anything, Mr. Winters, except not knowing what is happening to them." She brushed the tears away with the back of her hand. "Do you have children, Mr. Winters?"

He hesitated slightly, and his broad shoulders tightened beneath his sweatshirt. "No."

"Then you can't possibly understand the torture I've been living with." She raised her chin defiantly. "Usually I'm a proud woman, a woman who wouldn't beg a man for anything, but these aren't usual circumstances. I'm at the end of my rope, and I *need* your help."

He understood more than he wanted to admit. Zachary Winters had experienced more than one personal tragedy in his thirty-five years. He'd suffered the anguish of losing a loved one, had known the emptiness of living alone. But that had no bearing on this case. This time he wouldn't allow what had happened to him personally to affect his business.

His hands formed a tent shape under his chin. "I'd like to help you," he admitted with a hint of reluctance.

Lauren braced herself for the rejection she heard in his voice.

"But I seriously doubt that I can do what others haven't. I wouldn't want to mislead you, or incur expenses that may all be for the sake of a dead end...." *Or be the one who has to tell you that your children are dead,* he silently added.

"I don't care," she insisted, placing her palms on the desk and holding his intense stare.

"I understand what—"

"No you don't," Lauren cut in, her voice shaking as her palm slapped the corner of the desk. "No one can. No one who hasn't been a parent can possibly understand the loss—the pain—the agony of this nightmare I'm living.

"I was told by people I trust that you might be able to help me, and that's why I'm here, asking, *begging* you to help me. I love my children, Mr. Winters, more than I love anything in this life, and I'll do anything, *anything* to get them back!"

Chapter Two

Zachary watched the agitated woman in amazement. She rose from her chair and stood proudly before him. "I came here thinking that you were my last hope," she told him, her green eyes darkening with anger. "But maybe I was wrong. Because if you don't help me, I'll find someone who will. My children are alive, and they need me...and...and I need them. I'd go through hell and back to find them," she proclaimed, visibly trembling. "And I'll do it with or without you."

"I didn't say I wouldn't help you," Zachary said, his voice soft and calming. "I just wanted to point out the pitfalls we may encounter."

Lauren's heart was pounding so loudly it seemed to echo in the small room. "Does that mean you'll accept the case?"

"Let's just say I'll do some preliminary checking. If I think we have a chance of locating your children, I'll give it my best shot. If there's nothing to go on, I won't flog a dead horse." His dark eyes were sincere and honest, and they were sharply penetrating. "That is, I want you to know from the start that I'm not a magician. I can't make people appear out of thin air."

"Is that a kind way to tell me not to get my hopes up?"

"I just want you to be realistic."

"I am, Mr. Winters."

"A year is a long time," he pointed out. "And just for the record, the name's Zachary. Remember?"

"Zachary," she repeated. "Well, *just for the record,* I've lived that year, and it's been the longest of my life." Her voice had grown husky, but she firmly extended her hand toward the roguish lawyer with the windblown hair and worn gray sweatshirt.

He took her palm in his fingers as he stood, and the warmth of his hand filled her with renewed hope.

"I'm not making any promises, you understand."

"Of course." *How quickly he had interjected a legal disclaimer,* Lauren thought. Probably a habit of his profession. She withdrew her hand from his and rummaged in her purse. When she found the manila envelope, she handed it to him. In the slim packet were her only clues to the whereabouts of her children. "The reports from the private investigator and the lawyers," she explained, realizing how wretchedly thin the packet of information was.

Without examining its contents, Zachary placed the envelope on the desk. It blended with the rest of the clutter as if it were no more important than the legal documents littering his seldom-used desk. "I'll look over the reports, make a few calls and get back to you in a couple of days—or however long it takes. I'll need your phone number and address, and probably some more personal information from you, *if* I come to the conclusion that I'll be able to help you."

Some of Lauren's fear and anger slowly dissipated. She managed a feeble smile. "My phone number and address, along with my business number, are in the envelope."

"Good."

He seemed satisfied, and Lauren realized that the impromptu meeting was over. "Mr. Wint—Zachary?"

His bold eyes darkened in response, and he arched a brow inquiringly. In an unconventional way, he really was incredibly handsome. And though she hated to admit it, Lauren decided that the ragged sweatshirt, windblown hair and lines of cynicism bracketing his mouth only added to his rugged masculinity.

"Thank you." Quickly clutching her purse to her chest, she walked out of the law office with the feeling that, if nothing else, she had one reluctant ally in the bitter struggle to find her children. Once outside the building, she felt as if she could breathe again.

Zachary watched her leave and again wondered what had possessed him to agree with her request. He generally made it a practice to avoid sticky family disputes. At least he had since Rosemary's betrayal.

"You've gotten yourself into a helluva mess this time," he told himself before getting up from the desk, stretching bone-weary muscles and walking over to the lower cupboard of his bookcase, which a few years ago had served as a private bar. The bottles within the cabinet were dusty. He extracted a half-full fifth, studied the label and frowned.

Swearing under his breath, he grabbed an empty water glass from the shelf over the dusty bottles and splashed a stiff shot of Scotch into the glass. Taking an experimental sip of the warm liquor, he returned to the desk and only then noticed that it wasn't yet noon.

"Bad way to start the day," he warned as he cleared a spot on the desk and set the drink on the worn wooden surface. He reached for the manila envelope, opened it and began looking through the sketchy reports from the private investigator. He frowned darkly when he came across a letter from Pat Evans. There was nothing from Tyrone Robbins.

"Great," he mumbled to himself when he found nothing substantial in the first few pages.

But when his eyes encountered the last page, he felt an unwelcome emotion sear through his body. His lips thinned to a hard line, and he reached for the Scotch.

Attached to a plain piece of typing paper was a photograph of four people—the Douglas Regis family.

Zachary's gaze narrowed as he studied the photograph. He recognized Lauren. Though she seemed somewhat pale, her green eyes were filled with happiness. She was dressed in a loose-fitting sweater and comfortable jeans, and her auburn hair was pulled into a casual ponytail. Seated on her lap was a chubby, curly-headed baby of about six months. With rosy cheeks and two tiny teeth, the baby was laughing merrily at the camera. A little girl, the one he supposed was Alicia, stood near her mother and baby brother. Alicia had Lauren's fair skin, somber blue eyes and a shy smile.

Standing behind the small family, his hand poised possessively on Lauren's shoulder, was the man whom Zachary assumed to be Doug Regis. Of medium height, with curly brown hair, a tight smile and impeccable clothes, he seemed out of place in the photograph—a stiff interloper rather than an integral member of the family.

"You miserable son of a bitch," Zachary muttered before tossing the offensive photograph onto the desk and taking a long swallow of warm liquor. Every one of his razor-sharp instincts told Zachary that he was about to make a monumental mistake—one he might regret for the rest of his life.

The hell of it was that it wouldn't be the first time—and probably not the last.

With a sound of disgust, aimed primarily at himself, Zachary finished his drink in one swallow. It burned the back of his throat and did nothing to quiet the demons shrieking inside him.

Lauren felt drained by the time she made it back to the quiet, well-appointed trust department of Northwestern Bank. Located in the bank tower at Fifth and Taylor, the trust offices had been decorated in understated elegance. The furnishings hinted at a conservative opulence, from the brass lamps perched on the corners of the desks to the thick emerald-green carpet running throughout the sixth floor of the building.

Lauren paused by the receptionist's desk to pick up her telephone messages, then walked into her office. After hanging her raincoat on one of the curved spokes of the brass tree adorning her private office, she settled into the chair behind her desk.

She was just sorting through the phone messages when Bob Harding walked into her office and closed the door behind him.

"How'd it go?" he asked as he settled into one of the winged chairs near her desk and stuck two fingers behind his tight collar.

"All right, I guess," she replied with an uncertain smile. "What about here? Were you able to help Mrs. Denver?"

"No problem. She was just worried about the terms of her father's trust and the allocations to her children. One of the boys will be turning of age in February, and she doesn't want to see him get a lump sum of nearly two hundred thousand dollars."

Lauren nodded, understanding Stephanie Denver's concern. "Not much she can do about it, I'm afraid. When the kid turns twenty-one, he gets his share of his grandfather's trust. That's the way Mrs. Denver's father wanted it." Lauren settled back in her chair and arched a dark brow. "Anything else?"

Bob shook his head. "Nope. It's been pretty quiet around here."

"Good. Thanks for bailing me out."

"No sweat." Bob's eyes narrowed behind his thick glasses. "So what happened with Winters?"

"He agreed to take the case," Lauren replied.

Bob's round face sparked with enthusiasm, and he slapped his knee emphatically. "I knew he would."

"He wasn't all that anxious. And there's a catch."

"Oh?"

"If he doesn't think he can locate the children after he's done a little nosing around, he won't continue." Lauren couldn't hide the note of concern in her voice or the worry in her large green eyes.

Bob let out a long sigh. "Same old thing." He nervously ran his fingers over his mouth, then noticed the defeated slump of Lauren's slim shoulders. "Hey, look, what are you worried about? Zachary Winters said he'll take the case. You're on your way." He winked encouragingly. "He'll leave no stone unturned, let me tell you."

"God, I hope not," she said fervently, pushing her hair away from her face with her fingers. "I should have listened to you when you first brought up his name."

Bob shrugged. "Maybe. But you thought Pat Evans would find them."

"I hoped." Bob made a move to get out of his chair, but Lauren lifted her hand in a gesture to make him stay. "You said that Winters helped you find your aunt, right?"

Bob nodded.

"How long ago was that?"

After thinking for a moment, Bob replied, "'Bout eight years, I think."

"And how long did it take?"

"Six weeks—no, more like two months, I'd guess. We hired him in February, and Aunt Myrna was home by Easter."

Pensively, Lauren tapped her fingers on the edge of her desk. "Pat Evans also referred me to Zachary Winters," she mused aloud.

Bob nodded at the mention of the prestigious Portland attorney. The firm of Evans, Peters, Willis and Kennedy had referred many clients to the trust department of Northwestern Bank, and Evans sat on the board. Patrick Evans was one of the sharpest lawyers in the city.

"And?" Bob prodded.

"Patrick seemed to think that Zachary Winters wasn't quite as . . . dependable as he used to be. He said that he would have recommended Winters five years ago, but that things had changed for him." Lauren watched as Bob shifted uncomfortably in the winged chair near her desk. "And you said something about rumors surrounding the man and his wife—something about his being unethical."

"Unconventional is the word I used," Bob corrected with a frown. "You were the one discussing ethics. And I thought it didn't matter."

Lauren studied her friend and tapped her pencil on her lips. "It really doesn't. I'd just like to know what I'm dealing with," she explained with a smile. "So what are we talking about here? Idle gossip? Or fact? What happened to Zachary Winters?"

Bob hoisted himself out of the chair and paced between the window and the door. He was obviously uncomfortable with the conversation. "No one knows for certain...."

"But it had something to do with his wife."

"Right." Bob sighed, and his round shoulders tensed beneath his suit jacket. "Look, I don't really put much stock in rumors, and I don't know what happened...not for sure. I just know that Zachary Winters helped me when I needed him. As to all that business about his wife...it's just idle speculation in my book."

"But *something* happened to him. I was there, Bob. His office looked as if he hadn't been in it in days—maybe weeks. And his receptionist..." Lauren shook her head. "That poor girl didn't know whether she was coming or going. She was as surprised as I was when Winters literally jogged into the office."

"I told you—he's unconventional."

"That you did." Lauren looked up at him. "Now, are you going to tell me anything else about him?"

Bob shrugged. "I don't know much more. When I dealt with him eight years ago, he had moved here from Seattle. He'd been in Portland about two years, I think. He was married, had been for a while, seemed to adore his wife—'' Bob walked over to the window and stared at the gray clouds surrounding the west hills of Portland. Rain was slanting from the dark sky, and tiny droplets ran down the glass.

"The trouble started several years later, I guess. No one really knows what happened because Winters has been pretty closemouthed about it, but his wife died unexpectedly in a single car accident at three in the morning . . . somewhere on the coast."

"That must've been hard for him," Lauren whispered, feeling a sudden chill. At least she understood a little of the pain she had seen in Zachary's eyes.

"It gets worse."

"What?"

"Turns out his wife was pregnant."

"Oh, no." Lauren remembered the stiffening of Zachary's shoulders when she'd self-righteously asked him if he had any children. She closed her eyes against the image.

Bob turned back to Lauren. "It wasn't more than three weeks later that Zachary Winters's partner, Wendell Tate, was found dead in his home. Overdose of some prescribed medication, I think. No note, but the police thought it was probably suicide."

"Oh God," Lauren murmured, wishing she'd never pressed Bob for the truth. Zachary Winters had suffered his own private hell.

"You may as well know the rest of it," Bob continued. "Seems that somehow Zachary blamed himself for both deaths. Who knows why? Anyway, he took it upon himself to see that Tate's kid, Joshua, finished law school and became a full partner of the firm within three years of passing the bar exam."

Lauren let out a weary sigh and stared blankly at the neatly stacked account folders on the desk.

"You asked," Bob reminded her.

"And I'm sorry I did."

"Like I said, no one really knows how much truth there is to all the rumors surrounding the man. For reasons known only to himself, Zachary prefers to remain silent about the whole thing."

"And in the meantime, he's let his practice slide," Lauren said.

"I don't know. The only thing I'm certain of is that if I ever need any legal or investigative work again, I'll contact Zachary Winters."

Lauren smiled at the portly trust officer. Bob Harding was certainly loyal. And that meant a lot. Without Bob's friendship, Lauren wondered how she would have made it through the past thirteen months.

The telephone rang and Bob moved toward the door. "I'll talk to you later," he said as he left the room. Lauren paused before picking up the receiver. Slowly, she took a deep breath and forced all thought of Zachary Winters and her children aside . . . for now.

The clock on the bookcase indicated it was nearly seven when Lauren walked into her small house in Westmoreland. It was the same house she had shared with Doug and the children. From the living room and front porch she could watch the ducks gather on the man-made lake, witness a softball game in progress or see children playing under the fir trees that shaded the small creek running the length of the park.

Things had changed in the course of a year; the picket-fenced backyard still had a swing set, which had become rusty from the rain, and the boards in the sandbox were beginning to rot. Still, Lauren couldn't bear the thought of removing her children's playthings.

The day had been long and tiring. Because she'd been gone from the office for nearly two hours in the morning, she had decided to make up for it by staying late.

She didn't mind. The nights alone in the house were the worst. It had been over a year and she still found herself listening for the sound of Alicia's ever-racing footsteps or the soft gurgle of Ryan's laughter.

Lauren couldn't move out of the house. There was always the possibility that Doug might return with the children or that Alicia would remember her home.

After taking off her coat, she walked over to the fireplace and studied the portrait of her children that sat on the mantel. Looking at the portrait was a ritual she observed every evening, and though it brought tears to her eyes, she couldn't take the picture down. It would have been like giving up. And that, she vowed, she would never do.

How was Alicia doing in school? By now she would be starting first grade, learning how to read, would know how to ride the bus, maybe be able to comb her beautiful dark hair by herself. And Ryan. He would be walking and talking like a little boy, no longer a pudgy toddler. A painful lump rose in her throat, and she closed her eyes and sagged against the wall.

"Oh, dear God," Lauren murmured, "let them be alive and safe and...and please let me find them... please...." Her voice caught, and she thought of Zachary Winters. "He's got to help me," she whispered fiercely. "He's got to!"

Why had Doug taken them? she wondered for the thousandth time. The divorce was supposed to have been amicable, a friendly parting that wouldn't pit one parent against the other. Best for the children. *And a lie! Doug's lie.*

When she thought back to her marriage, Lauren shook her head in wonder. She'd been so young, and naive enough to believe in a romantic fantasy. It had all come crashing around her feet.

Lauren walked into the kitchen and put on a pot of tea. Her movements were automatic as she considered the unfortunate set of circumstances that had led her into marriage with Douglas Regis.

Lauren's parents had been happily married but poor. Her father was a vagabond who moved from city to city, always believing the grass would be greener somewhere else. Both her mother and father had adored their only child. Lauren never felt unhappy or unloved...until both Andrea and Martin Scott had died unexpectedly in a boating accident on the Willamette River.

Lauren, who was staying with a friend, had been told the news by the welfare authorities, since she was still a juvenile. Then she'd been unceremoniously delivered by a kind but busy social worker to her only living relative, a maiden aunt approximately forty years old.

Aunt Lucy hadn't been pleased to have a sixteen-year-old pauper dumped on her, and she'd made no bones about the fact. "It's just like your father to do this to me," the woman had complained, shaking her curly blond hair. Then, adding a heartfelt sigh, she'd said, "Martin never did have a lick of sense. Well, there's nothing I can do about it now, I suppose. Family's family."

Begrudgingly, Aunt Lucy had converted her small attic into a sleeping loft for her only niece, and Lauren moved in. Absorbed in her grief, Lauren didn't question what had happened to the few personal possessions left her. Much later she realized that Aunt Lucy must have sold everything and kept the money, which probably wasn't enough to cover the cost of raising a teenager for two years.

Lucille Scott was a flamboyant woman who despised responsibility and avidly pursued the good life, which was provided by several older gentlemen who were introduced to Lauren only by their first names. They provided Lucy with some relief from the boredom of a spinster's life and a low-paying government job.

It was obvious that Aunt Lucy didn't want or need an orphaned niece. Lauren promised herself that she would find a way to leave "home" as quickly as possible. She spent as many hours as she could at school, in the library or in her room with the books that were her escape. She applied herself to her studies with fervor, taking college courses offered by the high school while earning her diploma.

The scholarship she was awarded provided the funds for tuition and books, and with a part-time job, Lauren was able to move out of Aunt Lucy's house and into a small apartment near campus.

At the end of four years in college, Lauren not only had a B.A. but also was working on her master's. That's when she'd met Doug, an assistant professor of economics. And she'd fallen in love with his boyish smile and flashing gray eyes—or at least she thought she had. During high school and college, she'd rarely had time to date. Doug Regis was the first person since her parents had died who had told her she was loved.

When she and Doug were married, she felt as if the world were at her feet. She worked until Alicia came along and then felt the supreme joy of motherhood.

The marriage had started to deteriorate after the birth of Alicia. Without Lauren's income finances were tight, and to make matters worse, Doug lost his job at the university because of budget cuts. Two years and several jobs later, Doug had decided to move north.

With each employment failure, Doug had grown more bitter. The pattern was always the same—no matter where he worked, he was convinced someone in the firm was out to get him fired. No job lasted more than a year.

Then he began to drink.

The small family moved to Portland just after Lauren gave birth to Ryan. Lauren was incredibly happy with her two children. Though a little worried about Doug, she was certain that here, in a new city, they could begin again and find the happiness that had begun to elude them.

She'd been concerned about her husband's erratic behavior, of course, but was convinced that if given the right breaks, Doug would once again become the charming, self-confident man she had married.

When Doug found employment with an investment firm in downtown Portland, he and Lauren celebrated by uncorking a bottle of champagne, most of which Doug consumed himself. That night, while making love to Lauren, he unwittingly called her by another woman's name. The effect was chilling. For the first time, Lauren began to see Doug for the man he really was and not as the prince in a fairy-tale fantasy. He fell asleep, but she was haunted by the thought that once again she was unloved.

Doug's job with Dickinson Investments lasted less than six months.

When Doug came home with the news that he had been let go, he was already drunk. His tie was undone and hanging loosely around his neck; his jacket was slung carelessly over his arm.

Alicia was playing in the backyard, Ryan was napping and Lauren was preparing dinner.

She looked up from the stove when Doug noisily entered the room and slammed his briefcase on the small kitchen table.

"It happened again," he said flatly. "Goddamn it, I knew that Dickinson was out to get me from day one!"

Although Lauren no longer believed that it was everyone else's fault when Doug was fired, she tried to be understanding.

"You'll find something else," she said with a reassuring smile. "You always do."

"Well, maybe I'm tired of working my ass off!"

Surprised by his vulgarity, Lauren leaned against the kitchen counter and dried her hands. "I could get a job," she suggested.

"No!"

"I've got a degree—"

"And two kids!"

"It would only be temporary."

"I said forget it!" Doug raged. "It's bad enough that I got canned, but then you come up with some goddamned idea about going back to work."

"Just to help out—"

"My ass!" he exploded. "You've always expected so much from me. More money, bigger houses, more clothes—"

"That's not true, Doug. All I've ever wanted was for us to be happy... like we used to be."

His gray eyes narrowed. "Like hell!"

"I don't understand what's going on here," she replied to his sudden outburst. His face was flushed with anger, and he was nearly shaking.

"Oh, no? Then let me tell you. You're trying to emasculate me, that's what's going on."

"Oh, Doug, no!" she cried, hurt that he would think she could be so cruel. Despite the unhappiness, he was her husband, the father of her children. "Getting a job...it was only a suggestion...to make things easier."

"Sure."

"What do you want me to do?" she asked, refusing to release the tears of frustration stinging her eyes.

"Lay off, Lauren. Just lay the hell off."

He strode to the refrigerator and took out a can of beer. Pulling the tab and letting the foam spill onto the floor, he threw back his head and guzzled the cold liquid.

Lauren had never seen him so angry. It was as if he felt it was *her* fault that he'd gotten fired. Holding her temper in check, she grabbed a sponge and knelt to start wiping the floor where he'd spilled the beer.

She felt a numbing pain in her hand when Doug kicked the sponge away from her.

"Stop it," she hissed, holding her hand and looking up angrily at him. "Get a hold of yourself."

"Ha!" He laughed unevenly, and when she started to rise, he pressed a booted foot menacingly against her abdomen. She stared at him, aghast at the threatening glitter in his eyes. For the first time she was afraid—for her children as well as herself. Never before had Doug threatened her physically.

"Let me up," she demanded, "and don't you ever, *ever* do anything like this again."

The heel of his boot ground into her stomach. "You're no better than your Aunt Lucy," he spat out, crinkling the aluminum can in his fist and tossing it toward the garbage can. He missed, and the can rolled noisily on the linoleum floor to rest near the sponge. "You're a whore just like she was."

Lauren's temper flared and she tried to rise, but his foot dug deeper into her abdomen. Doug seemed to take immeasurable pleasure in watching her futile efforts. "She was always looking for an easy ticket, too," Doug continued. "Some old John to keep her in negligees—"

"Move your foot," Lauren said, her voice filled with anger and disgust.

Doug smiled and ground his boot heel into her ribs. "I don't think so."

Knowing that it might infuriate him further, Lauren took both her arms and swung at his leg. At the same time she tried to slither backward. Doug's drunken state was his undoing, and he lost his balance. His boot gouged her stomach, but Lauren was able to rise as he came crashing down on the linoleum.

"Mommy...." Alicia's worried voice and racing footsteps announced her entry, even before the screen door banged behind her. The little girl's eyes widened in fear as she noticed her father writhing on the floor, clutching his leg, his face white. When Alicia turned to Lauren, her lower lip trembled at the disheveled appearance of her mother.

"It's all right, honey," Lauren whispered, trying to sound calm as she reached for her daughter and held her tightly to her chest.

"I'm hurt, goddamn it!" Doug screamed.

With an effort, still carrying a sobbing Alicia, Lauren went to the phone and called for an ambulance while smoothing Alicia's hair and kissing the top of her daughter's head. Once she was assured that the ambulance was on its way, she offered Doug an ice pack for his rapidly swelling ankle. Not once did she let go of her trembling child.

"It's broken, you know," Doug accused, wincing against a sudden stab of pain. "All because of you...." He meant to say more, but the furious, indignant glint in Lauren's eyes stopped him. "I've lost you, too, haven't I?" he asked softly, and Lauren didn't have the heart to answer.

When the ambulance came, she clutched Alicia and Ryan to her as if fearful of losing them, whispering words of comfort that were meant for herself as well as her children. She waited nearly two hours before summoning up the courage to go to the hospital, where Doug was suffering from an acute ankle sprain.

It had been the first and last time Doug had threatened her physically. He had managed to get a job at Evergreen Industries a few weeks later, and Lauren sensed her marriage was slowly disintegrating. The new job wouldn't last; they never did. All the hope she had once harbored for herself and Doug was gone.

She had suggested that he get professional counseling, and he had scoffed at her and called her every kind of fool.

She had discovered that he was having an affair, and it didn't surprise her when he asked for a divorce. She didn't fight him. The marriage had been over for months. And despite all the pain, she had her children.

While the courts had allowed him some rights as a father, Lauren wouldn't permit him to be alone with Ryan or Alicia until he'd sought the services of a psychiatrist and apparently turned over a new leaf. She didn't doubt that he loved the children, and she knew that he would never hurt them. As he himself had said, they were all he had left in the world.

When he had come to take the children to the coast, supposedly for the weekend, Lauren had had no idea that he'd been fired from his job at Evergreen Industries.

She'd spent most of that Sunday working at the office, and when she'd returned home late that afternoon expecting Doug and the kids to be waiting for her, the house had been stripped of everything belonging to Alicia and Ryan—except for the one precious picture above the mantel on the fireplace.

That had been thirteen months ago....

"Damn you, Doug Regis, damn your miserable hide!" Lauren muttered to the empty house as the teapot began to whistle and bring her out of her unhappy memories. She brushed the tears away from her eyes. *I'll get them back,* she promised herself. *As long as there's a breath of life in my body, I'll keep looking until I find my children, and I'll bring them home!*

Chapter Three

On Thursday morning Lauren walked into her office and found a note on her desk stating that Zachary Winters had called. Her heart stopped for a moment as she stared at the slip of pink paper. Had he found something about the children, or was he merely calling to say that he'd had second thoughts and was dropping the case?

The phone number on the note wasn't the one she had called when trying to reach him at the office.

With trembling fingers Lauren dialed the number on the message and waited, eyes closed, silently counting the rings, until he answered.

"Zachary Winters." His voice was curt, authoritative and somehow comforting.

"Hi. This is Lauren Regis."

"Lauren." Did she imagine it, or did his voice soften a little? "I know this is short notice," he was saying, "but I thought it would be a good idea if we met soon. If possible, today. Maybe over lunch?"

Lauren's eyes slid to the calendar on her desk. She was scheduled for a trust board meeting at nine, and the remainder of the morning was filled with appointments. "Of course," she replied, mentally juggling the various meetings. "But I'm a little swamped. What time?"

"Whenever you suggest."

"I don't think I'll be able to get out of here until one or one-thirty," she admitted reluctantly. Her heart was thudding erratically with the hope that he had found something, *anything* that might lead to the children.

"How about one-thirty at O'Donnelly's?" he suggested. "Can I pick you up?"

Lauren hesitated. Zachary Winters's arrival at the office might cause undue speculation. After all, he *had* been one of the most sought-after lawyers in town a few years back. Lauren didn't like the thought of any idle gossip about her personal life by her co-workers. Bob Harding was the only employee of Northwestern Bank who knew everything about her past, and she preferred to keep it that way—at least until Alicia and Ryan were safely back with her. "I'll walk," she replied after an uncomfortable pause. "It's only a couple of blocks from here."

"See you then."

"Wait!" she pleaded, unable to contain her agitation. "Please, tell me. Have you found anything?"

"Nothing to pin your hopes on," he admitted, reluctance evident in his voice. "There's one more lead I want to check out before I see you. Maybe then I'll be better able to evaluate the situation."

A feeling of desperation seized her. "All right," she said. "I'll meet you at O'Donnelly's.... Right. Bye."

Softly she hung up the phone. Zachary Winters was going to drop the case; she was sure of it.

The door to her office burst open and Bob Harding walked in, making a great show of looking at his watch. "You'd better get a move on, girl," he suggested. "Zero hour is less than ten minutes away." If Bob noticed that she was preoccupied, he had the decency not to mention it.

Lauren managed a thin smile and tried to hide her depression. "You make it sound as if I'm walking into a lion's den."

"Near enough. It's D-day."

"Why so?"

"The Mason trust—remember? The heirs are suing the bank to the tune of two million dollars."

"Oh, of course. How could I forget?" she replied, shaking her head. Her telephone conversation with Zachary Winters had driven everything else from her mind.

"Anyway, rumor has it that the president of the bank is on the rampage and ready to fire anyone connected with the account."

Lauren eyed her friend suspiciously. "What are you trying to do? Scare me?"

"No." Bob shook his head. "I just want you to be ready for the grilling of your life."

"The investment mistakes in the Mason trust occurred because the heirs chose a disreputable investment firm. They wouldn't listen to the bank's advice," Lauren stated. "You know that as well as I do."

"You have the correspondence to back you up?"

Lauren picked up the Mason file, patted the cardboard exterior and tucked it securely under her arm. "Right here."

"Good. At least we have some ammunition. Let's just hope that you can convince our illustrious leader that we were in the right," Bob said as he opened the door with one hand. He made a sweeping, chivalrous gesture with his arm. "After you."

"Coward." Lauren laughed and walked out of her office toward the boardroom at the other end of the plushly carpeted corridor.

The board meeting went better than Lauren had hoped. As Bob had surmised, the small, wiry president of Northwestern Bank, George West, had been tight-lipped throughout the discussion of the Mason trust lawsuit. However, Lauren was able to placate him a little by giving him, as well as the other members of the trust board, copies of the correspondence that clearly proved the bank had not been negligent in handling the funds of the Mason trust.

Bob Harding had sat through the meeting alternately tugging at his tie and adjusting his glasses. He'd backed up Lauren's assessment of the situation, which had occurred three years ago, before Lauren was administrator of the account. To Bob's immense relief, Pat Evans, legal counsel for the bank, concurred with Lauren. George West relaxed as well when Pat convinced him that the plaintiffs didn't have a legal leg to stand on.

By the time the lengthy meeting had ended and Lauren had finished with two other short appointments, it was after one o'clock; Zachary was probably waiting for her. Quickly she forced her arms through the sleeves of her raincoat, grabbed her umbrella and raced out of the building into the Portland rain.

Lauren hurried along the redbrick-and-concrete sidewalk, unconsciously trying to sidestep puddles and slower pedestrians on her way to O'Donnelly's. She paused only to shake the rain from her umbrella before closing it at the door of the authentic Irish establishment.

Her cheeks were reddened from the brisk walk, and wisps of coppery hair had blown free of the sleek chignon coiled loosely at the nape of her neck. Disregarding her disheveled appearance and summoning her courage, she shoved open the cut-glass-and-oak door of the restaurant. The interior was dim and Lauren hesitated while her eyes adjusted to the light.

O'Donnelly's was a popular restaurant and bar in the heart of the city. Known for its spectacular clam chowder and imported Irish beer, the restaurant did a brisk business at all hours of the day. Today was no exception. Patrons crowded around the bar, and conversation hummed throughout the smoky interior.

Zachary must have noticed Lauren's arrival. Before she could explain to the inquiring hostess that she was looking for him, he strode up the front desk, took her arm and propelled her toward a private table near the windows.

Lauren couldn't help but smile as she sat down. Unconventional was the word Bob Harding had used to describe Zachary Winters, and it fit him to a tee. Lauren found it difficult to imagine this rugged man doing anything as confining as studying law journals, pacing in front of the jury or straightening an imported silk tie.

Once again Zachary was dressed down, wearing soft brown cords and what appeared to be a blue oxford shirt peeking up from the crew neck of a cream-colored sweater. His jacket, which was tossed over one of the unused chairs, was a soft brown tweed.

"What would you like?" he asked, motioning to the menu as a slim waitress came to take their orders.

"Just a bowl of chowder," she replied softly. Her stomach was in knots, and she didn't think she could swallow anything. Nervously Lauren twisted her linen napkin in her lap.

Zachary frowned at her response and looked back at the waitress. "Two bowls of chowder, two salads from the salad bar, whole wheat rolls and two beers—"

"No beer for me," Lauren broke in, turning to smile briefly at the waitress. "Water will be fine." At Zachary's questioning look, she replied, "I have to go back to work. Besides which, I want to keep a clear head while I listen to what you have to tell me."

Zachary shook his head, but he didn't argue, and the waitress disappeared after pointing in the general direction of the salad bar. Zachary forced a smile, stood and helped Lauren out of the chair.

"I really don't think I can eat all this," Lauren murmured as she placed various greens and vegetables onto her chilled plate and walked slowly around the spectacular array of condiments and specially prepared salads in the long, ice-covered carousel that served as "the bar."

"Sure you can," Zachary assured her matter-of-factly. He flashed her a rakish smile that nearly took her breath away. For the first time, Lauren realized that she was responding to Zachary as a woman to a man. *I can't let this happen,* she thought to herself as she walked back to the table, incredibly aware of his presence at her side. *This is the man who might help me find Alicia and Ryan— purely professional, strictly business. No other relationship can cloud the issue. No other emotions can be involved!*

Back at the table, she met his dark gaze steadily and tried to conceal the fact that he was having such an ef-

fect on her. "Tell me what you found out," she requested.

The corners of his mouth tightened as he took a swallow of beer. "Not much," he admitted. "I sorted
through all the reports you gave me."

"And?"

"And they're fairly complete. I looked for loopholes,
anything that Pat Evans or his investigator might have
missed. But—" he shrugged his broad shoulders "—as
usual, Pat was pretty thorough. I can't say the same for
Tyrone Robbins."

The bite of bread she'd just taken seemed to stick in her
throat. "Mr. Robbins was my attorney for just a few
months," she murmured unsteadily.

"Why?" It seemed an innocent enough question;
Zachary displayed only mild interest.

"It didn't work out. I didn't think he was putting all
of his efforts into locating my children." She kept her
eyes lowered, staring at her neglected salad.

"He probably spent more time trying to convince you
that it would help your professional relationship if you
got to know him better personally—dated socially, that
sort of thing." There was an underlying edge to his
words.

More than that, she thought, but resolutely pushed the
disturbing thoughts aside. "Something like that," she
said. "Sounds as if you know Mr. Robbins fairly well."

Zachary smiled grimly. "I've had the pleasure of
dealing with him in court a couple of times."

Swallowing hard, Lauren stared directly into Zachary's eyes. "So what does all this have to do with my
case?"

His dark eyes hardened with self-reproach. "Not
much."

"Meaning?"

"That I came up dry."

"Nothing new?" she whispered.

"Nothing." Zachary felt an overwhelming need to apologize and explain himself. A muscle flexed in the corner of his jaw.

"That just can't be...."

"Look, I'm sorry." He noticed the skepticism in her gaze. *"Really."* He tossed his napkin onto the polished wood of the table and took a long swallow from his glass mug before setting the beer back on the table. "I rechecked everything—even pursued a few new leads. I talked to the people who had worked where your husband worked, called the list of friends, visited the IRS. And—" he shook his dark head disgustedly "—nothing."

Lauren had trouble keeping her voice from shaking. "What about the new lead you were talking about this morning on the phone...? What happened?"

"Nothing's come of it." He folded his hands in his lap and studied her. "Why do you think your husband took the children from you?" he asked suddenly, his eyes returning to the elegant features of her face. God, she was beautiful. Escaping tendrils of red-brown hair framed her gently sculpted face, color highlighted the elegant curve of her cheeks, and her eyes... God, those intelligent green eyes seemed to reach into his mind and read his darkest thoughts.

"I wish I knew. I've asked myself the same question a thousand times...."

"Do you think he wanted them because he needed to be a part of their lives...or because he wanted to hurt you?"

"I don't know," she admitted, her voice rough.

Zachary's dark eyes held hers. "Do you still love him, Lauren?" he demanded softly. Though it had little bearing on the matter at hand, it was a question that had interrupted his sleep for the past three nights. He had to know what he was dealing with—what kind of emotions were involved.

Despite the urge to cry, Lauren managed a cynical smile. The question was so absurd! She shook her head, and the recessed lights of the restaurant reflected in fiery highlights throughout her hair. "No," she said quietly. "I wonder now if I ever did."

"But he hurt you?"

"Yes," she admitted, swallowing against the dryness in her throat. She lowered her eyes and pretended interest in her water glass. "There were other women...."

Zachary stiffened. "Do you know their names?"

Lauren shook her head. "I didn't want to—tried to pretend that they didn't exist." She shrugged slightly and met his concerned gaze. "It was stupid of me, I know...but at the time, with the kids, I preferred to bury my head in the sand." She reached for her water glass and found that her fingers were shaking. "My idea of fidelity in marriage and Doug's were worlds apart." She lowered her gaze and stared briefly at the linen tablecloth to compose herself. Then, managing a frail smile, she took a sip of water.

"I want to help you," he insisted quietly.

"But you can't," she finished for him, her voice toneless. The fire in her eyes had suddenly died, and she was left with a cold feeling of emptiness.

"I don't think it would do any good."

"A waste of your time?"

"And yours. Lauren, look at me." Slowly, her green, lifeless eyes lifted. One of his hands reached across the table and took hers. "You're a young, beautiful woman. Your whole life is ahead of you." The conviction in his voice pierced her heart. "You can't live in the past."

"I don't," she replied, her throat uncomfortably tight. She fought the tears stinging her eyes.

"Then accept the fact that your children are gone."

"No!" Her hand crashed into the table, rattling the silverware and plates. Eyes, sparked with fury, burned into his. "I'll *never* accept that." Her back was rigid, her head held high as she stood. "Obviously you don't understand that I'd be willing to pay any price to find Alicia and Ryan."

Zachary stared up at her and watched in silence as two tears trickled from her brimming eyes. Suddenly four years seemed to slip away, and he was transported back in time to a place where another woman had once stood, head held high, her eyes condemning and filled with hatred.

"I just don't think that I can find them for you," he said as the image of Rosemary faded. "I wish that I could tell you differently, but I won't lie to you or protect you."

"Protect me?"

"From the truth."

"Which is?" she asked.

Zachary rose slowly from his chair and placed a comforting hand on her shoulder. His eyes were kind, as if he understood her agony. "That I don't think you'll ever see those children again, unless your husband wants you to. And that, after a year, seems very unlikely. Whether he enjoys hurting you or is afraid to come back, I don't know. But it's obvious that he doesn't want to be found, and while your kids are minors there's not much they can do about it."

She suppressed a sob of anguish and turned to leave the cozy restaurant, but the fingers gripping her shoulder restrained her. "I can't believe that," she whispered, still trying to walk out with as much dignity as possible.

Zachary was at her side, still holding her arm, unable to break the fragile contact. "Or won't?"

"Doesn't matter. I intend to find them."

"And when you do? What will you do? Steal them away from your husband?"

She whirled to face him, determination flashing in her eyes. "If I have to."

"You think he'd allow that to happen after he's been so careful to cover his tracks? He's cut himself off from all of his family and friends, just to insure his secrecy. You don't have a chance."

"The courts are on my side. They gave me custody."

"*In Oregon.* Unless I miss my guess, he's taken them out of state—maybe out of the country."

She'd heard it all before. Within the restaurant she could hear the sound of muted laughter, merry conversation and glasses clinking familiarly together. The sounds were distorted and vague, in direct contradiction to her feelings of despair. Shaking her head, she turned to face him, her green eyes filled with pride and determination. "Whatever it takes, I'll find them, and when I do, I won't rest until I bring them home...for good."

"Lauren," he said sharply, "think about what you'll be doing to those kids if you uproot them."

She withdrew as if she'd been struck. "I think about my children every day. I *know* they belong with me. Not just for *my well-being, but for theirs as well*. No one can love them the way I love them. No one." She was shaking with the intensity of her conviction. "The courts will agree. My only mistake was thinking that you would help me." With that, she turned on her heel and strode out of the restaurant and into the slanting rain.

The pain of his rejection overwhelmed her. She thought she had prepared herself for the possibility that he might not help her, but his withdrawal from the case seemed to bleed her soul of all hope. She threw her coat over her shoulders, clutched the lapels together and opened her umbrella against the rain.

When she returned to the office, she repaired her makeup and tucked the untidy wisps of hair back into the neat coil at the base of her neck. It took all her concentration to return to the problems in the office. The Mason trust lawsuit paled in comparison to the problem for which she was steadily running out of solutions—that of finding her children.

It was nearly five o'clock when Lauren finally decided on a new, more visible way of locating her children. After looking up the telephone listing for KPSC television, Lauren punched out the number and prayed that someone in the news department would be able to help her.

What she was planning was a long shot, and if it blew up in her face, she would lose all chance of finding Alicia and Ryan again.

But without Zachary Winters's help, she had no other choice.

Chapter Four

Zachary had just stepped out of the shower when he heard someone knocking on his door. Swearing softly, he rubbed his hair with a towel, quickly smoothed the wet strands with the flat of his hand and stepped into his favorite pair of worn jeans. "Hold on a minute...I'm coming," he called in the direction of the front door as the loud pounding continued.

Who the hell would be stopping by his home? He could count on one hand the number of visitors he'd had since building the cabin four years ago...shortly after Rosemary's death. With the help of an able contractor he'd constructed a house better suited for the pine-covered slopes and sweeping farmland of Pete's Mountain, the edge of the grassland two short miles from the freeway leading to Portland.

He walked down the hall from the master bedroom toward the front door in his bare feet. The glossy hard-

wood floors felt cool and solid against his skin. Mutter-
ing ungraciously, he opened the door to find his partner
on the doorstep. Joshua Tate, dressed as always in a crisp
business suit and starched white shirt, was leaning on a
roughly hewn post supporting the roof of the porch. His
tawny eyes took in the state of Zachary's undress.

"Am I interrupting something?" he asked hopefully,
a knowing smile curving his lips.

"Only a shower."

"Alone?"

Zachary laughed mirthlessly. "Yeah. Alone." He
stepped out of the doorway to let the younger man inside.

"Aren't you supposed to be working?" Zachary inquired as he followed Joshua down the half flight of
stairs into the living room.

"I am." Joshua took a seat on the leather couch and
placed his briefcase on the coffee table. Snapping it open,
he withdrew a sheaf of papers.

"What's that?"

"The McClosky deposition. The one you wanted so
badly and then left on your desk last week."

Frowning at himself, Zachary shook his head. He
hadn't been thinking straight for the past ten days. Lauren Regis had not only stolen his sleep but had somehow
managed to muddle his usually clear thinking. He took
the papers from Joshua's outstretched hand. "Thanks."

"No problem. I thought maybe it was time we touched
base anyway." He tugged at his tie, tossed his suit jacket
over the arm of the couch and loosened his cuffs.

Zachary shrugged. "I suppose so." Joshua Tate had
learned his lessons from Zachary well, and despite
everything that had happened between them, the kid
seemed to like him. Zachary never really understood why.

By all rights, Joshua should hate him, regardless of the kindness he'd shown him after Josh's father's death.

"Have you eaten?" Zachary asked, watching as Joshua casually turned on the TV and began shucking peanuts, just as if he owned the place. Like a kid coming home. That's how Joshua acted whenever he dropped by.

"No. How about you? Want to grab a pizza?"

Zachary shook his head and smiled. Along with his jacket, Joshua had cast aside any pretense of sophistication. "I've got some leftover ham sandwiches...."

"Sounds great." Joshua was focusing his attention on the TV, catching up on the latest football scores.

McClosky deposition my eye, Zachary thought. The kid's lonely. And he'd probably hate being called "the kid." After all, Joshua had to be nearly twenty-seven. He'd passed boyhood years ago. And Zachary Winters was the only family he had left.

"Hey, Zack," Joshua called from the living room. "Ya got a beer?"

Zachary smiled to himself. Josh was so predictable. But smart. The kid had finished both high school and college early and breezed through law school—once Zachary had straightened him out. Joshua Tate wasn't much like his father.

At the thought of his ex-partner, Zachary's mood shifted. Scowling, he grabbed two beers and the sandwiches from the sparsely stocked refrigerator. He slapped the sandwiches onto a paper plate, tore off some paper towels from the roll and balanced the hasty meal in his hands as he returned to the living room.

"Take a look at this, will ya?" Joshua requested in mild admiration, eyes trained on the television set. "Isn't that the woman that Amanda was talking about—the one that wants to find her kids—what's her name? Regal, or . . . no, Regis—Lauren Regis.''

Already Zachary's eyes were riveted to the television. He set the food on the coffee table without breaking his stare. "What the devil is she doing?'' he demanded as he straightened again.

The television show was a half-hour program that usually dealt with some of the more pressing social issues of the day. At the end of the program, for one five-minute segment each week, the news team would explore a personal problem of a citizen who had not been able to receive help through the usual channels. With the power of the press behind it, KPSC news was sometimes able to get results for the victim. The problems televised had included discrimination, consumer fraud, grievances against government agencies and the like. Never before had Zachary seen a segment dedicated to finding a child abducted by a parent.

A muscle worked tensely in his jaw as he watched the raven-haired anchorwoman interview Lauren.

"So what you're saying, Mrs. Regis, is that your ex-husband, under the guise of taking the children for the weekend, took them away from you.''

"That's right.'' Lauren's hair fell to her shoulders in soft auburn layers, and her cheeks were highlighted by a rosy shade of pink. Her emerald-green eyes, partially hidden by the sweep of dark lashes, shifted uncomfortably from the reporter to the camera and back again. She was, without a doubt, the most beautiful woman Zachary had met in a long, long while.

"That was over a year ago and you still don't know where he is?'' the dark-haired reporter persevered.

"I have no idea.'' Lauren spoke softly, but Zachary recognized the underlying thread of steel in her voice.

"And no one has been able to help you find them?"

"Several have tried."

"Without any luck, I take it."

"None," Lauren replied softly.

Zachary's shoulders stiffened.

"And you feel like you have nowhere to turn."

Lauren hesitated, and her neck muscles tightened a bit, barely discernible on screen. But Zachary noticed, and his teeth ground together in frustration.

"Essentially, yes. I've tried the police, private investigators and lawyers. They've all attempted to help me, but so far...no one has been able to find even a trace of my children."

Her voice quavered, but she was able to hang on to her composure. When she looked into the camera, Zachary felt as if her incredible green eyes were reaching into his soul. "Damn," he muttered under his breath, his eyes fastened on the screen.

"What about the juvenile services?" asked the reporter, continuing the emotional interview.

Lauren smiled sadly and shook her head. The anchorwoman stared into the camera. "Mrs. Regis would like your help." The image changed and a picture of Lauren's children flashed onto the screen as the reporter spoke to the viewing audience. "Remember, this portrait is over eighteen months old. It's the last picture Lauren Regis has of her children. If you have seen either of these children, or have some information as to their whereabouts, please get in touch with your local police or call station KPSC at this number...."

"Son of a bitch!" Zachary cried as a telephone number for the television station flashed onto the screen.

"Is that the same woman?" Joshua asked, reaching for his beer and unscrewing the cap. "The one that got past Amanda—"

"Yes."

"And you turned her *down*?" Joshua didn't bother to hide his amazement. "Bad move, Zack." He lifted the bottle to his lips and took a long swallow, his tawny eyes never leaving the harsh features of his visibly irritated partner.

"There was nothing to go on."

"But a case like this—it could bring us a lot of recognition...publicity. Which, I might add, we could use. Find those kids and you'd be a hero. Maybe even get some national attention." Joshua Tate stared at Zachary over the top of the beer bottle.

"You're beginning to sound like a politician."

"Not yet, but just give me a couple of years." The cocky young attorney laughed, picked up his sandwich, then paused before taking a bite. His bright eyes narrowed pensively. "Seriously, Zack, I think you should call her and tell her you'll help her."

"Even if I can't?"

"Why the hell not? She's already been on television, for crying out loud. The media will jump on this faster than a flea on a dog. It could be worth a lot—and I'm not just talking about legal fees...."

"I know what you're talking about and I'm not interested."

Joshua frowned in frustration. "She's a good-looking lady, and the publicity surrounding her case could really give us some media attention. It'll be Christmas in a few months, and you know how the press loves a tear-jerker-type story at that time of the year. We could get a little recognition...."

"Which we don't need."

"That's the problem, isn't it?" Joshua demanded after taking a bite of his sandwich and washing it down with a long swallow of beer. "You really don't give a damn about the business. Or anything else, for that matter."

"I managed to save your scruffy neck, didn't I?" Zachary dropped wearily onto the couch and ran a hand over his suddenly tense shoulder muscles.

"You felt obligated."

Inclining his head in mute agreement, Zachary reached for his bottle of beer, discarded the cap and took a long swallow. It helped...a little. "Maybe so. Doesn't matter. If I hadn't bailed you out, you would have been working on the other side of the law by now. You were already on your way."

"Yeah, well, if I forgot it then, 'thanks.'"

Zachary grinned wickedly. "You're a mean bastard, aren't you?"

"Guess I've had a good teacher."

The two men laughed together and finished the haphazard meal in silence.

Hours later, once twilight had settled and Joshua had returned to the city, Zachary threw away his well-intentioned restraint and decided to visit Lauren Regis.

The television interview had been more difficult than she had imagined. By the time she got home that evening, Lauren was dead tired. After placing the portrait of the children back on the mantel, she took off her coat and sagged against the fireplace. "I hope I did the right thing," she whispered.

Then, trying to shake off the depression that had been with her ever since the interview at the television studio, she changed into her favorite pair of jeans and a soft lavender sweater before lighting a fire and preparing dinner.

By the time she had finished eating, the flames were beginning to crackle against the pitchy fir and the living room was scented with the odor of burning wood. She kicked off her boots and curled her feet beneath her in her favorite overstuffed chair. Tucking a faded patchwork quilt over her lap, she picked up the suspense novel she had just started reading and tried to concentrate on the book's reluctant hero.

Involuntarily, her thoughts wandered to Zachary Winters. What would he say if he had seen her plead her case on the news program? How would he react? Would he even care?

Probably not. He'd made it perfectly clear that he wasn't interested in helping her. He was probably glad to be rid of such a problem case.

But no matter how hard she tried, she could never convince herself that Zachary Winters was an arrogant, self-serving bastard so caught up in his own problems that he couldn't see his way clear to help someone else. She'd seen the regret in his dark brown eyes, the lines of pain bracketing his mouth when he'd told her that he'd found no new clues in the search for her children. He cared. Whether he admitted it or not, Zachary Winters cared!

With a start, she realized that she could fall for the handsome man with the roguish grin and the dark, knowing eyes. She'd been hurt and in despair when he'd dashed her hopes of ever finding Alicia and Ryan. But a part of her had been disappointed simply because his rejection meant she'd no longer be seeing him.

"Don't be an idiot," she admonished with a sigh. The feelings she had for Zachary were tied to the emotional situation regarding her children. She was confusing her hope that he would help her with something else. Because she needed his help so desperately, she had managed to convince herself that she was attracted to him. "You're a fool," she chastised aloud. "And you should know better—especially after Doug and Tyrone Robbins." At the thought of her ex-husband and the smooth-talking attorney who had turned out to be so much like Doug, she shuddered. It was ironic that she was attracted to Zachary Winters after her disgusting experience with Tyrone Robbins. "Damn it, Lauren, you're *not* attracted to Zachary Winters. You need him, yes, but *only* to find the kids!" *And he isn't going to help you, no matter how much you want him to.*

"No," she said aloud at the coldly betraying thought, as if by physically rejecting her feelings for him, she could expunge the frightening emotions from her heart. But even as she did so, she thought how easy it would be to fall in love with Zachary Winters. *You picked the wrong man once before. Whatever you do, don't make the same mistake again. It will only cause you more pain and won't help you find the kids. Besides which, he's out of your life. He made that choice, and he doesn't want to deal with you or your problems.*

A loud knock on the door caught Lauren off guard. She glanced at the grandfather clock mounted near the door just as it chimed half-past eight. She wasn't expecting anyone—who would be calling? And then she knew. It had to be someone with news of the children, someone who had seen her on television. Her heart began to pound in anticipation.

Tossing aside the quilt and suspense novel, she scrambled up from her favorite chair and forced herself to walk slowly to the door. Though she told herself to remain calm, she half expected a reporter from KPSC to be standing on her porch, ready to share the good news that the children had been located. Nervously she leaned against one of the long, narrow windows beside the door, flipped on the porch light and stared out.

Her heart nearly missed a beat as she recognized Zachary Winters. When he saw her anxious face pressed against the window, he smiled the same dazzling smile that had touched her heart before. Lauren returned his grin hesitantly.

Either he had seen the television program, or he had new information on the whereabouts of Alicia and Ryan. Lauren's pulse raced at the thought. Her fingers fumbled as she unbolted the door and opened it.

"Hello, Lauren," he said, his eyes resting on the elegant contours of her face.

His effect on her was immediate—and this time, undeniable. "Come in," she murmured, and stepped away from the door, leaving enough room for him to enter.

His friendly smile faded somewhat as he walked into the living room and scanned the modest interior. The small, one-story, 1920s vintage house was decorated with a blend of antique tables, overstuffed chairs and baskets filled with leafy green plants. A small, navy-blue velour couch rested before the glowing coals in the brick fireplace, and a brass kettle on the hearth was filled with pieces of oak and fir. A slightly faded, cranberry-colored chair sat near a window, and a worn patchwork quilt was tossed haphazardly over one of the overstuffed arms. Small calfskin boots were placed near a matching footstool.

It was a warm room, quietly intimate. Gleaming hardwood floors were visible around the edges of a well-worn Oriental carpet in soft hues of blue and dusty rose.

Zachary's eyes shifted from the floor to the mantel, and he noticed the portrait of the children. He walked over to the fireplace and studied the picture.

"I saw you on TV," he said, getting straight to the point.

"And—what did you think?" Lauren returned to her position in the chair, watching his reaction as she folded the quilt.

Turning slowly to face her, he leaned against the red bricks of the fireplace and felt the warmth of the flames heat his calves. "I think it was the most foolish thing you could have done."

Lauren's heart lurched. "Why?" Slowly, she placed the folded quilt in a wicker basket.

"Because you just gave your husband a warning. If he lives anywhere around here—or somehow saw you on television—he knows that you're still looking for him." Zachary rammed his hands into his pockets in frustration. "And even if he didn't see the program, you can bet that someone he knows did. He'll be warned."

"It was a chance I had to take," Lauren replied stubbornly. "I'm running out of options."

Zachary's shoulders sagged, and he closed his eyes as he leaned the back of his neck against the mantel. "Oh, Lauren," he whispered in a caressing tone. "I wish I had all the answers and that I could find those kids for you."

When she didn't immediately respond, he looked at her once again and she saw the agony in his eyes.

"I can't give up," she said, her throat tightening with emotion. She swallowed hard and crossed her arms under her breasts.

Impatiently he raked his fingers through his rich, sable-brown hair. "I don't expect you to."

"And what, exactly, is it that you do expect of me?"

"I wish I knew."

"That, counselor, is called hedging."

He shook his head and smiled sadly. "Wrong. It's called the truth."

"So why did you come here tonight?"

"To apologize."

She raised her eyebrows inquisitively and with a hand gesture encouraged him to continue. Having him here, in her home, was doing strange things to her. She had to force her eyes away from the strong, sensual line of his mouth.

"I didn't give you enough credit."

"I don't understand—"

"What I'm trying to say, Ms. Regis, is that I want another crack at finding your children." He turned his head to study the photograph again, then returned his eyes to her face. "Maybe I *can* help you."

"Didn't you insinuate that it would be a waste of time?" she asked, barely believing her ears. Not only was he here, but he was prepared to help her.

"It still might."

"Then forget it. I want someone who's dedicated, who'll leave no stone unturned, follow any lead.... I've wasted too much time as it is on attorneys and private investigators who squeezed me into their already full case loads."

"And I want a client who will put all her trust in me and not go spouting off to some two-bit reporter anytime the going gets rough. It's got to be my way or no way."

Lauren was held captive by the intensity of his gaze, mesmerized by the deadly gleam in his eyes. Someone had once said that he could be ruthless in pursuing the truth. She hoped to God that it was true.

"All right," she agreed suddenly. Instinctively she knew that he was the one man who could help her. "You'll call the shots and I won't do anything to sabotage you, even unintentionally."

Slowly he relaxed. "I'd appreciate that." Then, cocking his head in her direction, he asked, "Are you ready to get to work?"

"Now?"

"As soon as I get my briefcase out of the truck. Soon enough for you?"

She smiled in amusement. "You know how I feel about this. But before we get started, I want to know one more thing—what made you change your mind?"

He tensed slightly, and when his eyes searched hers, she felt as if he were reaching into her soul. "You did, lady," he said simply. His sensual gaze stripped her bare, and she caught her breath at the smoldering passion lurking within the depths of his eyes. "I want to help you. I fought the attraction I've felt for you and I lost the battle."

"Then . . ." she began, her voice a hoarse whisper. "It wasn't because of the television interview."

"That was the catalyst, but I would have been back, anyway." He thought fleetingly of Joshua's remarks about the publicity surrounding Lauren's case, but kept silent. In all truth, that had nothing to do with his reasons for driving to Westmoreland this evening.

"What made you think I'd agree?"

"Because you need me."

She couldn't deny what was so patently obvious. "All right, counselor," Lauren said with a smile intended to break the tension in the room. "How do we start?"

"It's simple. You make the coffee, and I'll get my notes and tape recorder."

"Tape recorder—why?"

"We're going to start at the beginning," he declared, his jaw tightening in resolve.

"But I've gone through this all before. You have the reports from Pat Evans and—"

"And I prefer to do things my own way. Now, do you want to find your children or not?" Without waiting for her response, he walked across the small room and went outside to his truck.

When Lauren returned to the living room with the coffee, Zachary was waiting for her. What was it about him that made her little house seem like home? Was it his dazzling smile, the bold thrust of his chin or his eyes, first compassionate and kind, then sensual and intimately dangerous?

He was kneeling on the hearth and placing fresh logs on the fire. The light, worn denim stretched across his buttocks, and his shirt tightened over his shoulders as he adjusted the logs with a poker. His masculine presence seemed to fill the room. When the flames began to crackle, he dusted his hands and positioned himself on the floor, his back braced against the bricks. "Not bad for a guy who never made it to an Eagle Scout," he said with a smile.

She laughed. "Not bad at all."

"Sit down, sit down, let's get on with this." He patted one of the cushions of the couch and accepted the mug of steaming coffee she offered.

"Cream? Sugar?"

He smiled. "Black."

Lauren sat on the couch facing him. She tucked her feet under her and watched as he took an experimental sip.

"Okay," Zachary said, crossing his legs. "Let's get started." He flashed her a disarming smile before assuming an expression of intense interest. "Why don't you start by telling me a little of your background and then explain how you met your husband, where he was from. I want to know where you met, who your friends were, who *his* friends were, where he comes from... everything."

She hesitated slightly as she realized how difficult it would be to talk about her personal life. With the other attorneys, telling her story had been strictly a matter of business, but she sensed that with Zachary Winters it would be different. With all of her efforts to convince him to take her case, she had begun to know him—more than she wanted to. Perhaps more than she should.

She held on to her cup and stared into it as she began to talk. She told Zachary about her parents' death, living with Aunt Lucy, going to college in Medford, and meeting Doug when he was an assistant professor of economics and she a graduate student. Tears filled her eyes when she told Zachary about the birth of her first child, and the happiness she experienced at becoming a mother. Then she explained about Doug's inability to hold down a job. She mentioned his feelings of inadequacy. The beginning of his drinking problem. The fact that he blamed her for his failures. Finally she explained about Ryan's birth and the move back to Portland.

She tried not to leave anything out. Though her eyes burned when she explained about the frequent arguments, it wasn't until she repeated the story of the terrifying day Doug had lost his job at Dickinson Investments, when he had pressed his boot into her abdomen, that tears began to slide down her cheeks. And when she spoke haltingly of the day she'd come home to find that he had stolen the children, her shoulders began to shake and she could fight the stream of tears no longer.

Zachary had been quiet throughout most of her story, only interjecting questions to clarify something he didn't understand. He'd watched her fight a losing battle with the emotions ripping her apart, but he'd pressed her further, hoping to find anything that might lead him to her children.

She wiped her eyes and took a deep breath. "That was the last time I saw them—or heard from them," she said.

Zachary set his pad on a table nearby and crossed to her, placing his hands on her shoulders. "It'll be all right," he promised, tilting her trembling chin with one strong finger and forcing her to look into his eyes. "We'll find them."

"How...how can you be sure?"

He hesitated only slightly. Then his rugged features hardened with emotion and his eyes glittered. Lauren could feel the tension in his touch. "We'll find them," he repeated, his voice steely with resolve, "because I won't rest until I do."

A small, thankful cry broke from her lips as his strong arms gathered her close.

Chapter Five

At last, Lauren thought, *at last I've convinced him to help me.* Tears of gratitude welled in her eyes. For the first time in weeks, she was filled with hope.

Zachary held her gently, pressing his comforting lips to her forehead and gathering her close. She felt his strong arms around her and the seductive tease of his breath on her hair. She didn't withdraw from the embrace but accepted the strength he offered. It had been years since she had leaned on a man. Usually she hated the thought of it, but with this enigmatic lawyer, her feelings had changed. Intuitively, she knew that accepting his strength wasn't a sign of weakness. For over a year she had depended only upon herself, and now, at last, she had a friend…an ally in the struggle for her children. Tears of relief slipped from the corners of her eyes.

Zachary's arms tightened around her slim shoulders. It was as if he were suddenly aware of the intimacy of the

embrace and was struggling within himself to let her
go.... Lauren recognized the signs of his conflicting
emotions; they mirrored her own inner turmoil.

Zachary tried to restrain himself, but the feel of Lauren's body pressed against his chest brought back sensations he had thought long dead. *What the hell are you
doing?* he asked himself. He wasn't usually a stupid
man—he'd earned a reputation as an intelligent, sharp-
witted lawyer by proving himself to be shrewd, intuitive
and incisive. He recognized that holding Lauren was
nothing short of lunacy; yet he couldn't release her. As
crazy as it was, he wanted her, more desperately than he
had ever wanted a woman before.

The salt taste of Lauren's tears lingered on Zachary's
lips; the fragrance of her hair drifted into his nostrils; her
soft breasts pressed intimately against his chest, forcing
sensually erotic images to his mind—dangerous images
that burned in his brain and would not be ignored.

The sobs that had been racking her body eased a bit as
he held her, but still he found it impossible to let her go.
His fingers slid up from her neck and wound in her thick
auburn hair. God, he couldn't let himself get involved
with her....

Lauren must have felt the tension in his muscles, because she began to draw slowly away from him. What
was it about her that made him react so irrationally?
True, Lauren was a beautiful woman, but he couldn't
afford to get involved with any woman, especially a
client. In all his years of practicing law, he'd never suc-
cumbed to even the most tempting of advances from
women who had employed him. Usually the ones who
threw themselves at him were suffering emotional crises
of their own, and in any event Zachary considered him-

self smart enough to avoid emotional entanglements with his clients.

Until now. But then, Lauren wasn't throwing herself at him. If anything, she seemed to be experiencing the same conflict that was slowly ripping him apart.

Lauren took a shuddering breath. "I'm...I'm sorry," she apologized, wiping the tears from her eyes with her fingers. "I didn't mean to get so upset."

"It's okay."

"You've had your share of emotional clients?" she asked, attempting to lighten the mood and dissipate the tension clouding the air.

The corners of his lips twitched. "A few. Comes with the territory."

Lauren nodded, once again experiencing the urge to weep. Her voice broke as she explained, "It's just that usually I'm a fairly rational person—"

"Except where the kids are concerned."

"Yes," she whispered. "Except where the kids are concerned."

Zachary cleared his throat. Thinking it would be best to put some distance between her body and his, he walked across the room to lean against the warm bricks of the fireplace. "Look, maybe we should call it a night," he said as he reached for his tape recorder and placed it, along with his legal pad, into his briefcase.

Anxiously, she searched his face for a clue of what he thought of her story, but his expression was unreadable. Now that she had explained everything, perhaps he could find the children.... She forced herself to ask the question. "Do you have enough information to go on?"

"No." He rubbed the tension from the back of his neck, and his thick brows knotted together in concentration. "But it's late."

Then he couldn't leave. Not yet. "I can make some more coffee. Please stay until you find something, *anything* that might help."

A look of tenderness crept into his eyes, and Lauren suddenly realized how desperate she must sound...how desperate she had become.

Zachary walked back toward her, reached forward as if to touch her shoulder, then let his hand drop before shoving it into the pocket of his jeans in frustration. "I'll come back," he said, fighting the urge to stay with her, "after I've gone over my notes and double-checked some of the places that Evans and his private investigator looked into."

"Will that do any good?"

His lips compressed angrily. "Probably not."

"Then why waste your time?"

"Because we don't have a lot to go on, Lauren," Zachary replied honestly. "I want to make sure that no one, including Evans, made any mistakes—overlooked anything."

"Surely Patrick Evans can be trusted."

Zachary glanced skeptically in her direction. "Can he?"

Suddenly Lauren felt uneasy. Zachary didn't seem to trust anyone.... But maybe that was good. "He's on the board at the bank. He recommended you," she pointed out. *For God's sake, Patrick Evans is a respected member of the Northwestern Bank Board of Directors as well as legal counsel for the bank. His reputation as a lawyer is beyond reproach!* "His reputation is—"

"A lot better than mine," Zachary finished for her. He scowled and his eyes locked with hers. "What about Tyrone Robbins?"

Lauren drew in a quick breath. "That was a mistake," she admitted, hoping to close the subject. "*My* mistake."

Zachary muttered something unintelligible that Lauren deduced to be profane. "And I'm just trying to be careful, so that *we* don't make any more mistakes. Doing things my way might take a little more time, but it'll be worth it."

"You're sure?"

"No, but I'll do my damnedest to get those kids back to you," he promised with a slow, genuine smile that concealed all his reservations. "Trust me."

"I do," she replied, adding silently to herself, *whether I want to or not. You're my last hope. I hope to God that you're as good as Bob Harding and Pat Evans think you are.*

"Good. Then I'll call you in a couple of days." He strode to the door, and she followed him, placing a hand on his arm.

"Zachary?"

"Yes."

Lauren smiled, though her sea-green eyes still glistened with tears. "Thank you."

His shoulders tensed slightly. He looked as if he were about to say something, and for a moment his eyes embraced hers. Then he opened the door, stepped into the night and was gone.

Lauren waited until the sound of his truck faded into the darkness. Then she locked the door and sagged against the smooth wood. Between working most of the day, being interviewed by the news reporter at KPSC and recounting her life to Zachary Winters, Lauren was exhausted. Ignoring the stack of dishes in the kitchen sink, she headed for the bathroom, pulling her sweater over her head as she went. Once there, she knelt by the tub and turned on the water, testing the temperature now and then by running her fingers through the clear liquid, as she had done hundreds of times while preparing a bath for her small children.

She could almost see Ryan's cherubic face as he splashed in the water, his blond curls becoming dark ringlets as he played. He kicked his legs, thinking proudly that he was swimming as he crawled along the bottom of the white enamel tub.

"He's not swimming," Alicia had said as she looked disdainfully down at her younger brother splashing happily in the water. The little girl had sat on the linoleum floor surrounded by a mound of dirty clothes. As Alicia tugged on her dusty socks, she'd frowned disapprovingly at Ryan.

"He thinks he is," Lauren had replied. Ryan squealed happily, put his face in the water and then lifted it up again, his blue eyes shining.

"Good boy."

The pudgy baby grinned, showing off his two teeth.

"But his hands are touching the bottom of the tub," Alicia pointed out with all the wisdom of a four-year-old.

"That's the way you used to swim, too." Lauren pulled the hooded pink sweatshirt over her daughter's head and dropped it into the growing pile of dirty clothes.

"When I was a baby?" Alicia's round, earnest eyes delved into her mother's, and Lauren laughed at her daughter's serious expression.

"Yes, honey. When you were a baby."

The memory was so vivid that Lauren smiled to herself. Suddenly she noticed that the tub was nearly overflowing; she turned off the water and took a long, steadying breath. "I'll find you," she whispered fiercely.

"I promise. This time, I'll find you, both of you, and I'll bring you home! This time I've found someone who will help me."

Zachary's fingers tightened over the steering wheel and he cursed himself for being the worst kind of fool. For the first time in four years he had let his emotions get in his way and cloud his judgment.

"Son of a bitch," he muttered angrily. How could he have been such an idiot as to promise that he would find those kids? Hell, it was probably impossible. Doug Regis probably had them stashed away in the wilds of British Columbia or maybe even in the desert in Mexico. Or, worse yet... for all Zachary knew, the lot of them could be dead. And he'd been foolish enough to promise Lauren that he'd locate them!

His fist slammed into the steering wheel in frustration, and his eyes narrowed against the darkness. He had turned off the freeway and was winding his way up the familiar, unlit country road that curved up the gradual slope of Pete's Mountain toward his secluded cabin.

Why had he been such a damned fool? Maybe it was seeing Lauren on television, or maybe it was because Josh was right—Lauren Regis's case could be news. Big news. Or perhaps it was a chance to get back at Tyrone Robbins one more time. Whatever the reason, Zachary had made promises that would probably prove impossible to keep. Unless he got lucky.

"Boy, you've got it bad," he muttered to himself, diagnosing his problem as an unwanted attraction for Lauren. "Why should you think you can succeed when Patrick Evans gave up?" *And why did Evans recommend you in the first place?*

He turned on the radio, hoping that the throbbing beat of a sixties rock classic would drown out the unanswered questions spinning crazily around in his mind. It didn't. Zachary's thoughts flitted uncomfortably to Lauren Regis, her husband and her first attorney, Tyrone Robbins. How the hell had Lauren gotten involved with the likes of Robbins? he wondered, frowning. He told himself it didn't matter, but he could still recall Tyrone's smug face and the satisfied gleam in the younger man's eyes when Tyrone had served Zachary with the divorce papers four years ago. Robbins had had the audacity to come with the court-appointed messenger, just to witness the shock in Zachary's expression as he was handed the documents that had shattered his life.

"Happy anniversary, Zack," Tyrone had taunted, knowing that he had timed it so that Zachary was served the papers on the fifth anniversary of his stormy marriage to Rosemary. Tyrone had sauntered back to his car, smiling to himself as Zachary had stared numbly down at the documents in his hands, unable to believe that Rosemary actually planned to go through with the divorce. Less than a month later she was dead. Zachary wondered if Tyrone had taken the news any better than he had.

That's what you get for defeating the poor bastard so many times in the courtroom, Zachary thought. *And now it's your chance to get even—to get back at Robbins by succeeding where he's failed.*

So where was the sense of satisfaction, the lust for revenge that should be coursing through his veins?

He downshifted and turned into the lane that led to his house. His headlights caught the interlaced branches of the fir, maple and oak trees that grew naturally along the gravel drive. Finally he pulled the truck up near the garage and hopped out, angrily striding up the two steps to the front door.

Just what the hell am I doing?

He had no more chance of finding Lauren's children than the proverbial needle in the haystack. The odds were stacked against Ms. Regis, and in all honesty, Zachary seriously doubted that he could help her.

Then why all the promises?

Because I'm a fool; a goddamned hypocritical fool who's attracted to a beautiful, intelligent woman. Just like before. With Rosemary!

He walked inside the house, kicked the door shut behind him and headed straight for the liquor cabinet.

The next morning, as she walked into the suite of offices of the trust department, Lauren saw several of her co-workers staring curiously at her. Obviously, more than one of the employees of Northwestern Bank had seen the television program. She was reminded of Zachary's warning that Doug may also have seen the show. Going public with her personal problems may have been a horrible mistake. Lauren braced herself for what promised to be a long, uncomfortable day.

Don't second-guess yourself, she thought as she picked up her messages from the receptionist and smiled at the petite blonde, who quickly returned the smile and then avoided any further eye contact.

So it's already started. Lauren groaned inwardly and turned toward her office. *If you hadn't done the television show, Zachary wouldn't have accepted the case. And then where would you be? Back to square one.*

As she was about to enter her office, Lauren was confronted by Della McKeen, the securities cashier for the trust department. Della was a quick-witted, petite woman in her late fifties who'd worked at several brokerage houses before coming to work for the bank. She smiled sincerely and ran nervous fingers through her curly gray hair as Lauren approached.

"Good morning," Lauren said.

"Same to you." Della looked a little self-conscious. "I . . . I, uh, well, I saw you on the news last night."

"You and half the staff. I suppose I'm the main topic of conversation in the lunchroom," Lauren replied with a good-natured grin. This was going to be harder than she had imagined, but she tried to look unruffled.

"I—" Della shrugged "—I don't really know what to say. I had never guessed that your husband took the kids from you." She shook her head. "It's just awful. That's what it is. Gawd-awful. I've got two kids of my own. They're grown now, but I can't imagine what it would have been like to lose them. . . ." Realizing that she'd blundered and inadvertently voiced Lauren's fears, Della quickly added, "But don't give up, mind you. If I were you I'd hire the best attorney in town and chase that husband of yours down!" Della's small brown eyes blazed furiously from behind her silver-rimmed glasses.

"That's exactly what I'm trying to do."

"Good!" Della replied emphatically. "I hope it all works out for you. If there's anything I can do—"

"I'll let you know. But I doubt that anyone can help now." *Except Zachary.*

"But maybe someone who saw the program?"

"Maybe," she murmured. But she didn't have much hope of that.

"Well, honey, if it's any consolation, I think that husband of yours should be strung up by his. . .hamstrings." The cashier patted Lauren affectionately on the arm and continued talking under her breath as she stalked down the long corridor.

"Yep. It's going to be a long day," Lauren muttered, glancing at her watch and noting that it was barely eight-thirty. She walked into her office, hung her coat and umbrella over the brass hall tree and sat down at her desk. She had just begun to check her appointment book when Bob Harding strolled leisurely into the room. He closed the door behind him, placed a cup of steaming coffee on the corner of the desk and then did a quick double take as he looked at Lauren.

"I didn't expect to find you here."

"What?" Good Lord, what was Bob talking about? Lauren put down her pen and focused her attention on her friend. He was still gazing at her with overly dramatized awe and a twinkle in his myopic eyes.

He shrugged. "I thought someone else must be occupying this office."

"Someone else?" she repeated. "Why?"

"I have it on good authority that some infamous Hollywood star is supposed to be here."

"Don't I wish!" She shook her head and rested her chin in her palm as she eyed her friend. "Are you going to tell me what this is all about?"

"You first. I caught your act on television last night, and from the sound of all the gossip ripping through the lunchroom, a few others saw you, too."

Lauren groaned as she imagined the excited knots of bank employees sitting around the Formica-topped tables and whispering about her. "Is it that bad?"

"Not really." He settled into one of the chairs near the desk and dropped his teasing facade, to Lauren's immense relief. "Actually, from what I understand, everybody feels sorry for you. You know, they're all wondering what they can do to help. That sort of thing."

Lauren was touched, but she was also realistic. "I don't need sympathy, Bob, just answers."

"I hear that the operations staff is taking up a collection—"

"What!" Her bright eyes impaled her co-worker. "Tell me you're kidding."

"Okay. I'm kidding." He shrugged his round shoulders and sipped his coffee.

"Not funny, Bob," she told him, chuckling. She reached for her cup and cradled it in her hands. "Thanks," she said, indicating the coffee.

Bob rested his elbows on the arms of the chair and placed his hands over his belly. "I just thought you could use a laugh or two."

She smiled. "You thought right."

"Don't I always?"

"Most of the time. Say about seventy percent."

"At least you think so," he replied. "The powers that be might disagree." He frowned into his cup, and Lauren had a sudden, chilling premonition. All of Bob's teasing was to get her to relax because the ax was about to fall. She could sense it.

"Meaning?"

He waved away her obvious concern, but the lines of worry creasing his forehead didn't disappear. "I'll get to it in a minute. Tell me, what's really going on with you? Why did you agree to be on that program yesterday?"

Lauren set her cup on the desk and rotated her pen between her fingers. "To find my kids."

"Because Zachary Winters wouldn't take your case," her friend deduced. He studied her closely, and Lauren suddenly felt he was keeping something from her, to protect her.

"Right," she agreed somewhat hesitantly. "But it seems that he's changed his mind."

Bob took a deep breath. "I don't know if that's so good," he said.

"What're you talking about?" Lauren stared at Bob incredulously. "You're the one who recommended the man to me. You've been insisting for the past six or seven months that I should switch attorneys and try to get Winters interested in my case."

"That was before."

"Before what?" Her voice had risen and she had to force herself to remain calm. "If this is another joke—"

"No joke, Lauren." The eyes behind the thick lenses saddened slightly. "I still think that Zachary Winters is the best attorney in Portland . . . maybe even the entire West Coast."

"But?"

He cleared his throat. "We've had some bad news," he said with a grimace. "The date of the Mason trust lawsuit is on the docket."

"What does that have to do with retaining Winters as my attorney?"

"I'm getting to that. The heirs of the Mason trust are out for blood."

Lauren was having trouble switching gears. What did the Mason trust have to do with Zachary Winters finding her children? Trying to keep her patience, she began tapping the tip of her pen on the polished surface of the desk. "So they're really going to take this to the limit?"

"The bank won't settle, and the heirs have hired another lawyer on a contingency. He's pushing it through, hoping that all the bad press will force the bank into settling out of court." Bob slid photocopies of the documents across her desk. "We're in court on December fifth, unless the bank decides to settle, which we won't. George West has decided to fight the suit with all we've got. He figures that if we lose this, it will open doors for lawsuits of a similar nature. And that could be bad."

"You're telling me." Lauren could envision the result. Anyone who'd ever lost a dime on an investment—even one initiated by an adviser the account holder himself had hired—could try to sue the bank. Even if Northwestern Bank won the case, the legal fees would be enormous.

"So who's the brilliant attorney who decided to put the bank through the wringer?" she asked.

"You're not going to like the answer to this one."

Lauren's heart skipped a beat. "Who is it, Bob?"

"Joshua Tate. Zachary Winters's partner."

Lauren felt as if she were suffocating; she couldn't seem to breathe properly. "When...when did he take the case?"

"Just last week."

"After I'd met with Winters?"

Bob rubbed the top of his bald head. "Looks that way."

"So Zachary may have accepted my case just to get close to me and find out what the bank was planning," she said slowly, numb at the insinuations in her mind. After all, she was the administrator of the Mason trust. Why else had he decided to help her after telling her that locating the kids was next to impossible? Lauren stared at the desk and felt all her hopes slowly die.

Bob was shaking his head. "I don't think so. The man is basically honest."

"With more than a little dirt on his reputation," Lauren murmured. How could she have been so foolish as to believe that he cared about her or the children?

"Gossip."

Lauren sighed and placed her head in her hands. The morning had barely started and already she had a blinding headache. "No one knows for sure."

"Except Winters."

Lauren closed her eyes and thought about the enigmatic man with the dark brown eyes and cynical smile. She knew he was the only person who could help her, and that thought rekindled her determination. "I won't let him go," she said, half to herself.

"Pardon me?" Bob shifted in his chair and tugged at his collar uneasily.

Lauren lifted her head, her green eyes glittering with resolve. "He said he'd take my case, and he meant it. I'm not taking him off it."

"I agree with you. You know that."

"But?"

"If George West finds out about it, he might go through the roof."

Lauren's jaw tightened. "What I do with my life outside the office is my business. It has nothing to do with George West or Northwestern Bank."

"Except that now you've made a public issue of your life by going on that television show last night. And to top things off, you've hired Zachary Winters as your lawyer."

"Just following your advice," she reminded him.

"I know. I know." Bob got up and paced restlessly to the window to stare at the overcast sky. "But now his partner has taken on a case against the trust department of the bank you work for. More than that, the Mason account is under your administration. Whether you were handling the account when the alleged investment errors were made is irrelevant. The important thing is that there seems to be a conflict of interest. The law firm attacking the bank is the one you've hired for your own personal use.''

"And I'm the administrator for the Mason trust," she said softly, her heart thudding irregularly.

"Yes." Bob frowned as he noticed how pale she had become.

"I can't . . . won't believe it's all that cut and dried."

"God, I hope not," Bob said worriedly as he wiped his sweating brow. "Because, despite everything, I still think Winters is the right man to locate those kids."

"So do I."

"Let's just hope George West agrees."

"It's none of his business," Lauren said firmly.

"Yet."

Bob checked his watch, then straightened his jacket and walked to the door. "If it's any consolation, I'm on your side."

"I know."

"Well . . . good luck."

"Let's just hope I don't have to rely on luck." She took a sip of her cold coffee as she watched Bob disappear from her office. *Yes,* she thought again, *it's going to be a long day, and it's probably going to get a lot worse.*

Chapter Six

You did *what!*" Zachary demanded incredulously. He was seated in his desk chair, glaring at his partner past the various law books, journals and documents that littered the scarred oak desk. Joshua Tate, his crisp three-piece suit, gold cuff links and satisfied smile smugly in place, returned the older man's stare as he dropped into the leather chair nearest the window and watched the first drops of rain drizzle down the glass.

"I agreed to represent the Mason trust beneficiaries in their lawsuit against Northwestern Bank," Joshua replied. Gold eyes filled with challenge, he rotated to face Zachary and braced himself for a dressing-down.

Zachary leaned back in his chair, took off his reading glasses and rubbed his temples, as if to ease a suddenly throbbing headache. Sweat trickled down his temple and stained the front of his sweatshirt in a dark V, evidence of the exertion of his recent run along the waterfront.

He'd only stopped by the office to make a few calls. Just for fifteen minutes! Then Joshua had calmly sauntered in and dropped this—this *bomb*.

"You can't represent Hammond Mason or the trust," Zachary declared wearily. He was familiar with the Mason trustees. The most vocal of the angry heirs, Hammond Mason, was the kind of man who would never be satisfied, no matter what. If Hammond had been left two million dollars from a relative he'd never known existed, it wouldn't be enough.

"Of course I can."

"It's a no-win situation," Zachary cut in impatiently.

"Maybe...." Joshua let his voice trail off suggestively.

"Just what the hell are you trying to prove?" Zachary asked tiredly as he pushed aside a stack of mail and leaned his bare forearms on the desk.

Josh's eyes darkened. "I'm trying to prove that Winters and Tate is still a firm to be reckoned with. Look around you. Haven't you noticed what's been happening here? We're dying on the vine! We're supposed to be in the business of practicing law, Zack—something you've been avoiding for some time."

Zachary couldn't argue with that one—the kid was right. "Go on," he said quietly.

"And I thought—no, make that you told me, very emphatically, I believe—that you weren't interested in taking on Lauren Regis's case or looking for her kids."

"I wasn't."

"But you changed your mind?"

"Yeah." Zachary got out of the chair and stretched. He thought about pouring himself a drink, then decided against it. Alcohol wouldn't help. Not much would. The whole set of circumstances—Lauren, her children and her position at the bank as administrator of the Mason trust—was a mess, a damned bloody mess.

"And now you expect me to drop *my* case because of a *possible* and highly unlikely charge of conflict of interest." Joshua crossed his arms over his chest, awaiting further battle.

Zachary realized that arguing with Josh would get him nowhere. Josh was a master at verbal attack and defense. So he decided to change tactics. "Why didn't you bother to tell me about your discussion with Hammond Mason?"

"I meant to."

"When?"

Joshua shrugged and looked away. "Oh, hell, Zack. I don't know. Like I say, I intended to—"

"Yeah, well. It's a little late."

"It's not like you hang around here much, y'know," Josh pointed out, knowing he was hitting a sensitive nerve. He cleared his throat and the angle of his jaw hardened determinedly. "I'm not letting go of the Mason case."

"Why?"

Josh rolled his eyes heavenward. "You haven't been listening to a word I've said, have you? We need a case, Zack, a strong case that will get us a little publicity."

"Even if we lose?" Zachary rubbed his hands together and guiltily eyed a stack of unanswered correspondence on the corner of his desk. Maybe the kid was right. Maybe he didn't spend enough time in the office and therefore had no right to exercise his prerogative as senior partner of the firm. In all honesty, Zachary had to admit that Josh had been all but running the firm for the past couple of years.

"We won't."

Josh was sure of himself; Zachary had to give him that. "You don't have a prayer."

"Old man West will settle."

"I doubt it." Zachary folded his hands behind his back and stretched, attempting to relieve the tension in his shoulders. As he shook his head, he leaned one hip on the window ledge. "He's out to beat you, Josh, and he's got Patrick Evans on his side."

"Evans is over the hill."

Zachary's eyes narrowed. "No way." He frowned slightly. "I thought the first lesson I taught you was never to underestimate the opposition. As for Evans, he's the best Portland has to offer."

"Since you gave up."

Zachary tensed, and the muscles between his shoulder blades knotted uncomfortably. "Evans has always been good."

"Then it's time he came down a peg."

Zachary sighed and studied the angry planes of Joshua's even-featured face. "When are you gonna get rid of that chip on your shoulder?" he asked. "It's not doing either one of us a damned bit of good."

"As if you care." Joshua pushed himself out of the chair. "You haven't given a damn about anything for four years." He made a sweeping gesture with his arm that encompassed everything in Zachary's office—the seldom-used law journals, the stack of mail, unanswered letters and dust-covered volumes on the shelves. "Look at this mess! You call this an office?" Sarcasm edged his words. "I remember the way it used to be, Zack. Y'know, when Dad was alive and Winters and Tate was the most sought-after law firm in the Pacific Northwest."

Zachary's eyes glinted at the mention of Wendell Tate. "That was a long time ago."

"Not so long."

"But I let it slide." Zachary's dark brows lifted challengingly.

Joshua backed off a little. "Lots of things happened. Rosemary and Dad dying...well, no one blamed you for packing it in, but now—Christ, Zack, it's been six years! With the right case we could have it all again." He held out his hand and curled his long fingers into a fist, as if he were reaching for something tangible.

"And what would it be worth?"

Josh's gold eyes glittered. "It's what it's all about, old man, money and prestige."

"Whatever happened to justice?" Zachary asked cynically.

"If we're good enough, justice will come along for the ride."

Zachary smiled sadly and shook his head. "Just like that?"

Josh grinned—a flash of white teeth and good humor. "I didn't say we didn't have to work at it."

"And in the case of the Mason trust?"

"I plan to wait and see, but I'm willing to bet that justice will prevail."

"In the form of a huge out-of-court settlement."

Joshua's grin broadened.

"You could lose big," Zachary warned.

"And you think you've got a better chance with Lauren Regis and her kids?" Joshua folded his arms over his chest and eyed his partner skeptically.

"It won't be easy," Zachary admitted, raking his fingers through his damp hair and staring out the window at the drizzly autumn day.

"So why'd you agree to do it?"

Zachary raised an eyebrow. A sticky question. He considered lying to Josh, but he'd never yet had to resort to dishonesty with his younger partner, and he didn't want to start now. "The lady needs help," Zachary finally responded. That much wasn't a lie.

"And she was on television the other day," Josh thought aloud, grinning as he looked at his partner. "We're already talking about major publicity, aren't we?"

"Nothing to do with it."

"It could be big, Zack." Joshua pursed his lips and his eyes narrowed into speculative slits.

"And it could blow up in my face."

"Maybe. But life's a gamble," Josh pointed out. "At least that's what you've always told me."

"And you insist on throwing it back in my face every chance you get, don't you?"

"Only when you need a kick in the ass."

"Like now?"

Josh glanced at Zachary, and a slow-spreading smile inched across his face. "Yeah," he replied with a quick nod of his head. "Like now." He started to leave the room, but Zachary's voice stopped him.

"Drop the Mason case, Josh. It won't work."

Zachary very rarely issued orders, at least not since making Joshua a full partner, and the ultimatum rankled. "Can't do it, Zack. The challenge of it all, y'know." He turned and faced the man he'd come to think of as a second father. "I'll never know that it won't work until I've tried," Josh stated evenly. "After all, I've got nothing to lose but a little time."

"And Northwestern Bank?"

"Can afford it."

"Even if they're in the right?"

"Then George West will have the chance to prove it, won't he?" He reached for the doorknob.

"What about Lauren Regis?"

Josh turned and again surveyed Zack calmly, shrewdly. Suddenly a glimmer of understanding flickered in his eyes. "That's what this is all about, isn't it? The woman herself, not her case. Lauren Regis. She's gotten under your skin. That's why you took her case."

"One reason," Zachary drawled.

"And the others?"

Zachary's mocking grin slowly widened. "Maybe I think that you're right—it's time I took a little interest in the office."

Joshua snorted in disbelief and opened the door. "Maybe," he said, shaking his head as he gazed at the clutter in Zachary's office. "But then again . . . maybe not."

Lauren was snapping her briefcase closed when the intercom buzzed. She glanced swiftly at the clock. Six-thirty. Most of the employees had already left the bank, and Lauren was about to join them. It had been an exhausting, disappointing day. She was anxious to get home to see if she'd received any calls on the answering machine concerning Ryan or Alicia's whereabouts. After that, a long, leisurely bath and a glass of wine, not necessarily in that order.

When the intercom buzzed again, Lauren frowned but pressed the button on the receiver and answered, "Yes?"

"Ms. Regis? Mr. West would like to see you," the receptionist said.

Lauren's throat tightened with dread. "When?"

"In about ten minutes, if you're not too busy."

Lauren smiled despite her unease. George West was nothing if not a gentleman, but whenever he issued a polite request, he expected it to be followed through as if it were an imperial command.

"I'll be there," Lauren said as she clicked off. Great. So even the president of the bank had seen or heard of her television appearance. He probably knew that she'd hired as her personal attorney the senior partner in the firm that was attempting to sue Northwestern Bank to the tune of two million dollars on behalf of the Mason trust beneficiaries.

Her heart was pounding irregularly by the time she had slipped on the jacket of her wine-colored business suit and was heading for the elevator. Once inside the confining car, she punched the button for the eleventh floor, where the bank's corporate headquarters were located.

George West's secretary, a competent, unsmiling woman in her midforties, escorted Lauren into the large corner office which faced both south and west. A bank of ceiling-high windows on the outside walls of the office offered a panoramic view of the west hills of Portland. Modern skyscrapers, Gothic church spires and elegant old hotels rose in the foreground. In the distance were the lush, forestlike grounds of the gently sloping west hills. Some of the most expensive homes in the city were hidden behind a private curtain of regal Douglas firs and autumn-burnished maple and oaks. Tudor and Victorian mansions peeked through the colorful trees from their lofty vantage points.

George West was sitting at his desk, which was angled in the corner of the room, with the commanding view of the city at his back. Thick imported carpet in a subtle shade of ivory silenced Lauren's footsteps. Spiky-leaved green plants sprouted from porcelain vases, and gold plaques awarding honors of city consciousness adorned the two mahogany-paneled walls.

"Lauren," George West said familiarly, rising from his padded leather chair as Lauren approached. "Please...take a seat." He motioned toward one of the winged chairs near his desk and dropped back into his own chair to survey her shrewdly with eyes that for sixty-two years had seen life solely from the viewpoint of the very rich. George West had been born with the proverbial silver spoon in his mouth, and had managed first to double, then triple his family's fortune by investing wisely in real estate.

As Lauren lowered herself into the oxblood leather chair, the president of the bank checked his watch and then got straight to the point. "I heard that you were on the KPSC news program last night...what's it called? *Eye Contact*?"

"Yes."

"Didn't see it myself, but Ned Browning did."

Ned Browning was vice-president in charge of personnel. Lauren's heart sank as she realized she'd already been the subject of at least one closed-door upper-echelon meeting. She managed a stiff smile but didn't comment on George's observation, preferring to wait until he asked her a question.

"I didn't realize what had happened between you and your husband," George explained with a thoughtful frown. "Of course, I knew that the kids weren't with you, but I just assumed that your husband had custody." His frown deepened. George West prided himself on knowing his officers fairly well, but this was becoming increasingly difficult as Northwestern continued to grow. "This is a nasty business," he stated.

"Yes," Lauren agreed, wishing that the uncomfortable interview were over. She shifted uneasily in her chair but held her head high, waiting for a direct question—or command—from her boss.

"Browning said you'd hired several attorneys and a private investigator."

"That's right. I worked with Tyrone Robbins and then Patrick Evans."

"And?"

She shook her head. "Nothing. At least not so far."

"Pat Evans couldn't help you?" George asked, clearly skeptical.

"No," she responded, waiting for the ax to fall.

"And now you've hired Zachary Winters."

Lauren nodded.

George thoughtfully drummed his fingers on the mahogany desk. "Did he suggest you go on television?"

The question surprised her, especially considering Zachary's reaction to the program. Still, she was careful. Something in the set of George's jaw discouraged confidence. "No, actually, he hadn't accepted my case at that point."

"He accepted *after* you were on last evening's show."

Lauren folded her hands carefully in her lap. "Yes."

George thought for a minute, scratching his temple pensively. Then he said, "You know, of course, that Winters and Tate are attorneys for the Mason beneficiaries."

"I found out about it this morning. Bob Harding brought me all of the documents from Winters and Tate. I looked them over carefully and found no evidence that Zachary Winters is involved in any way. Joshua Tate is the attorney of record. I'm working solely with Mr. Winters."

George shook his head and discounted her excuse with a wave of his hand. "All the same outfit," he muttered, as if to himself. "You can see what we're up against, can't you? Whether Winters intended it or not, it *appears* that he took your case knowing that his firm was representing the Mason trust. Sticky business, if you know what I mean."

Lauren saw no reason to hedge. "You think there may be a conflict of interest?"

"Appears so." He patted his hands together, pleased that she had caught on so quickly. Lauren Regis was as smart as she was attractive, he decided. "Winters knew you were an employee of Northwestern Bank?"

"Yes."

"In the trust department?"

She nodded, her face losing some of its color.

"Did he have any idea that you were the administrator of the Mason trust?"

Lauren had anticipated the question; she had been asking it of herself for most of the afternoon. "I don't think so. No, he couldn't have. At least not from me."

"But the beneficiaries of the trust—who's the guy that's spearheading this suit—Hammond Mason? Yes, that's the name. He could have talked with Winters before he did business with Tate. Or, for that matter, Winters could have talked to Joshua Tate himself or even seen some of the documents. No doubt your name appears on various correspondence from the bank."

Lauren placed her hands on the arms of the chair and curled her fingers around the padded arms. "Yes."

George took off his glasses and tiredly rubbed a hand over his face. "You see what we're up against here, don't you? The bank's position is clear—we have to go to court and prove that we weren't the least bit negligent, in order to discourage these ridiculous lawsuits.''

"And you're afraid that if it ever leaked out that I was using Zachary Winters as my counsel, the members of the board and the stockholders of the bank would be upset.''

"To put it mildly.'' He straightened his tie. "They'd be out for blood.'' He didn't have to say whose blood. "If we lost, which I admit is highly unlikely, but still a possibility, the bank would lose two million dollars plus the cost of the trial. There might be an investigation.''

"All because I hired Winters,'' she finished for him.

"Precisely.'' George seemed pleased that she understood the bank's position so well.

"You want me to find another lawyer.''

George smiled a little. "It would make things much easier.''

Lauren could feel herself breaking out into a cold sweat. She couldn't fire Zachary as her attorney. *Wouldn't*. He was reputed to be the best, and she couldn't believe that he would use her. He wasn't like Doug or Tyrone Robbins. He couldn't be!

"Legally, you can't ask me to fire Winters,'' she managed to say calmly.

"I realize that.''

"Are you saying that my job is on the line?''

He shook his head slowly, as if he were extremely tired. "I just want you to think, Lauren. You've made an excellent career for yourself here at Northwestern Bank. You have a brilliant future as well. I wouldn't want you to make any rash decisions that might jeopardize it. You're up for a promotion within the next few months, and I see nothing that should affect it . . . so far.''

Lauren began to tremble in frustrated rage. Sometimes it seemed as if the entire world were against her, all because she wanted to be with Alicia and Ryan. "We're talking about my children," she said. "You have to understand, Mr. West, that I'll do anything to get them back. They're the most important part of my life."

"And your job with the bank?"

"Is secondary," she admitted without hesitation.

George sighed and looked at the framed photograph of his granddaughter on the corner of his desk. "That's how it should be," he agreed. "I understand your feelings . . . and I admire them, but I can't run this bank on emotion. I have stockholders who expect me to protect the bank's reputation and get the best performance I can from each of its employees."

Lauren stared at the small man seated at the big desk, her heart pounding with dread. "So you are suggesting . . ."

"That you find yourself another attorney."

Even though she'd been expecting the president of the bank to say just that, she felt betrayed; trapped. "Patrick Evans referred me to Winters."

George's eyes rounded and he rubbed a hand over his chin. "I see," he said, frowning. "Then I imagine that you know all about Winters and you're not worried about the scandal that surrounded him a few years back."

"No." Her green eyes blazed defiantly. "I don't know all about it, but I don't really care what happened. His personal life doesn't concern me. All I want from Zachary Winters is for him to locate my children and bring them back to me."

"Whatever the cost?"

"Whatever the cost!" she repeated, her voice shaking with emotion. "You know that I would never do anything to jeopardize Northwestern's reputation or undermine the bank's defense, but I have to do everything in my power to find Alicia and Ryan."

"Yes. Well, I suppose you do." He pressed his hands flat on the desk and smiled slightly as he stood, indicating that the interview was over. "Thank you for talking with me."

"You're welcome," Lauren replied dully as she straightened from her chair, smoothed the hem of her skirt and headed toward the double doors of the opulent office. Anger seethed through her at the unfairness of it all, and she had to force herself to walk proudly, to keep the slump of defeat from her shoulders.

"I hope you find your children, Lauren," George said as she reached the doors.

She turned back to face him and noted that he was still standing in front of the large plate-glass windows. Threatening storm clouds, dark with the promise of rain, had begun to gather over the west hills. "Thank you. So do I." With that she slipped through the heavy doors and hurried away.

In the elevator, she thought back on the interview. If nothing else, she'd been honest with the president; now it was up to him to decide how to deal with the problem. Sighing, she stepped out of the car, returned to her office to pick up her things and hurried out of the building.

Thank God it's Friday. She had two free days before she had to return to the bank. Maybe by then the gossip about her appearance on television would settle down. Maybe she would know something more about Alicia and Ryan. And maybe she would be out of a job.

The downpour had just begun as she walked out of the building. A heavy breeze caught in her umbrella, and the rain began in earnest, chilling her face and hands as it slanted down from leaden skies.

"Damn!" Lauren muttered as she dashed across the wet pavement of the parking lot and unlocked the car door. She slid her hands over the wheel and fought to quiet the rage storming in her heart.

All she wanted was her children. Was that so much to ask? Tears gathered in her eyes, and her small hands, curled into impotent fists, pounded mercilessly on the steering wheel.

She'd fight them. She'd fight them all! Douglas Regis, George West, Joshua Tate, even Zachary Winters if he tried to thwart her. She was the woman who had given birth to Alicia and Ryan, and if she accomplished nothing else in her life, she would find her children, no matter who stood in her way.

Chapter Seven

Zachary's pickup was parked on the street in front of her house. Lauren's fingers tightened on the steering wheel in tense anticipation. Maybe he'd already found out something, anything, about her children!

Or maybe he'd come to report that he had to drop the case because Joshua Tate had already agreed to represent Hammond Mason. Fleetingly, she wondered if he had come to extract information from her, then discarded the idea. If gaining some sort of advantage in the Mason trust trial had been his objective, he would have tried to pump her for information already, before the bank caught on to his scheme.

As she turned into the driveway and parked, she realized her feelings for Zachary ran deeper than anxiety over the children or worry about the Mason trust lawsuit. Yes, she desperately wanted to know about the kids, and the bank's attitude about her attorney concerned her. But she was also glad that Zachary had come to the house searching for her. Somehow it eased her earlier doubts about his integrity.

Silently chastising herself for her foolish thoughts, Lauren climbed out of the car, dashed to the mailbox and hurried up the wooden steps to the front door, sifting through the bills and various pieces of junk mail as she ran. Wet leaves in hues of orange and brown littered the steps and caught on the heels of her boots.

Zachary watched Lauren approach as he stood lazily on the small veranda that ran the width of the cream-colored house. Wide pillars supported the roof, and a half wall constructed of the siding that covered the house afforded the roomy porch some privacy. Cobalt-blue shutters and trim provided a striking contrast to the ivory exterior. All in all, the small house seemed cozy, well kept and inviting, to Zachary's way of thinking. But maybe that was because of the intriguing woman who lived there.

Lauren forced a wary smile as she approached the enigmatic man she had hired as her attorney. His legs were stretched out in front of him, his ankles crossed, and he was supporting his weight with his hands on the half wall. He wore a bulky-knit camel-colored sweater, tan cords and soft leather loafers. A slight breeze caught his dark hair, mussing it and softening the harsh angles of his face. He was still dressed down, but his casual attire and unconventionality only added to his sensuality. She felt comfortable with Zachary, relaxed. Maybe even the clothing was part of an act to gain her confidence. He'd acquired a reputation as a roguish lawyer, she reminded herself, and wondered just how unconventional, even dishonest, he might be if pushed.

At the sight of Lauren, a grin spread slowly across Zachary's face to display straight white teeth and the traces of what had once been a dimple in his cheek.

Despite the scandal of Zachary's past, and George West's doubts about his integrity, Lauren found that there was something reassuring about coming home to him. It seemed so natural and comfortable; she felt he was a man she could live with and enjoy. The mystery surrounding him and the seldom-seen twinkle in his eyes intrigued her. If it hadn't been for the fact that he was her attorney, hired for the specific purpose of finding her children, she could imagine herself falling for him. *Crazy,* she chided herself. *You're thinking like a crazy woman.*

Before she could say anything, he pushed away from the short wall and reached for the briefcase she had been juggling between her umbrella, her purse and the mail. "I thought I'd better come over and explain a few things," he began.

"A few things?" she echoed, attempting to keep the indignation out of her voice as she recalled her uncomfortable meeting with George West. "Like Joshua Tate and the Mason trust?" she asked, fumbling in her purse for her keys and finally unlocking the door.

Zachary averted his gaze. "For starters."

"Good." Her emerald eyes darkened with reawakened anger. "Because I've been hearing about it all day, and I hope to God that you've got some answers for me. Everyone at the bank thinks I'm out of my mind for hiring you!" She opened the door and tried to remind herself that this man was only her attorney, nothing more. If he was really interested only in using her, she'd have to get rid of him. *And then where will you be?* Her heart filled with desperation at the thought, and unconsciously her eyes moved to the portrait of Alicia and Ryan on the mantel.

"And do you think you're...uh, 'out of your mind'?" he asked.

"I don't know what to think. The way I've been treated the last few hours, you'd think I'd changed my name to Benedict Arnold!" She saw the unconscious tightening of his jaw and immediately felt remorseful. Unsteadily, she pushed aside the windblown wisps of hair that had pulled free of her chignon. "Oh, God, Zachary, I'm sorry," she said, her chin trembling slightly. "I didn't mean to take it out on you.... It's just that today has been a total disaster. If people weren't smothering me with sympathy, they were treating me as if I were some kind of traitor." She shook her head and closed her eyes wearily. "Dear Lord, I've made such a mess of this. I guess I shouldn't have gone on the air last night...."

"You did what you had to," he replied as he touched her shoulder reassuringly. "Now, what about you? Are you all right?"

The concern in his brown eyes touched her, and she nodded mutely, struggling to maintain her poise. "Yes...or I will be, once I calm down."

After she had tossed her coat over the back of the couch and set her briefcase on the rolltop desk, she quickly rewound the tape on the recording machine and listened for her messages. There was only one—it was from Zachary, explaining that he wanted to see her and felt it would be better if he came to her home rather than meet with her at the bank.

"I didn't think George West would appreciate my visit," Zachary said when Lauren turned off the machine.

"You thought right," she agreed with a mirthless laugh.

"I was surprised that you weren't here when I drove in, but I waited, figuring you'd show up."

"I had an unscheduled meeting with the president of the bank."

"Let me guess—the Mason trust."

"And the attorney representing it," she replied distractedly. Her thoughts weren't on George West or the Mason trust as she rewound the tape and turned off the recording machine. There was no call about Alicia or Ryan. No one who'd seen the program had contacted her. For a few seconds she couldn't turn around and face Zachary. She was bitterly disappointed—and angry at herself for putting too much confidence in the broadcasting of *Eye Contact*. Airing her problem had been a long shot, but Lauren had prayed that someone who had seen the show would be able to help her.

"It's only been one day since the program was aired," Zachary said quietly, as if reading her troubled thoughts.

"I know, but I thought—well, I hoped—that I'd hear something by now, while the program was still fresh in the audience's mind. I expected a quick response. The more time that goes by, the sooner the public will forget and the less likely I'll hear anything." She raised her hands, then let them fall limply to her side in a gesture of frustration.

"You don't know that," he said softly.

"It's been a long day, Zachary," she replied, shaking her head. "I just hoped—"

"That someone would call with information about your kids," he concluded, touching her gently on the shoulder.

"Yes." Tears threatened, but she refused to release them. She would not break down in front of him again. "I don't suppose you've come up with anything?" she asked.

"Other than a pain in the neck from my partner, no." He noticed that beneath the rich weave of her burgundy jacket, her shoulders sagged a little. Her fingers played distractedly with the silky tie of her pale pink blouse.

Zachary reached forward and tilted her chin up with one finger, forcing her to stare into his eyes. "It's only been one day for me, too," he told her, determination flashing in his eyes. "Give it a little time."

"Oh, Zachary, I have—it's been over a year!"

"Come on, let me buy you dinner."

Her frail smile faltered. She didn't want his sympathy or his kindness. Her feelings about him were confused enough as it was. Slowly, she shook her head. "I don't think so."

"You're beat."

"I know, but I think we have things to discuss."

"And we could just as well talk over dinner. I don't know about you, but I'm starved."

She hesitated. "What about the phone? Someone may call about the kids." Even as she said it, she realized that pinning her hopes on *Eye Contact* was probably foolish.

"Put on your answering machine again."

"Yes, I suppose you're right. There's no sense in waiting around for someone to call," she replied, and turned on the recorder. Zachary grabbed her raincoat from the back of the couch and slipped it over her shoulders as he led her back out the door.

The restaurant, which proudly boasted an authentic German cuisine, was a small, turn-of-the-century home that had been converted into an eating establishment.

Large maple trees still stood in what had once been a front yard. A redbrick path led to the open porch of the gray house, where an elegant hand-painted sign displayed the hours of operation in black letters. The entrance was softly illuminated by sconces mounted on either side of the narrow windows surrounding the carved oak door.

Zachary and Lauren were seated at a private table near the fireplace in what appeared to have been the living room of the cozy home. Glossy wooden tables were covered with ivory-colored linen cloths. The elegant wallpaper, frilly Austrian shades covering paned windows and hand-painted ceramic tiles over the fireplace were all a beautiful moss green. Fresh-cut flowers and brightly polished oak floors gave the restaurant a certain old-world charm that was enhanced by the softly glowing fire.

A waiter with a trim, waxed mustache, laughing blue eyes and a thick Bavarian accent brought the food and wine to the table. Lauren began to relax over the meal of thick brown bread, lentil soup and fresh trout. The conversation remained light and companionable, as if both she and Zachary were deliberately avoiding anything serious.

The tension Lauren had experienced all day seemed to drain from her as she sat with Zachary in the intimate surroundings of the restaurant. After a dessert of cinnamon-flavored apple strudel, Zachary ordered brandied coffee for them both.

"So," Zachary began as he settled back, cradling his warm drink and studying Lauren intently, "you already knew that Joshua had agreed to represent the Mason trust."

Lauren shook her head. "Not before I walked into the bank this morning. Apparently, George West received notice of the change in attorneys just yesterday."

Zachary observed Lauren over the rim of his cup as he drank. "And George guessed that I was your attorney?"

"Yes."

"How did he know?"

Lauren shrugged, and her finely arched brows drew together pensively. "Probably from Patrick Evans or Ned Browning in personnel. I suppose it really doesn't matter, though. When he asked about you, I told him that you had agreed to represent me . . . as of yesterday evening."

"*After* he'd learned that Joshua had taken on the Mason trust," Zachary muttered. "Great! He probably thinks I planned it that way. I don't suppose that West wants you to find another attorney?" he asked sarcastically.

"As soon as possible."

The muscles around Zachary's mouth tightened. "And?"

"I told him I wouldn't," Lauren replied softly, holding his gaze with her own.

Zachary smiled. "I doubt if he liked that."

"Not much he could do about it."

"He could fire you," Zachary said carefully, watching her reaction.

Lauren winced a little at the thought. She couldn't afford to be out of a job. "Not legally."

Zachary shook his head, and firelight reflected off the sable-brown strands of his hair. "He could find a reason, have your supervisor make the appropriate notes in your file, make it look as if you were doing unsatisfactory work."

"Sounds as if you've had some experience yourself in this type of deception, counselor," she observed uneasily. Just how ruthless was he?

"I've practiced law a long time. It wouldn't be the first case of fraudulent employee records I've come across."

Lauren held on to her cup with both hands and watched as the fragrant steam rose from the dark liquid. "I don't think George West would resort to those kinds of backstabbing tactics. Too obvious," she mused. "I've had good employment reviews so far. Besides, it's not his style," she reasoned, trying to convince herself as well as Zachary. "He's not the sneaky type, and I think he genuinely likes me. It would be my guess that if he felt he was being backed into a corner, he would transfer me to another department rather than do a hatchet job on my employment records. He would have it seem as if the transfer were a promotion and then make damned sure I had absolutely no access to any records surrounding the Mason trust."

"Except that you already have had access," Zachary reminded her. "If you wanted to give me any information on the Mason trust, you could have done it already."

Something in Zachary's tone struck a nerve. Lauren forced herself to look directly into Zachary's dark, probing eyes and ask, "Is that what you expected of me when you took my case?"

A muscle throbbed in the corner of his jaw. "Of course not. Last night I told you why I took your case."

"And I believed you," she replied, her face taut. "But you have to admit, it looks bad...very bad...for everyone involved."

"I know."

"And now that I've made the search for the kids a public issue, the press is involved," she continued, lowering her voice slightly.

"So what do you want to do?" Zachary asked.

"What I've wanted for more than a year," she replied softly. "I want to find my kids. And I want you to help me."

"What about the Mason trust?"

She glanced at the ceiling and shook her head. One hand lifted in a gesture of bewilderment. "I don't know," she answered honestly. "I guess I'll have to cross that bridge when I come to it."

Zachary was silent for a long, tense moment, and Lauren wondered what was going through his mind. Finally, he sighed. "I don't want you to risk your career, Lauren," he said, his voice grave with concern.

"There are other banks in Portland."

"But you're happy with Northwestern."

How well he could read her. Already. After knowing her only a few short weeks. Zachary Winters was more than shrewd—he was insightful, and this worried her a little. "Yes, I'm happy at the bank. At least I was."

"If it's any consolation, I tried to talk Joshua out of handling the Mason trust."

"And?"

"He flat-out refused, accused me of pulling rank on him."

Lauren set down her cup and smiled cynically as she remembered the first time she had set foot in Zachary's seldom-used office. Zachary's neglect and disinterest had been obvious. Joshua Tate had probably decided to take the bull by the horns. "Do you blame him?"

Zachary shook his head. "No. He's been waiting a long time for a big case—a chance to prove himself—and he sees the Mason trust as just that opportunity."

"He'll lose," Lauren predicted.

"Maybe so, but he's willing to gamble." Zachary's brown eyes burned into hers. "Just like you."

"Maybe he feels like me. That he's really got nothing to lose and everything to gain from the lawsuit."

"Maybe."

"Then I guess there's nothing either of us can do," she said. "I want you to find my children. And I trust you not to weasel information out of me about the Mason trust." Her green eyes suddenly turned cold. "It certainly wouldn't do any good to try."

She was about to get up from the table when Zachary's hand reached out and caught her wrist. His dark gaze burned with honesty, and in a low, intense voice he said, "I want you to know Lauren, that whatever else happens, I would never... *never* use you."

Her gaze moved from his face to her wrist and back again to the conviction in his dark eyes. Her heart began to pound.

"If you don't believe anything else," he continued, "know that you can trust me. Otherwise we have no reason to continue the search for your children. If I'm going to work with you, I'll have to know that you're with me—not against me."

She slipped her hand away from his. "All right, Zachary," she agreed, wondering how many words of his impassioned speech were sincere and how many were the well-rehearsed legal theatrics of a convincing trial lawyer.

In the end it didn't matter, she supposed, as long as Zachary continued to help her find Alicia and Ryan.

The short drive from the German restaurant in Sellwood was undertaken in a strained silence that made it impossible for Lauren to relax. Night had descended upon the city and the interior of the pickup was dark, illuminated only by the flash of oncoming headlights, or by the ethereal streetlights, which gave the city and the cab of the truck a bluish tinge. Rain poured from the heavens, spattering against the windshield before being pushed aside by the rhythmic wipers.

The subject of Joshua Tate and the Mason trust lawsuit had been left at the restaurant, and Lauren was too tired now to think about how the situation might affect her or her job. There was no point in spending her weekend second-guessing George West. Monday would come soon enough, whether she worried about her job or not.

Zachary braked slowly and parked the pickup by the curb in front of her house. He let the engine idle for a minute, his hand cocked over the ignition before he turned the key and allowed the rumbling motor to die.

In the silence that followed, rain began to collect on the windshield. "Would you like to come in?" Lauren offered, knowing that her business with him wasn't concluded and unable to face the cold, dark house alone. Once she had loved the little cottage across from Westmoreland Park, but now, without the sounds of the children's laughter and their high-pitched arguments, she could barely stand the place. The nights were the worst. She turned to face Zachary, the invitation still in her eyes.

God, if she only knew what she did to him, Zachary thought. "I do have a few more things to discuss," he admitted, avoiding her eyes and rubbing his hand around the back of his neck as he watched the headlights of an oncoming car. It roared past and sprayed the truck with water from the street. "But the questions won't be too pleasant."

"Will they help me find the kids?" she asked.

"I hope so."

Lauren supposed that was all she could expect. She didn't hesitate, despite the uneasiness she saw in the tense lines of his face. "Then, of course I'll answer them. Come on, counselor," she said, trying to dispel the growing tension between them, "just give me a few minutes to change and I'll make you a cup of coffee."

He smiled tentatively. "I can't turn down an offer like that," he said with a trace of reluctance as he grabbed his briefcase and helped her out of the pickup.

Once inside the house, Lauren quickly put on the coffee, then stepped into the bedroom. She took off her wool suit and donned a blue sweater and a pair of soft gray corduroy slacks. By the time she had changed, the water had run through the coffee maker and the kitchen was filled with the enticing aroma of freshly ground coffee. Zachary had taken it upon himself to start a fire in the living room, and as she poured the coffee into ceramic mugs, she could hear the pleasant sound of crackling flames igniting against mossy wood.

Zachary was on his haunches, leaning into the fireplace, when Lauren entered the living room. His sweater had pulled away from the waistband of his low-slung cords, and she stood there for a few moments, fascinated by the play of muscles in his back and thighs as he placed a chunk of oak onto the fire.

Suddenly he straightened, and the intensity of his stare told her that he knew she had been watching him. He dusted his hands together but didn't comment as she blushed and handed him a steaming mug. Sitting cross-legged on the floor near the warmth of the fire, she peered at his handiwork. "You sure you weren't an Eagle Scout?" she teased, trying to disperse the tension in the intimate room.

"Not on your life. My folks had a wood stove to heat their cabin in the Cascades. It was my job to start the fire every morning, and I learned quickly. It's pretty cold in the mountains at five in the morning. Even in June."

She laughed a little, enjoying the easy feeling of companionship. Then, deciding that she couldn't put off the inevitable any longer, she looked up at him through the sweep of long, black lashes and said, "Okay, counselor, what's up? You said you had questions."

"I need some more information," he replied, staring at her steadily as he sipped his coffee. He was leaning against the fireplace, one shoulder propped on the mantel.

As long as the questions don't have anything to do with the Mason trust. "Shoot." She took a long sip of her coffee and waited.

"I've started checking over everything I got from Patrick Evans and his investigator. So far I haven't found anything that will do us much good, I'm afraid. Evans is still the best in town, and his investigator was thorough."

"Oh." She couldn't hide her disappointment. "Nothing?"

"Not so far."

"Then what about the information from Tyrone Robbins?" she asked reluctantly, the name of the arrogant attorney nearly sticking in her throat. It was a long shot, but she had to make sure that Zachary had looked over every piece of evidence she'd given him.

Zachary snorted disgustedly. "What Tyrone Robbins came up with isn't worth the price of a snowball in Alaska."

Lauren felt her tired muscles stiffen. "I guess I already knew that much," she admitted.

"So why did you hire him?"

"A friend of mine gave me his name."

"Some friend," Zachary replied sardonically.

"You have to understand that I had never dealt with any lawyers, aside from those I knew from the bank, and I didn't think it would be wise to deal with someone in my capacity as a trust administrator as well as on a personal basis."

"As you're doing with me, because of the Mason trust."

"Exactly." She looked up at him apprehensively. "You have to admit, everything's become more complicated now that Tate's representing Hammond Mason and the rest of the beneficiaries."

His dark eyes glittered. "Go on. How did this 'friend' of yours come up with Robbins?"

"Sally, a girl I used to go to school with, gave me his name. He'd helped her with her divorce, and she claimed that he was... 'terrific,' I think was the term she used."

Lauren shuddered a little as she thought about Sally's earnest face. "Tyrone Robbins is the best in Portland," Sally had promised. "And his fees are... negotiable." The brunette had smiled knowingly, but Lauren hadn't questioned her words. At the time, Lauren had been frantic; Doug had just taken off with the kids. She'd needed a good attorney quickly and had latched on to Tyrone Robbins like a drowning woman to a life raft.

"Terrific?" Zachary shook his head. "You don't strike me as the naive type, Lauren. You work with lawyers every day."

"That was the problem."

"What about the guy who handled your divorce?"

"He moved out of the state," she answered, frowning. "Look, you have to understand that I was desperate and . . . well, I went to see Robbins. As far as I knew, he didn't represent any of the trust accounts I was overseeing, and he didn't have any ties with Northwestern Bank."

"And?"

She looked away from Zachary and stared into the fire. The flames crackled and hissed, and the scent of burning wood mingled with the aroma of the coffee. "Robbins seemed interested in helping me and . . . and . . ." Lauren's voice caught at the vivid memory of Tyrone attempting to unbutton her blouse after their second meeting, which had turned out to be an intimate dinner instead of the business meeting that had been planned. The turquoise silk had ripped as she'd pulled away from him, but neither that nor her violent protests had deterred him. If anything, her rejection had seemed to backfire, making him more bold. She still shivered as she thought about his soft hands clutching her bare shoulders. "It . . . didn't work out."

From the ashen color of Lauren's face, Zachary could well imagine what had happened. He knew from his own experience that Tyrone Robbins was a snake of an attorney who didn't deserve his license to practice law. Tyrone had twice been before the bar on charges that hadn't stuck. Somehow the slimy lawyer had always managed to avoid disbarment. Zachary felt the muscles at the base of his neck tightening in sudden rage at the thought of Tyrone's slippery hands on Lauren. He had to force himself to appear calm. "Do you want to talk about it?" he asked.

"Not particularly," she admitted, composing herself. "Let's just say that Tyrone Robbins seemed to think that he could help me find my children, or at least relieve some of my tension and lower his attorney's fees by seducing me. I didn't see it that way. When I finally convinced him he was wrong about me, he nearly tripped over himself with apologies, but I'd already decided to find another attorney."

"You could have sued him for malpractice," Zachary suggested darkly, imagining his fingers around Tyrone's throat.

"But that wouldn't have helped me find Alicia and Ryan." Lauren's color returned. "What happened with Tyrone was . . . an unpleasant situation that I decided to chalk up to experience."

"So that's when you hired Evans."

"Right. At that point I didn't care that Patrick worked with the bank. At least he was someone I could trust. I . . . well, I practically begged him to take my case." She set her cup on the hearth and leaned back against the couch. "That's why it took me over a year to end up with you; when Patrick couldn't find the kids, he recommended you."

"With some reservations, I'll wager."

"A few," she conceded. "So now, counselor, you know all of my darkest secrets, right?"

"Not quite."

"Pardon?" She heard the hesitation in his voice. "What're you talking about?"

"Your secrets. I need to know more about them."

"I don't understand."

"Specifically about the other people in your life—that is, the friends you had when you were married to Doug. It doesn't seem likely that he would disappear without a trace and not contact one single person in the last year. There must be someone he befriended, cared about enough that he would keep in touch."

"I already explained about our friends...."

"What about *his* friends? The ones you didn't meet."

Her blood turned cold as she realized what he meant.

"The other women, Lauren," he said, kneeling next to her. "Can you tell me the names of any of the women your husband was involved with during your marriage—or better yet, after the separation?"

"I don't know them," she replied, burying her gaze in the bright, hungry flames of the fire. "I told you that much last night. It was just easier if they remained nameless and faceless."

"But you're sure he was unfaithful?"

"Yes." Dear God, she was certain. Even when she'd tried to believe that Doug was not involved with other women, she'd known her hopes of his fidelity were futile and naive.

"How?"

Lauren shifted her eyes to his. "A woman knows," she said. "I... Look, I don't see what this is going to accomplish."

"Lauren, think! One of those women might know where Doug and the children are." Zachary's face was grim, as if he knew the pain he was putting her through. "Think back. Certainly you had your suspicions."

"Nothing I can prove."

Now he was getting somewhere. "Did you mention them to either Tyrone or Pat?"

"No... well, yes, but nothing came of it...."

"And you're sure you can't remember any names?"

Lauren looked away. "This—this isn't my favorite subject," she faltered, avoiding his gaze.

He reached out and grasped her shoulders, forcing her to face him. "Dammit, look at me," he ordered, his fingers tightening over her sweater. "I'm trying to help you. But I can't, not unless you tell me *everything*."

"I have."

His fingers continued to grip her upper arms, and his dark eyes pierced hers. "Then give me a name. You said yourself that a woman knows when her husband is having an affair. Surely there was one woman you think may have been involved with Doug." He pressed his hand against her cheek. "I know this is painful, but I don't have anyone else I can ask, Lauren. I have to trust your intuition."

As all the old memories, filled with torment and fear, resurfaced, Lauren found she was having trouble breathing. "Doug was very discreet," she said, her hands curling into fists of frustration as she forced herself to recall what she'd sought to blot out for so long—the grim, deceitful side of her marriage. "I never caught him...not on the phone, not going out." She paused for a moment. "Once, a woman called when he wasn't home, and I wondered... Well, nothing came of it."

"Did she leave a message or her name?" Zachary persisted, hoping for any shred of evidence, just one tiny lead.

Lauren shook her head. "No...she wouldn't say who she was. That's why I became suspicious."

"Damn." His hands fell to his sides. "I know this is hard for you," he murmured, pinching the bridge of his nose thoughtfully. "I wouldn't ask if I didn't think it would help, but it might be our only chance of finding your children.''

Lauren stared into the fire, trying to reconstruct the painful nights when she'd been alone in the double bed, waiting for Doug, knowing he was with another woman. In the beginning, she hadn't been sure he was lying to her. She'd forced herself to believe his excuses of working late, but eventually she'd been faced with the simple truth that he was having an affair, one of many.

Her hands twisted uncomfortably in her lap, and she had to clear her throat as she began to speak. ''There was one time,'' she whispered.

Zachary's eyes narrowed. ''What happened?''

Lauren fought to control the tears that were forming behind her eyes. She'd sworn that night nearly two years ago that she would never cry another tear for Doug Regis. It had been a promise to herself that she'd broken time and time again.

''Lauren?'' Zachary prodded, his voice filled with kindness.

''Doug had just gotten the job with Dickinson Investments,'' she began. ''He was ecstatic and came home with a bottle of champagne to celebrate the occasion. I thought…anyway, I *hoped* that this job would be a new beginning for us.'' She closed her eyes and forced her voice to remain steady. ''We drank the champagne and went to bed…and while we were making love…he called me by another woman's name.'' A solitary tear slid down her cheek, and she hurriedly brushed it aside. *No more tears, not for Doug.*

Zachary gritted his teeth as he saw the anguish in her glistening green eyes. All because of a bastard by the name of Douglas Regis. ''What was her name?'' he asked, tenderly touching her chin with the tip of his finger.

"I can't remember," she replied, pursing her lips. "Maybe I never wanted to know."

"Lauren, please. *Try*."

She sighed. "I don't know." Closing her eyes, she could almost see Doug's face, flushed from the alcohol in his bloodstream, as he bent over her and placed a sloppy kiss on her neck. "Oh, baby," he'd whispered thickly, stretching anxious hands over her abdomen and breasts. "Please..." And then, as painful as if he'd slapped her face, he'd called her by another woman's name.

Lauren's stomach knotted as she tried to concentrate. "I can't remember, but I think it was something common like Susan or Sandra or Sharon." None of the names sounded quite right. But then it had been several years ago, and she'd tried hard to forget that night.

"When you heard the name, you didn't connect it with any of the women you knew or that Doug may have worked with?"

"No." Every muscle in her body was taut with the memory.

Zachary rubbed his thumb tenderly along her jaw. "I'm sorry," he murmured, watching her reaction. Her cheeks were flushed, and the dark twist of her hair had begun to fall free, framing her face in tangled burnished curls that reflected the firelight. Her green eyes were filled with pain. It occurred to Zachary that Lauren might still be in love with her ex-husband, and that thought only served to harden the set of his jaw.

"It's okay," she said, sniffing a little and trying to regain her composure.

"Lauren, are you sure you want to continue looking for your children?"

"What?" Her head snapped up, and she saw that he was serious. "Of course I do."

"How will you feel when you see your ex-husband again?" he asked, damning himself for needing to know.

"Angry," she replied without hesitation.

"You're sure?"

"He's put me through hell. Every day I wake up wondering where Alicia and Ryan are, if they're all right, if they'll remember me, if I'll ever find them . . . if they're alive."

Zachary's eyes narrowed as he studied her. "I just want you to be certain that you're not in love with Doug, or out for revenge; that you're only thinking of the children."

"Of course I am," she snapped. "But if I weren't, would it matter?"

"It would to Alicia and Ryan."

She pointed a condemning finger directly into his face. *"What kind of a mother do you think I am?* All I want is to get my children back. What happens to Doug I don't care, except for how it will affect Alicia and Ryan."

"You're certain of that?" He leaned against the couch and searched the soft contours of her angry face.

"Yes."

"And the love you once felt for your husband?"

"Is dead. He killed it." Lauren took a deep breath, then returned her gaze to Zachary. It was imperative that he understand her. "I know that probably sounds callous, Zachary, but I loved Doug once, trusted him, dreamed with him, planned my life with him, and he didn't want me or the kids. That's what came as such a shock, I suppose, that he would take them away from me.

I *never* thought he would do anything so horrible. I didn't even think he wanted the kids, but I guess I was wrong. It was just me he didn't want.''

Zachary felt the need to comfort her, but she faced him dry-eyed. ''Don't get me wrong, I'm not feeling sorry for myself because I lost Doug; he and I were never right for each other, and I should have been smart enough to realize it before I married him. But I wasn't, and in one respect I'm glad I married Doug—because of the kids.'' She leaned back on the couch and ran her fingers through her hair. ''If only I could find them.''

She felt the hot tears begin to slide down her cheeks. How could she hope for Zachary to understand? ''Maybe you should go,'' she whispered. But when his strong arms encircled her waist, she didn't resist. She swallowed hard and tried to stop the tears. ''Look, Zachary, I can't wind up crying on your shoulder every night.''

''Sure you can,'' he said fervently, the passion in his voice startling her. ''Every night if you want.'' He kissed the top of her head tenderly, and she felt the warmth of his lips against her hair. She clung to him, glad of his strength and warmth. Her body was touching his, her hips and thighs fitting snugly against his muscular legs. ''You don't have to worry, lady,'' he said, ''I'll be with you . . . help you. . . .''

The doubts that had lingered with her for the better part of a day faded away silently. ''I trust you,'' she whispered, touching his rough cheek.

''That's how it's supposed to work between client and attorney.'' His lips brushed hers tentatively, and the tenderness of the gesture brought fresh tears to her eyes.

''You're almost too good to be true,'' she murmured.

''I bet you weren't thinking that this afternoon.''

''No . . . my thoughts about you were rather unkind.''

"I'll bet." His fingers reached up and slowly removed the pins from her hair. The auburn twist gently unwound to fall in a thick braid at her shoulders. Zachary's fingers twined in the red-brown silk and brushed against the curve of her neck. When his lips touched the hollow of her throat, she shivered with pleasure.

This can't be happening, she thought, but she couldn't find the words to halt what her body longed to feel. The pliant pressure of his tongue as it lazily rimmed her collarbone should have sobered her—should have reminded her of Doug, of Tyrone Robbins, of all the men who had used her—but it didn't. She was aware only of awakening feelings of desire, and she moaned Zachary's name in response.

His lips found hers and softly molded to her mouth. She reached forward and wound her arms around his neck, drawing him closer as the magic of his tongue gently urged her lips apart to taste the liquid warmth within. Gladly she opened to him, her blood beginning to race wildly through her veins, her heart pounding erratically.

You're a fool, she thought as the weight of his body pressed solidly against hers, forcing her to the floor in front of the fire. She felt his chest crushing her breasts and became vaguely aware that her sweater had slipped up as she felt the rough texture of the faded carpet rubbing against her skin.

Zachary saw the parted invitation of her mouth before he lowered his head and took her lips with his. Warmth invaded her body, filled her soul with yearning. It had been so long since she had been with a man, years since she had wanted to be caressed. But now she ached for more, wanting to be fulfilled by this man who had such power over her—over her future, over her happiness. Perhaps that was it—the danger of it all, the intrigue of becoming involved with the one man she shouldn't. Every instinct screamed that she was making a monumental mistake, but when she looked up and stared into the mystery of Zachary's eyes, she knew that she was lost to him....

He groaned her name aloud, an ancient agony ringing in his voice. His hand brushed over her ribs to capture one straining breast, and the silky fabric of her bra rubbed urgently against the budding nipple.

Dear God, how desperately she wanted him. Her skin was flushed from the fire in her blood, her lips were swollen with the sweet torment of his kisses. When he lifted the sweater over her head, she didn't resist, anxious to touch him, to feel his body molding to hers.

He tossed her sweater onto the couch and quickly added his own. When he once again faced her, his torso was bare. Dark hair curled over rock-hard muscles and arrowed downward to his belt, emphasizing the flat, rippling muscles of his abdomen.

He looked down upon her, his eyes smoldering. "God, you're beautiful," he murmured. His gaze lingered at the gentle swell of her breasts, the creamy skin rounding over the edge of the sheer bra. Beneath the white lace, rose-colored nipples protruded deliciously, invitingly. With tentative fingers, Zachary outlined the beautiful buds, his eyes returning to Lauren's heavy-lidded gaze. Tangled red-brown hair framed her face, and desire darkened her intriguing green eyes. Zachary had to fight the urge to strip her of the rest of her clothes and take her at once.

"I don't want you to do anything you might regret," he said, his voice husky with desire.

"I won't."

"You're certain?"

She hesitated, then sighed and slowly shook her head. "Oh, Zachary, I'm not certain of anything right now," she admitted.

Gently he kissed her forehead and twined his fingers in her long, shining mane. The flames from the fire reflected in his brown eyes, and Lauren wound her arms around his chest, holding him close, as if she were afraid he might vanish into the stormy night.

The feel of her pressed against his bare flesh made him groan in frustration. "If only you knew what you do to me."

When she tilted her face up to look at him, he brushed gentle lips across her cheeks and tasted the salt traces of her tears. She felt his muscles, taut with restraint, press against her thighs and hips.

He wants you, she thought, *with as much passion as you feel storming through your veins. He wants you. Tonight.*

"Lauren," he murmured against the fiery curtain of her hair, "I'm sorry."

She sensed his battle, knew that he was trying to restrain himself, and her heart wrenched at the desperation in his apology. Still, he didn't let go but held her more closely, his arms tightening around her as he willed the tides of passion to subside. "I . . . I shouldn't have let things go so far," he said softly.

With more strength than she thought herself capable of, Lauren pushed him gently away, hoping she would find the courage to tell him that what had happened tonight would never be repeated. But she couldn't. It would have been a lie.

Chapter Eight

Zachary kissed her forehead softly, his lips lingering against her skin. "I'll wait for you, Lauren," he promised, "until you realize that what I feel for you won't interfere with locating Alicia and Ryan, and you can give me some sort of commitment. I think you know how I feel about you."

Dear God, what was he saying? "I really can't think about any commitments other than that of finding the children," she said softly, hoping that he would understand.

Involuntarily, her eyes lifted to the mantel, to the picture of the two smiling children. God, what she would do just to see them again, talk to Alicia, watch Ryan smile.

"I just need time," she said, wondering if she were releasing the one man who might change her life. She knew that Zachary was asking for more than a simple night of passion; his feelings for her ran far deeper than a casual one-night stand. But Lauren wasn't ready for an affair—not when her life was so unbalanced. Loving Zachary and knowing that someday they would part was more than she could handle at the moment. Everyone she had ever loved in her life had abandoned her—first her parents, killed in the boating accident; then her husband, lost to fate and the wiles of other women; and now her children, taken from her so heedlessly by a man she had trusted. She couldn't bear the thought of learning to love Zachary only to have him leave her as had all the other people she'd loved.

That she was beginning to love him came as a surprise, and she told herself she was confusing love with dependence. She *needed* Zachary to help her find her children, not as a woman needs a man. She reached for her sweater, but Zachary's hand clamped firmly over her wrist.

"I want you, Lauren, but I won't push. I have to know that my feelings are returned."

"You know I care about you."

"Do you? Is it me or the fact that I might be able to find the children?"

"Both."

His thick brows drew together, and his eyes reached into hers, searching. "I won't push you, Lauren," he promised, relaxing the fingers on her wrist slightly, "but I'm not a patient man."

"And I'm not a patient woman."

His lips quirked in the hint of a warm smile. "Thank God for small favors."

She retrieved the sweater and pulled it hastily over her head, lifting the thick curtain of her hair through the neck and looking from Zachary to the picture on the mantel. Zachary saw her contemplative expression as she gazed at the portrait of the children. *First things first,* he reminded himself. Gently, he drew away from her and stretched his aching back and shoulder muscles. Then he stood and grabbed his sweater.

He hesitated a minute before dressing hastily. "I'd better go," he said when he saw the reluctance in her wide eyes, "while I still can."

She attempted a smile but failed. "I'm not trying to drive you away, you know. It's just that..." She lifted her palms expressively.

"You're going through a difficult period in your life. And you don't want anything to interfere."

"Yes." She caught her lower lip between her teeth. "I didn't think that you'd really understand."

He made a deprecating sound. "Oh, I understand, lady, probably better than I should." He picked up his briefcase and notepads and stuffed them under his arm. "Good night, Lauren." He turned on his heel and walked to the door. By the time that Lauren had managed to stand, he was gone.

Saturday and Sunday passed quickly but quietly. The phone didn't ring and Lauren didn't hear anything about the children. Nor did Zachary call or come over. The small house seemed strangely quiet and cold. When Zachary had finally left her on Friday night, Lauren had felt lonelier than she'd ever thought possible. Without the children the little house seemed gloomy, but without Zachary it suddenly felt like a cage without a key.

Lauren couldn't shake her dismal mood, and the weather didn't help. Throughout the starless night the rain had pelted the windows and gurgled through the overflowing gutters. Lauren had tossed and turned until early morning, caught up in restless, unresolved dreams of Alicia, Ryan and Zachary. In retrospect, the next morning, Lauren thought it odd that Doug hadn't been in the dream at all. Maybe subconsciously she'd decided that Douglas Regis no longer had rights as a husband *or* a father.

Trying to shake her moodiness, Lauren spent most of the rainy weekend inside the house, working on a project she'd been putting off for weeks—wallpapering the kitchen. Now that she'd been able to locate an attorney who had the expertise and desire to help her find the children, she could dedicate some time to the repairs and renovations the little house so desperately needed.

If the weather permitted, she also intended to stack the cord of wood lying haphazardly against the garage onto the back porch out of the rain.

"That's a tall order," Lauren told herself as she threw on a pair of her favorite faded jeans and a sweatshirt that still had splotches of house paint on it from the last project she'd completed. Eyeing the drizzly day outside, she started gluing wallpaper to the kitchen walls.

As she applied wet paste to the strips of wallpaper, Lauren considered the fact that she had been willing, even eager, to make love to Zachary the night before. Never had she wanted a man so desperately. Her feelings were completely irrational, she decided, and the sexual attraction she felt for him had to be ignored, at least until he'd located the children. She had to get Zachary Winters, the man, off her mind and concentrate on him only as the attorney she'd hired to find her children. The task proved impossible. She found that she was humming to herself and thinking of Zachary as she worked.

It took most of the weekend to finish the wallpapering, but by late Sunday afternoon it was done and most of the mess had been cleaned. Lauren looked at her han-

diwork with a practiced eye and smiled to herself. The
new print, a muted gray with a striped basket weave design in cream, tan and blue, gave the kitchen a much-
needed face-lift. She decided that next weekend she
would tackle painting the scratched wooden cabinets in
the kitchen. A solid ivory color would brighten the room
and complement the steel-blue counters. Her conscience
bothered her a little at the thought of the firewood still
lying on the wet ground, a tarp thrown hastily over the
top of the mound to protect it from the rain. *So much to
do,* she thought while sipping the final dregs of her cold
coffee and setting the cup aside, *and never enough time.*
"Oh, well, Rome wasn't built in a day," she told herself
philosophically as she headed for a hot shower to re-
move the dirt and relieve the aches in her tired muscles.

She'd showered, combed out her hair and was sipping
a mug of steaming hot soup when the phone rang. The
clock had just chimed five o'clock. Her first thought was
that the caller had to be Zachary, and her pulse began to
race as she answered the telephone.

"Hello?" she called into the receiver.

"Mrs. Regis?" asked an unfamiliar, weak female
voice.

*Someone who knows something about Alicia and
Ryan.* Her heart skipped a beat. "Yes?"

"My name is Minnie Johnson," the elderly voice said.
"I saw you on that program, *Eye Contact,* the other
night."

Lauren's palms began to sweat and her fingers curled
around the phone until her knuckles whitened. "And you
think you know where my children are?" she asked anxiously.

There was a pause. "Well, that's just it. I'm not sure,
but there are a couple of kids in this neighborhood, liv-

ing with their dad, about the right ages, y'know, and I thought that they might be yours. I really didn't know how to call you or whether I should, but I called the television station, couldn't get an answer and found your number in the book."

Lauren's thoughts were spinning crazily. This was the first positive piece of information she'd received in over a year. Though she knew that it might turn out to be only a coincidence that didn't involve Alicia and Ryan, she couldn't help the anticipation she felt. "Where do you live, Mrs. Johnson?"

"Out here in Gresham. East County."

Oregon. Less than thirty miles away. Tears began to gather in Lauren's eyes, and she had trouble keeping her voice steady. "Do you know the family?"

"Not much. Keep to myself most of the time, don't y'know? I don't get out much...." The old voice faded and then returned, with more conviction. "But I've seen the neighborhood kids."

"And they look like mine?"

"Yep. A girl 'bout seven or eight, I'd guess, and a boy a couple of years younger. The dad, he goes by the name of Dave Parker, but well, I figured that husband of yours could have changed his name easy enough."

Alicia will be seven in three weeks. Lauren's heart was thudding so wildly, she had trouble hearing the woman's soft responses. "And the children? Do you know their names?"

"No. I'm sorry. Like I said, I don't pay much attention, at least I didn't until I saw you on TV and put two and two together."

"I understand," Lauren replied, her hopes soaring. *Was it possible? Could Alicia and Ryan be barely a half hour away? All this time? Oh, God.* "But you think this boy and girl might be Alicia and Ryan?"

"That's why I called. Look," said the elderly woman, "here's the address." She repeated the street and cross street where the Parker family resided, and Lauren scribbled the information on the notepad near the phone.

"Thank you so much for calling," she said with heartfelt enthusiasm.

"You're welcome. I just hope those kids are yours, or if not, I sure hope you find yours soon. It's not right, a mother being away from her kids like that." There was a short pause in the conversation, as if the elderly lady wanted to say something more and then thought better of it. "Please let me know how it all turns out."

"Thank you, I will."

"I'm praying for you."

Tears of gratitude for the woman's kindness streamed from Lauren's eyes. "Thanks."

Lauren replaced the receiver and stared at the single piece of paper with the vital name and address. *Please,* she prayed, *let me find them.*

She dropped into the chair at the old desk and picked up the receiver again, anxiously punching out the number of Zachary's home. When he answered, she closed her eyes in relief.

"Hello?"

"Zachary, it's Lauren. I've got wonderful news! A woman just called and she thinks the kids might be in Gresham. She gave me the address. A man lives alone with two kids, about the ages of Alicia and Ryan. Can you believe it, right here in Oregon—"

"Hold on a minute," Zachary interrupted, then hesitated. He hated to burst her frail bubble of anticipation, but he had to be realistic. It was more than his job. He cared about Lauren and didn't want to see her hopes crushed again. "What makes the woman think they might be your kids?" he asked.

"She saw the picture of Alicia and Ryan on *Eye Contact*."

Zachary hesitated, and Lauren could sense his reluctance to share her enthusiasm. "That picture was nearly two years old," he reminded her.

"Just the same, she thinks Alicia and Ryan are there."

"I think it's highly unlikely that Doug is in Gresham."

Lauren knew that Zachary was just trying to force her to remain calm and prepare her for a possible—make that probable—disappointment. But this was her first real lead as to the whereabouts of her children! "We have to check it out," she said, her voice rising a little.

"Of course we do. In the morning—"

"Now!"

"Lauren, think about it. You can't go barging into a man's house at six o'clock at night, demanding to see his children. What if your information is wrong?"

"I have to know!"

"What you've got to do is keep things in perspective. Even if we go to Gresham and this guy, what's his name—"

"Dave Parker," she supplied impatiently.

"Even if Parker turns out to be Regis, which I doubt, what would you do?"

"Oh, God, Zachary, I'd hold my children," she said, her voice cracking. "I'd call the police, steal the kids, do *anything* I had to and then take them home with me."

"I don't think—"

"You don't *understand*!" she cried passionately. "It's been over a year since I've seen them, Zachary. *A year!*

I'm going out to that address and I'm going to find out if my children are there. I'm going with you or without you. Your choice.'' She tapped her foot angrily on the carpet, waiting for his response.

He muttered something unintelligible, then let out a breath of air exasperatedly. "All right. Wait for me. I'll be at your place in about . . . forty minutes."

"Good. I'll see you then." Lauren hung up and dashed into the bedroom, stripping off her robe and pulling on her favorite cream-colored slacks and a rose-hued sweater. After combing her hair until it shined, she repaired her makeup and then paced from the living room to the kitchen and back again, constantly checking the time while she waited impatiently for Zachary.

When she heard the familiar sound of his truck in the driveway, she grabbed her jacket and dashed out of the house clutching the precious piece of paper.

Zachary was halfway up the rain-slickened stairs and waited on the third step while Lauren locked the door. Her fingers were shaking and her cheeks were flushed. "Maybe you should stay here and wait," he suggested, seeing the hope shining in her beautiful green eyes. She was setting herself up for a monumental fall. He could feel it in his bones.

"Not on your life, counselor. I've waited over a year for this moment, and I'm not about to let you go alone." She was already down the short flight of stairs and striding toward his pickup with purposeful steps. He had to jog to catch her. When he was within arm's length, Zachary reached for her arm and twirled her around to face him, his fingers wrapping possessively over her coat sleeve. Zachary hated himself for what he had to do.

"I want you to be realistic, Lauren," he said as he felt the rain slip down his face. "This may be a disappointment, you know."

"I know that." She jerked her arm free. "But I can handle it," she assured him, turning back to the car. She was wasting precious time, time she could be spending with her children.

Lauren climbed into the pickup and slid to the passenger side of the cab. Zachary reluctantly followed her and shut the door. "You're sure...that you'll be okay—if this turns out to be a bad lead?"

Her green eyes burned into his. "I know the chances of this working out are slim, Zachary. But I can't help the fact that I'm as nervous as a cat about the possibility of facing Doug again and seeing Alicia and Ryan." In the fragile light of evening, her eyes narrowed into angry slits. "You can't possibly imagine the hell it's been for me this past year. Now, maybe—just maybe—I'll see Ryan, talk to Alicia, hold them both again . . . forever."

"If they're really in Gresham."

She smiled uncertainly, her incredible eyes darkening somewhat. "I can handle it if this all blows up in my face," she promised, her lower lip trembling.

Zachary sighed and settled behind the wheel. He could tell that there was no changing Lauren's mind. "Okay, I just have one condition."

She turned her head in his direction. "What's that?"

"That I go to the door, ask the questions." His dark eyes impaled hers. "Without you."

"Why?" she asked suspiciously.

"If Doug sees you, he may decide to bolt. And that's the last thing we'd want, considering what you've already been through."

"How could he?"

"The same way he did last time. He might get scared, pack the kids in the car tonight and run. Are you willing to take that gamble?"

"No," she whispered. She didn't think she could face losing the children a second time.

"Okay. So I'll go to the door. You stay in the truck and we'll see if the old lady knows what she's talking about."

"You're saying that even if my children are there, I won't be able to see them."

"I think it might be best," he agreed as he inserted the key into the ignition. "It's more important that we get them back to you for good rather than just for a quick look. Agreed?"

"Agreed," she said, wondering how she would be able to restrain herself if, indeed, the children were her beloved Alicia and Ryan.

Dave Parker was not Douglas Regis. Not by a long shot. As Zachary stared into the inquisitive brown eyes of the short man, he knew without a doubt that Lauren's hopes would be cruelly dashed once more. Silently, he cursed himself for letting Lauren talk him into bringing her out to Gresham on this wild-goose chase.

"Yes, I'm Parker," the man had replied to Zachary's inquiry. Dave Parker's face was honest; he didn't seem to be hiding anything, and Zachary had seen enough bluffs on the witness stand to recognize honest curiosity. "And I've got an eight-year-old daughter and a four-year-old son." Parker frowned a little at the visitor's unlikely questions. "Why are you interested in Ellen and Butch? What's all this about?"

"A mistake, I'm afraid," Zachary admitted with a disarming grin. He caught a glimpse of a red-haired girl standing behind her father. The girl bore very little resemblance, if any, to Lauren's Alicia.

Zachary explained that he was a local attorney who was representing Lauren Regis, a woman who was desperately searching for her lost children.

"And you think I could help you?" Parker was clearly dubious.

Zachary shifted from one foot to the other. "We're checking out every possibility, no matter how remote."

"But I've never heard of this guy—Regis, or whatever his name is, and the kids don't have any classmates by the names of Alicia or Ryan...." He lifted his shoulders. "Sorry. I'd like to help the lady, but I can't."

Parker followed Zachary back to the pickup, his children following happily in his wake despite the rain and their lack of jackets.

"You kids go inside," he growled good-naturedly as he approached Lauren's side of the truck, "before you get soaked to the skin. Go on. Scat." The children ignored their father, and Parker turned to Lauren as she rolled down the window. She looked into the curious faces of the two small children and realized with a severe sense of disappointment that she was no closer to locating Alicia and Ryan than she had been a year ago.

"Hate to disappoint you," Parker said regretfully, "but I've never heard of your husband or your kids. Whoever told you that I might have some information about them gave you a bum steer."

"It's okay, Mr. Parker—"

"Dave."

"Dave," she repeated with a courageous smile. Her eyes returned to Parker's children. Though the girl held no resemblance to Alicia, the blond boy with the round blue eyes did have facial characteristics similar to Ryan's. Lauren's heart began to ache all over again.

The two kids scampered around the back end of the truck after Parker glared at them in mock anger.

"Sorry I can't be of more help," he concluded as Zachary opened the door of the truck. "I can't imagine why anyone would think that I would be able to help you."

"Just an anonymous tip," Zachary replied, handing the short man his business card. "If you do learn anything, please call me, either at the office or home."

"Will do." Dave smiled at Lauren and then turned his attention to his children. "Come on, you two, dinner's probably burned already. We'd better eat and then you've got some homework to attend to." He patted his daughter's head affectionately.

Lauren watched the retreating figures wearily. She leaned her head against the back of the seat and fought the urge to cry.

"I should have listened to you," she said, forcing her gaze out the window as Zachary started the truck and eased into the uneven flow of traffic. He shifted gears, and then his large hand covered hers.

"You couldn't. You were too excited."

"And foolish."

"It's not foolish to want to see your kids, Lauren," he said, his voice soothing, "but you've got to face the fact that this is just one of what might be a long string of false starts. Your ex-husband is clever, and he definitely doesn't want to be found. Unless I miss my guess, he's in another state . . . or country."

Lauren shook her head despondently. "We may never find them," she whispered as the black void of uncertainty loomed before her.

"Sure we will." He lifted his hand to the side of her face and gently brushed aside a tear with his thumb. "It's just going to take time, that's all."

The next two weeks were tedious. The tension in the bank was so thick that at times Lauren felt as if she would scream. On the first Monday back on the job, she'd been informed by George West that due to the circumstances involving her relationship with Zachary Winters, the Mason trust was no longer under her administration. From that day forward, Bob Harding would be in charge of the account.

Bob had regarded her with woeful eyes, knowing that she saw the transfer of authority as a slap in the face. Lauren tried to tell herself that it didn't matter, that the Mason trust was more trouble than it was worth, but she felt a little disappointed that the president of the bank had so little faith in her integrity.

"Be thankful you've still got a job," she told herself two weeks later as she reflected on the last several days.

After Minnie Johnson's call, what had started out as a trickle had quickly become a flood. Lauren was deluged with messages on her recording machine from people who were certain they had seen her children. Both she and Zachary sifted through the information, sorting fact from fiction, fantasy from truth, crank calls from sincere offers of help. Nothing had come of any of the leads, and with each passing day Lauren had grown more dejected. Sometimes the enormity of the task made finding her children seem impossible.

Working so closely with Zachary had been difficult. The attraction she felt for him continued to grow steadily, though, true to his word, he'd made no more advances upon her. She watched him while he sat at her kitchen table, and a warmth spread through her. His glasses were perched on the end of his nose as he meticulously went over each piece of information that came in. His legal pads were filled with notes to himself, clues to check, ideas beginning to hatch. *If nothing else,* she thought, *he's thorough.* And that's what she wanted. Lauren didn't doubt that, given enough time, Zachary would find the children. Her fears rested on the length of time involved. As each day slipped into the next, she felt the chasm between herself and the kids widening. Would they remember her? Would they run and hide when she opened her arms to them? When, oh, God, when would she see them again? Only time would tell.

Despite the worries clouding her mind, Lauren found that the conversations and quiet time she shared with Zachary had come to mean a lot to her. She welcomed the sound of his voice, smiled when she heard his truck in the driveway. And Mason trust or not, she was glad she'd hired him as her lawyer, for he was fast becoming her friend. Occasionally an unspoken invitation lingered in his dark eyes; she knew she had only to accept and they would become lovers.

The hours they spent together seemed to strengthen a bond between them. Lauren began to feel as if Zachary were as committed to finding the children as she was. She also knew that once the children were safely home, there would be no reason to see him, and his interest in her would certainly wane. Today she represented a challenge; once the children were found, he would go on to the next seemingly impossible task.

Though he was still kind to her, it seemed to Lauren that he'd purposely built a wall around himself...and under the circumstances, she thought it was a wise precaution. She reasoned that he'd finally realized an affair with her would be too sticky, what with the Mason case and all. Only once in a while, when he thought she wasn't looking, did she catch him staring at her with a flame of passion in his intense brown eyes.

Friday didn't come soon enough to suit Lauren. The hours at the bank were torture. Though she still worked on the private trusts, the fact that she was excluded from all conversation regarding the Mason trust drove her to distraction. Bob Harding would still drop by her office to chat, but even he seemed distant, nervous whenever the conversation strayed to the forbidden territories of Hammond Mason, Zachary Winters or Joshua Tate.

For once Lauren was relieved to return to her lonely house in Westmoreland. She didn't mind that the weekend stretched before her. Anything was better than the tension at the bank. She kicked off her shoes, rewound the tape on the recording machine and was disappointed that no one had called with information about the children.

After changing into comfortable jeans, a thick plum-colored sweater and worn tennis shoes, she stood in her bedroom and began extracting the pins from her hair. She was just shaking it loose when she heard the familiar rumble of Zachary's truck. Glancing into the mirror, she noticed that she was smiling. Like it or not, she was falling in love with the man.

She was already at the front door when Zachary knocked.

"I didn't expect you tonight," she said, not bothering to hide her pleasure at seeing him.

"I thought it was time for a change," he replied cryptically, and for the first time in two weeks, he drew her into the possessive circle of his arms.

"A change, counselor? What kind of change?"

"Of scenery."

"Oh?"

"Pack your things. We're going to the coast," he said, kissing her lightly on the forehead.

"Tonight?"

"Right now."

"But I can't," she replied, trying to pull out of his persuasive embrace.

"Why not?" He nuzzled her neck and a tingling sensation whispered across her nape. "I've been as patient as I can, lady, and I won't take no for an answer."

A dozen excuses formed in her mind, all of them sounding incredibly frail. "I might get a call—"

"The machine will take care of it."

"Someone might come by—"

"They'll come back or leave a message."

"But Alicia and Ryan. Maybe someone is bringing them home to me right now...."

Zachary tightened his arms around her and lifted his head to gaze into her eyes. "You and I both know that's not going to happen." One finger reached up and traced the worried arch of her brow. "What are you afraid of, Lauren? Is it me?"

"Of course not."

"Did Doug hurt you so badly that you're afraid to be with another man?"

"No."

"I promise that I won't ask you to do anything you don't want," he vowed, his dark eyes gazing intently into hers.

"I know that." For two weeks he'd kept to himself, treating her casually, remaining distant. She knew she could trust him with her life, but she wasn't so certain about her own feelings.

"We both need a break," he reasoned persuasively. "You more than I. The sea air will give us each a chance to think differently, more clearly, and when we get back, who knows? Maybe we'll just solve this riddle."

"You don't believe that any more than I do," she challenged.

"You won't know until you give it a try."

He was trying to buoy her spirits, and they both knew it, but Lauren couldn't fault his judgment. "All right, counselor," she said with a coy toss of her head, "you've got yourself a deal."

"Finally," he groaned, and released her. "So come on, get a move on. I'd like to get to the cabin before midnight."

Without further argument she went into the bedroom, threw a few things into her overnight bag and paused only for a moment to consider the fact that she was about to spend a weekend with a man for the first time since she'd been married. She should shrug it off, she thought, be a little more avant-garde, but she couldn't. She was falling in love with Zachary Winters, and the decision to spend a weekend alone with him couldn't be made lightly. Though it wasn't as if she were a seventeen-year-old virgin dashing off to a midnight rendezvous with her college boyfriend, Lauren wasn't the kind of woman who could sleep with a man and forget him overnight.

"Second thoughts?" he asked, suddenly standing in the doorway to the bedroom, leaning one shoulder against the jamb.

"A few."

His shoulder slumped a little, and he raked his fingers through his sable-dark hair. "You want to talk about them?" he asked, his eyes kind and understanding.

She gathered her courage and faced the obvious—she was falling in love with Zachary Winters. Avoiding him or denying her own physical urges wouldn't stop that. "Sure. But let's wait till we're at the beach," she replied, caressing him with her eyes. With renewed determination she snapped the overnight bag closed and lifted it from the bed. "After you, counselor."

Chapter Nine

The small cabin was positioned on a cliff high above the ocean offering what Lauren supposed was a commanding view of the stormy Pacific Ocean. As Zachary drove down the short lane to park near a dilapidated garage, Lauren squinted through the windshield for her first peek at the rustic coastal retreat.

"Here it is," Zachary announced as he stared at the cabin in which he had last seen Rosemary alive. "Home away from home." He turned off the ignition and looked at Lauren. "I guess we'd better go inside."

Though she detected a note of reluctance in Zachary's voice, Lauren was anxious to see the cabin and get a glimpse of the personal side of Zachary's life. Although she had spent as much time with him as was possible in the past two weeks, she realized that she didn't know much more about him personally than she had on the first day she'd entered his office nearly a month before.

Grabbing her overnight bag, she dashed through the slanting rain and down a slightly overgrown path. Zachary was right behind her. He carried his canvas bag as well as the sack of groceries they'd purchased at the market in Cannon Beach. He also managed to train the beam of a flashlight onto the sandy path leading to the front door of the cabin.

The wind blowing off the ocean howled and threw Lauren's hair into her face. Raindrops fell heavily from the black sky and splashed against her cheeks to chill her skin. The salty smell of the ocean permeated the air. Lauren paused for a moment to scan the dark, westerly sky and listen to the roar of the surf, but Zachary nudged her forward.

"I just want to see the ocean," she said over the sound of the ocean and rising wind.

"It's too dark. Wait till we're inside and I'll try to switch on the exterior lights."

With one last glance at the inky, raging ocean, Lauren followed Zachary to the door.

After several attempts, he was able to turn the key in the seldom-used lock and reach inside to snap on the lights. He propped the door open with his body and cocked his head toward the brightly lit interior. "Go on in. It's not much to look at, but at least we'll be alone."

That thought was all the encouragement she needed to carry her over the threshold. Two solid days alone with Zachary. No phones, No Mason trust or Northwestern Bank, she thought gratefully. Then she realized that also there were still *no children*. Despondently, she walked through the doorway and into the tiny cabin overlooking the ocean.

The furniture was worn, but sturdy; a few mismatched pieces seemed to blend into a comfortable eclectic design. The walls were yellowed pine, the ceiling boasted exposed beams and the windows were composed of small panes, most of which faced west toward what she suspected was a panoramic view of the ocean. A corner fireplace of blue stone was blackened and empty, and the cabin felt cold, as if it hadn't been lived in for years.

Zachary tossed his overnight bag onto the couch and set the paper grocery sack on the counter separating kitchen from living area. "I haven't been here in a while," he admitted as he watched her look around.

"How long?"

He shrugged as if her question were insignificant, and his lower lip protruded thoughtfully. "I don't know—four, maybe five years."

"Why not?" She eyed the cabin discerningly. It could be a warm, comfortable home away from home, and she would have expected Zachary to spend quite a bit of time here.

"I don't know," he replied. "Too busy, I guess."

"With all the work at the office?" she quipped, not intending to sound sarcastic. He looked up sharply and impaled her with dark, knowing eyes. "I'm sorry," she said quickly. "I didn't mean it the way it sounded." She tossed her jacket over the back of the couch.

"This place brings back a lot of unpleasant memories," he admitted, obviously uncomfortable with the subject. His gaze moved familiarly over the objects in the room; the slightly worn, wine-colored couch, an overstuffed tan chair, two scratched end tables.

For the first time Lauren realized that Zachary was referring to his dead wife. Hadn't Bob Harding told her that Rosemary, Zachary's wife, who had been pregnant at the time, had been killed in a single-car accident near the coast? It had probably happened while she and Zachary were spending a quiet weekend together. No wonder he hadn't returned to the little cabin overlooking the ocean. Rosemary, the beautiful wife he had adored, had died not far from here.

Lauren rubbed her hands over her forearms as if experiencing a sudden chill. "I didn't mean to pry."

"You didn't." He started toward the door. "Why don't you try to find your way around the kitchen? I'll work on the fire, if I can find any dry wood."

"Just like home," she said, thinking about the comfortable routine they'd established together the past couple of weeks at her home in Westmoreland.

Zachary hesitated at the door, his gaze momentarily locked with hers, and he flashed her an endearing smile that warmed her heart. "Yeah, just like home."

She familiarized herself with the rustic kitchen as she reheated the Irish stew they'd purchased at a restaurant near the grocery store in Cannon Beach, warmed French bread and tossed a salad. Zachary worked at the fireplace, alternately cursing the poorly functioning damper and stoking the sodden logs that had to be coaxed to ignite.

An hour later they had consumed the hearty meal and were sitting together on the floor of the living room, boots discarded, bare feet warming on the stone hearth. Zachary's arm was around Lauren's shoulders, and her back was propped against the burgundy couch as she sipped clear wine from a cut-glass goblet.

When the conversation began to lag, Lauren listened to the storm and imagined she heard the powerful breakers pounding the rocky beach with thunderous intensity. The wind whipped noisily around the tall grass surrounding the cabin and through the contorted pines that clung to the rocky cliffs.

"So who keeps this place up for you?" Lauren asked as she sipped her wine.

"There's a maid service in Cannon Beach. Someone comes in once a month, more often if I request. I called them early in the week and asked that someone clean the place before we arrived. I didn't think you'd want to spend the weekend dusting furniture and mopping floors."

"Oh, I don't know. I'm pretty good at it. Lots of practice, you know," she said, smiling. "Besides, the company would have been great." She looked at him, her eyes twinkling. "And you would have gotten all of the hard work. I don't do windows."

"What you do, lady," Zachary said, his voice low, "is fascinate the hell out of me."

Caught off guard, she looked into his eyes and was lost in the depths of his dark, omniscient gaze. She twirled the wineglass nervously in her fingers. Reflections of the fire's shadows caught in the glass, seeming to turn her wine golden. "What would you have done if I'd had other plans this weekend?" she asked.

"I thought about that." He turned his gaze back to the quiet flames. "I decided to come back here anyway."

"Alone?"

He looked up sharply. "What kind of question is that?"

"I just wanted to make sure that I wasn't the third or fourth woman who was offered an invitation."

Zachary laughed hollowly and shook his head. A lock of sable-brown hair fell over his eyes, and he pushed it away. "You shouldn't have to ask."

"I don't know much about you," she said. "And you know everything about me. My life is a series of files, cross-files, notes on legal pads and tapes. You've examined my work record, my marriage, even my sex life."

"Does that make you uncomfortable?"

"A little."

Zachary studied her luminous green eyes and frowned. "I had to ask all those questions. I needed to know everything about you and your family life in order to start searching for your children."

"I know, but in the process you've managed to avoid any questions about *your* private life."

"I'm the attorney, remember?"

She set her empty glass on the raised hearth and turned to look at him. "But not tonight, right? Tonight has nothing to do with finding the kids, or the fact that I hired you. Tonight we're here as friends."

"At least," he replied, smiling.

"Then you understand."

"What? That I should tell you everything there is to know about me? I'm afraid I'd bore you to tears."

"Not a chance, counselor," she disagreed with a cautious grin. "And I don't want to know everything, I suppose," she pointed out, catching her lower lip between her teeth. "Though it would be nice. I guess what I really wanted to know was that you weren't seriously involved with another woman."

He laughed. "Keeping up that kind of relationship would be a little difficult, don't you think, considering the amount of time I've spent with you lately."

Lauren knew she was blushing and wished there was a way she could stop. "I just wanted to be sure."

"Oh, Lauren, if you had any idea what I've been going through the last couple of weeks . . . seeing you, talking with you, working with you and not being able to touch you." His dark eyes searched hers. "I thought I'd go out of my mind."

"That works two ways, counselor," she said, smiling uncertainly.

"You're a tease, you know," he remarked, setting down his empty glass.

"Hardly."

He brought his face close to hers and looked deeply into her eyes. "I should have ignored all your ridiculous reasons for keeping me at arm's length."

"I don't remember saying anything ridiculous." Lauren swallowed with difficulty. His warm breath caressed her face, and his eyes—God, his gentle brown eyes!— seemed to be looking into her soul. Her heart began to pound.

"I'm too old to play games," he said.

"I don't think you're exactly over the hill."

"But I'm tired of playing cat and mouse with you. It's child's play. Both of us have been married before. We know what it means to be intimately involved with someone who is important to us." He shifted a little and settled back, caressing the nape of her neck with his fingers.

She forced her eyes to meet his directly. "What are you asking, Zachary?"

"Only that you accept your feelings for what they are and that you don't hide behind any excuses—your marriage, your kids, the Mason trust lawsuit. All of that is back in Portland. This weekend, it's just you and me."

"Naked to the world?" she asked, trying to dispel the tension in the room.

"To each other." He brushed her lips softly with his, and Lauren closed her eyes. She felt him shift his weight and realized that she was slipping backward onto the heavy braided rug. She didn't care.

The pressure on her lips increased as Zachary's passion intensified. His kiss deepened, and willingly she parted her lips to the supple invasion of his tongue. The pounding of her heart echoed in her ears, and she felt the dormant fires of womanly need ignite deep within her.

His hands found the hem of her sweater and he slid it slowly up her back, warming her skin, fanning the restless flames of her desire. She felt his thumb outline the back of her ribs, tracing sensual circles against the muscles of her back.

"Let me love you," he whispered into her ear. He lifted the sweater over her head and stared down at the beauty of her breasts straining against the sheer lace of her bra. His head lowered, and he kissed the dusky hollow between the luscious mounds, letting his tongue slide up to press against the hollow of her throat. Her pulse quivered expectantly.

Deftly, he unbuttoned his shirt and tossed it aside. Lauren feasted her eyes on his rock-hard abdomen and chest, bronzed and glistening in the golden glow of the fire. Beads of sweat had collected on his forehead, and his corded shoulder muscles vividly displayed the restraint under which he held himself.

Lauren twined her fingers in the thick waves of his dark hair, and she moaned his name when his fingers found the catch of her bra and released it, allowing her breasts to fall free. The tip of his tongue touched one dark peak and then the other, the nipples hardening expectantly. Lauren had to fight the urge to plead for an end to the exquisite torture, to beg him to fill her aching body with his.

"I love you," he whispered, and Lauren found herself wanting desperately to believe his words. No one, except perhaps her two small children and her dead parents, had ever loved her. Certainly no man had ever really cared about her.

Gently, he rotated their bodies, positioning her above him. His hands gently massaged the muscles of her back as he stared into her flushed face. He pressed her forward with his palms, took one taut nipple between his lips and slowly suckled.

Lauren was supporting her weight with her hands placed on the carpet on either side of Zachary's face. As he filled his mouth with the ripeness of her breasts, she threw back her head and let the exquisite sensations overtake her. While he feasted from one creamy mound, his hands massaged the other ripe peak, preparing it for the plundering of his lips and tongue.

A sheen of sweat dampened his skin and reflected in the fire's glow; every muscle of his body was taut. Her fingers traced the outline of a male nipple, and Zachary sucked in his breath.

"Oh, God, Lauren," he murmured, his eyes closing with the feel of her fingers against his skin. "Let me love you and never stop."

He touched the waistband of her jeans, and his fingers pressed urgently against the velvet-soft skin of her midriff. She heard the zipper slide down, felt the gentle tug of her jeans as they slid over her hips and down her calves.

Her heart was throbbing by the time he'd removed her jeans and his own. Then his lips captured hers once again. His arms encircled her waist, pressing her against him, letting her feel the urgency of his need. Touching her intimately, he pushed her to the floor and covered her yielding body with his own.

His fingers caressed her thighs and kneaded her buttocks until she groaned in exquisite agony.

"Zachary, please," she pleaded. "Please, love me."

"I do, sweet lady," he replied, lowering himself upon her and gently urging her legs apart with his knees. "I'll love you forever, if you let me."

"Oh, God, yes," she cried, as she felt the warmth of his body gently pierce hers. She gasped as he settled upon her and began to fill her with swift, sure strokes of love that urged her higher, forced her soul to soar in physical and spiritual ecstasy.

Moist heat surged within her, urged forward with the possessive thrusts of Zachary's body. Her breath came in short, shallow gasps until she felt the splendor of his lovemaking explode in a series of earth-shattering waves that ripped through her body as well as her mind.

He fell against her, crushing her breasts with his weight, pressing her back into the soft coils of the rug. In the fire's glow, with the sound of the sea thudding tirelessly against the beach, they lay entwined in spirit and body, one man and one woman.

Lauren had never felt more secure with a man in her life.

"I do, you know," he said at length as he gazed down upon her and stared into her intense green eyes. Her hair fanned seductively over the tan carpet, framing her face in long, fire-gilded curls.

"Do what?"

With a reluctant shake of his head, he rolled to his side, one hand resting possessively at the bend in her waist. "I love you." He said the words sincerely, all the while staring into her eyes. Lauren didn't doubt that at this moment, while they were away from the strain of the city, locked in intimate embrace, Zachary meant what he said; he truly loved her.

"And I love you," she whispered. *Only it isn't just for this night, or for the weekend, or a year. I'll love you forever.*

He smiled softly. "Then I think we should do something."

"Do something?" she repeated. "What're you talking about, counselor?"

"I think we should consider the fact that you could get pregnant."

She nodded absently. "I'd thought of that."

"And?"

"And I'm not ready to raise a child alone...at least not until I can find my other children. It would be...like giving up, almost...betraying them somehow."

"Shh." He took her hand in his and held it. "That's not what I meant. I would never expect you to care for my child, our child, alone." He nodded slightly, as if emphasizing his words. "When the time comes, I want to be a part of his or her life; but right now..."

Obviously, Zachary was caught up in the moment, and Lauren couldn't find the strength to bring him back to reality. "I understand," she murmured.

"I don't think you do," he said, his eyes never leaving hers. His hand moved upward to stroke her cheek. "I love you, Lauren. And I want to marry you."

For a moment she was silent. He couldn't mean it! "Just because we made love, you don't have to propose," she said with a tremulous smile.

"Making love has nothing to do with it," he said. "Being in love does. I'd ask you to marry me tomorrow if it weren't for the fact that I want to find your kids, resolve the problems with the Mason trust lawsuit and put all the past behind us before we start a future together. I think we should start out on the right foot."

God, how desperately she wanted to believe him. "I...I don't think we should...spoil this weekend with what-ifs and maybes and whens," she said. "Let's just take one day at a time and forget about all the problems in Portland. That's what this weekend was all about, wasn't it, counselor? No heavy stuff?"

He smiled that special, rakish smile that touched her heart, glanced at the ceiling and back to her again. "Right, lady. No heavy stuff. At least not tonight."

He tugged gently on her arm, forcing them both to stand, and kissed her passionately. Then, lifting her off her feet, he headed for the small alcove that served as a bedroom—the bedroom he had shared with Rosemary.

Lauren tried to forget her jealousies of a wife long dead, but she couldn't quite shake the feeling that she was trespassing on private property.

"What's wrong?" Zachary asked as he gently lowered her onto the bed. The ice-blue comforter was cold against her bare skin.

She looked at him with eyes filled with love. "Just hold me, darling," she murmured, clutching him to her and ignoring her doubts. Tonight she was with Zachary, and nothing else, save her concern for her children, would disrupt the bliss she felt in his arms.

"Willingly," he said as his lips claimed hers in a kiss that promised to last all night long.

Lauren awoke to the odors of perking coffee, sizzling bacon and burning wood. She was alone in the bed but could hear Zachary rustling around in the kitchen. She smiled to herself and stretched, looking around the bedroom for the first time. The gray light of morning filtered into the room through lacy curtains. Near the sturdy maple bed, there was an antique dresser with an oval mirror, and a small desk was pushed into a corner of the room. The walls were the same yellowed pine as the rest of the cabin, but the plank floor was bare and felt cold to her feet as she lowered herself from the bed.

Zachary had placed her overnight bag near the foot of the bed, and she zipped it open, threw on her robe and reached for her brush. After cinching the tie of the royal-blue robe around her waist, she stood before the mirror and tried to brush the tangles free from her long auburn hair. She stared at her reflection and wondered just how many times Rosemary Winters had stood before this very mirror.

Tossing off her morbid thoughts, Lauren headed for the kitchen. Zachary was busy at the stove. A smile tugged at the corners of her mouth when she noticed that he was dressed in the same gray sweatshirt and navy running shorts he'd been wearing the first time she'd seen him. The sleeves of the sweatshirt were pushed up to expose his forearms as he poked the bacon. Sweat was running down his face and had collected in a dark V on his chest as well as his back, discoloring his shirt. A fluffy orange towel was looped over his neck. It was obvious that he'd just returned from a long run along the beach.

Realizing he was being watched, he looked up and offered Lauren a devastating smile. "About time you woke up," he said as he walked over to her and circled his arms around her small waist. "God, you look good."

"And you look like you're on the way to work," she joked, eyeing his lean frame.

"Not funny, lady," he replied with a wave of the spatula, his dark eyes sparkling. "Any more talk like that and

I'll wreak my vengeance on you and have my way with you right here—on the kitchen floor.''

"Promises, promises." She laughed, and Zachary thought it was the most precious sound he had ever heard.

"I'm warning you," he said as he dropped the spatula and gripped her shoulders, pulling her unresisting body against his. Lazily his lips claimed hers, and she parted her mouth, ignoring everything but the tides of desire beginning to flood her senses. His fingers undid the tie at her waist to explore the hidden valley between her breasts. "You make me crazy, y'know," he whispered against her hair, gently caressing a soft, rounded breast.

She laughed a little and slowly drew away. "If we don't stop this right now, your bacon will burn."

"Who cares?" he murmured, nuzzling her neck.

"I do. I'm always starved when I wake up."

"So am I." His hands slid under the lapels and lowered to the soft hill of her hips. She moaned and he knelt on the floor, working at the knot of the robe with his teeth, letting his lips brush lightly against her abdomen as he parted the soft barrier of cloth. Finally he pushed the robe down to the floor, letting his tongue and lips caress the soft skin of her abdomen. She quivered with longing.

"Zachary—" She gasped as he nipped her lightly, his hands dancing lightly across her buttocks. Then he stood, turned off the stove and pushed the bacon off the burner.

"No more excuses," he said, and reached beneath the bend of her knees to carry her back to the bed. Lowering her slowly onto the comforter, he shed his running clothes and placed his long, hard body next to hers.

Sweat glistened on his chest, abdomen and thighs, and she ran her fingers over his damp skin as he closed his eyes and moaned her name. She touched him boldly then, making him growl deep in his throat in anticipation.

"I love you, Lauren." He swallowed with difficulty as her fingers caressed his chest, traced the length of his lean torso, dug into his buttocks. "You're a fascinating, teasing witch," he muttered, "and I love you."

He pulled her on top of him and stared at her with smoldering brown eyes. "Make love to me," he ordered, lifting his hips off the bed and rubbing sensuously against her. "Make love to me all morning."

She felt the soft hair on his thighs brushing against her legs, watched as his abdomen rippled when he pushed up to her, saw the passion glazing his eyes. "Anything you want, counselor," she whispered, lowering her head and touching her lips to one dark male nipple.

He groaned and his fingers twined in the fiery curls of her hair, holding her head against him as he moved beneath her.

"Lauren, please," he begged, his voice raw with passion.

Slowly, she lowered her body, sliding over him until with one sharp thrust he entered her. Then his hands, pressing against her upper thighs and buttocks, started the sweet, gentle motion of love.

"I want—"

"Shh," she whispered, closing her eyes as the tension within her mounted. She rocked in rhythm to it, her mind soaring, her body propelled by the driving force of Zachary's love. "Oh, God," she moaned as the spasms of love burst within her. Her body bent over his, and she felt him stiffen, then explode in a series of shock waves of hot passion. "I love you, Zachary," she cried, wondering why the words sounded so tormented.

His hands reached forward and twined in the curling silk of her hair, forcing her to lift her head and stare into his eyes. "Then marry me, Lauren. When we find your children, please, marry me."

Tears gathered in her round green eyes as she witnessed the tenderness and sincerity in his gaze. She smiled. "Of course I'll marry you, Zachary." Bending forward, she placed a kiss on his forehead while her hands brushed a lock of hair away from his face. "And once I do, I'll never let you go."

He returned her smile. "You couldn't shake me if you tried, lady. When we get married, it's forever." He shifted his weight slightly. "Now, how about a shower?" he asked.

"With you?"

"Why not?" His dark eyes twinkled mischievously. "I don't know about you, but I certainly could use one."

"Lead on." She laughed, rolling off him and standing by the bed. His gaze slid sensuously up her body.

"This could be interesting," he announced devilishly. "Very interesting."

Two hours later, the shower and breakfast were finished. Lauren felt more satisfied than she had in years. It was as if the woman she'd hidden away for so long had finally emerged.

After the dishes were done, Zachary suggested they go for a walk along the beach, and Lauren didn't disagree. He helped her down the slightly unsteady steps that led to the stretch of beach far below the face of the cliff.

The sand was moist and the fog that had settled after the storm was beginning to lift. The horizon wasn't yet visible, but dark, black rocks near the shoreline loomed in the gray tide pools. Foamy waves slipped onto the wet sand, trying to retrieve the lost treasures they had deposited the night before during the fury of the midnight storm.

Sea gulls dipped and arced over the water, their lonesome cries piercing the air above the soft roar of the now quiet surf. Broken shells, sodden driftwood, near-black seaweed and shiny pebbles littered the sand. The salty smell of the sea lingered in the air.

Lauren was walking with Zachary, her arms linked with his, the wind pushing her hair away from her face. The only other impressions in the sand were the footprints from Zachary's early-morning run. "It's beautiful here," Lauren observed with a sigh.

"I like it."

"But you don't come here often?"

"Not anymore." He stopped and stared out to sea. The happy light faded from his eyes and his jaw hardened as if he were experiencing some inner turmoil.

"Because of Rosemary?" she asked.

His dark eyes sharpened, as if focusing on some distant object on the horizon. "Yes."

"You don't have to talk about it."

"No, it's time." He looked back to her and smiled sadly. "And it's not fair to you. It's not that I have any great secret, you know, just something I'd rather forget."

"I understand." She had only to consider her painful marriage to Doug.

He placed his arm gently around her shoulders and continued walking north along the beach. "Rosemary and I had been having problems off and on. I don't think she was ever happy living in Portland. While we were in Seattle, everything was fine, or at least I thought it was.

But once we moved to Portland and uprooted her, well, things were never the same. She was . . . restless.''

"You loved her very much, didn't you?" Lauren asked, hating the question and wrapping her arms around her waist as if to brace herself for the truth. Suddenly, her suede jacket didn't seem to be withstanding the chill of the raw morning.

"Yes, I did. At least in the beginning. But once we were in Portland . . . hell, who knows? I was probably as much to blame as she was. My career, you know. Rosemary didn't know very many people in town and she was alone a lot of the time. That was my fault.''

"And you've been blaming yourself ever since.''

He frowned, then nodded slowly. "That's the way I see it, I guess. Rosemary was unhappy, and I didn't do my best to help her. That's why I bought this cabin; I thought we could spend some time alone together.'' His jacket was open and it caught in the sharp morning breeze.

"But it didn't work out?''

He shook his head and the breeze ruffled his hair. "It only added to the problem," he admitted. "She saw it as just one more way to isolate her from the life she loved.''

"Which was?" she asked.

"Rosemary was a very social person. She was born beautiful, an only child of wealthy parents. She had been adored and fawned over all of her life. It was to her credit that she wasn't spoiled, I suppose, but she needed a certain amount of attention as well as a social life, I guess. And I failed to provide her with those particular things that were so necessary.''

He rammed his fists into the pockets of his jeans. "At first, while we were in Seattle, she tried to include me in her wide social circle, and I went along with it. But once we moved to Portland, and I buried myself in my work, trying to establish a practice with Wendell Tate, I didn't have time for the parties. On the weekends, all I wanted to do was come here and unwind. Rosemary was bored out of her mind and she told me so. She even went so far as to file for divorce once, just to shake me up, or so she claimed. She never went through with it."

"I'm sorry. . . ."

"Don't be. Maybe things would have worked out better if she'd gone through with the divorce. At least then she might still be alive." He massaged the bridge of his nose as if warding off a headache. "Rosemary was just bored and was trying in her own way to make me wake up to the fact that she was terribly unhappy."

"I take it she didn't work," Lauren said, studying the strained lines of his face before looking away and watching the graceful flight of a marauding sea gull. It was evident to her that Zachary was still a little in love with his wife.

"She tried several things—interior decorating, owning an art gallery, even writing. But nothing ever worked out for her. She blamed it on my lack of interest and support; maybe she was right." He shrugged and let out a long, weary sigh. "I should have seen it coming. . . ."

"What?" Lauren asked.

He stopped to stare at the distant horizon. As the fog lifted, dim silhouettes of small boats and larger ships had become visible in the gray morning. "I came home early one day, and apparently she didn't hear me come into the house. Anyway, she was talking with a friend, discussing the fact that she was pregnant."

Lauren remembered her discussion with Zachary the night before about the possibility of pregnancy. Was it possible that Zachary, caught up in his practice, hadn't wanted the responsibility of a child? "What happened?" she pressed.

"Nothing." His voice was emotionless. "I went into the den and she came in later." His eyes darkened with the memory. "She was carrying a tray of drinks and offered me one. Stupidly, I thought it was to celebrate the pregnancy, but she didn't mention one word of it to me. In fact, she seemed distant, reserved . . . wouldn't let me near her."

"Didn't she want the baby?" Lauren asked, appalled at the image he was painting. Lauren's children were the single most important part of her life.

"I don't know. At least I didn't, not then." He paled a little as the first rays of a frail autumn sun pierced the gray clouds. "Rosemary became moody and I attributed it to the pregnancy. I thought she was waiting for just the right moment to spring the news on me." His lips twisted cynically as he considered what a fool he'd been. "So I brought Rosemary here."

"To the beach cabin."

"Right. That was a mistake, not my first by a long shot and unfortunately not my last."

"She wasn't happy."

"That's putting it mildly. She paced around the cabin restlessly, as if she were looking for an excuse, any excuse to leave. She began to drink too much, and I was concerned for her as well as the baby. Finally, I asked her about it."

Zachary remembered the stricken look in Rosemary's round, violet eyes. She had accused him of murderous deeds, and she had lost her battle with hysteria.

"How did you know?" Rosemary had gasped, the blood draining from her lovely face.

"I overheard a telephone conversation last week—"

"You *bastard!*" she'd exploded, pushing her hair away from her forehead in nervous agitation. "Is *that* how you get your jollies? By eavesdropping, for God's sake?" she'd accused with a sneer.

Zachary shook his head and tried to dispel the vivid image.

"What happened?" Lauren asked, afraid to hear but fascinated nonetheless. What had happened to scar him so badly?

"Rosemary became hysterical and she swore that she was going to get rid of the child," he said.

"An abortion?" Lauren felt sick inside and watched Zachary's dark eyes as he recalled the painful past.

"I'm not about to have this baby," Rosemary had sworn. She'd worked herself into a frenzy. She was drinking from a half-full bottle of wine and staring at Zachary with eyes that glittered with malice. "I've already talked to a doctor."

"I won't let you do it," Zachary had responded. "I have some say-so in this, you know, seeing as I'm the father."

"Ha! You think!" she'd cried, laughing viciously. "Think about it, husband dear. How long has it been since you've been in my bed?" He'd stopped walking toward her as the meaning of her words became clear. "That's right, Zack. The baby isn't yours."

"I don't believe you," he'd replied weakly. But the satisfied smile on her lips convinced him.

"You haven't had time for me, have you? I couldn't possibly be pregnant with your child. It's been over two months since you've been near me...not that I'm counting, mind you."

"Then how?" His eyes had grown incredibly dark. *"Who?"*

"Wouldn't you like to know?" she'd taunted, lifting the bottle of wine to her lips and taking a long swallow. His hands had clenched into tight fists of fury, and for the first time in his life he wanted to hurt her. "Well, what do you suppose your partner has been doing while you've been building up the reputation of your firm?"

"Wendell Tate?" he'd said incredulously.

"Who else?"

"You're lying."

Rosemary had smiled, her amethyst eyes dancing. "Sure I am." She tilted the wine bottle to her lips and took another long drink. He could see the movement of her throat as she swallowed. His stomach turned over and he thought for a moment that he was going to be sick.

"I don't believe it."

She shrugged her slim shoulders indifferently. "Suit yourself. You always do anyway."

Zachary stalked across the room, grabbed the wine bottle from her hand and threw it into the fire. The green glass burst into shards that glittered among the blood-red coals. Burgundy wine drizzled down the charred logs, causing the fire to sputter and hiss.

Zachary's fingers tightened around Rosemary's arms. "You're lying," he accused, his voice raspy with the hate blackening his heart.

Her dark, expressive brows arched. "If you don't believe me, ask Wendell."

"Oh, God, Rosemary." He released her, as if suddenly finding her repulsive.

"Save the wounded hero routine, Zack. It's not as if you've been faithful to me, you know."

His brown eyes impaled hers. "Since I've known you, I've never been with another woman," he said, his dark, horrified stare filled with honesty and despair. "I've never wanted anyone else."

"Save it, Zack."

"It's true and you know it."

The facade of mockery and indifference slipped a little as she believed him. "But you haven't wanted me, either. Oh, God, Zachary, all those nights you said you were working late...."

"I was."

"You can't expect me to believe that you haven't had a lover.... You certainly haven't been interested in *me*." She was pale now, and her lower lip quivered. If he'd been more of a man he would have taken her into his arms and comforted her.

"I've been tired, Rosemary, and ... well, you haven't been interested much yourself." He looked at her pointedly. "I guess we know why."

"I've always loved you, Zack," she protested, tears beginning to slip from her eyes. "You've just never seemed to find the time to be with me.... Oh, God, what have I done?" she said, burying her face in her hands.

A little of his anger faded. He placed a hand on her shoulder comfortingly. "Come on, Rosemary, you'd better go to bed—"

"Alone?" she cried. "Won't you come with me?"

He hesitated. "I've got a lot to think about."

"Don't hate me, Zack, please, just don't hate me."

"I don't hate you, Rosemary," he whispered, most of his impotent anger turned now toward himself.

He helped her to the bedroom and tucked her into bed. When she reached out to him, he folded one of her hands in his own and turned away. "I just need a little time to think," he said, not knowing those words would be the last he would ever say to her.

In the past four years he had relived the nightmare of that night a thousand times.

Lauren, raw from a year of living without her children, couldn't believe that Zachary's wife would want to destroy her own child. "Why didn't she want the baby?" she asked.

"Because it wasn't mine. She was having an affair with Wendell Tate."

"Your partner?" Lauren closed her eyes in horror at the image. No wonder Zachary was reluctant to talk about it. "Oh, God, Zachary, I'm sorry—"

"It's over," he said. "She thought I was involved with someone else, and that was my fault. As I said, I hadn't been particularly attentive to her needs. Anyway, she was immediately contrite. When we were through talking I put her to bed, thinking that with all the wine she'd been drinking she would fall asleep right away. I checked on her once; her eyes were closed and her breathing was regular, so I went out for a long run along the beach. It was midnight and raining, but I didn't care; I needed to think and work out my frustrations.

"I was just climbing the stairs back to the cabin, and I'd decided that I'd let Rosemary make the decision. If she wanted a divorce, I'd grant it; if she wanted to start over, I'd try. That's when I heard the car. I raced up the remaining stairs and heard her roar out of the driveway. First I double-checked the cabin, to make sure that she was really gone—I had trouble believing that she'd be so reckless—then I called the police. It turned out to be the longest night of my life."

Lauren wrapped her fingers around Zachary's arm, but he didn't seem to notice. "That was the night she died," she whispered.

Zachary nodded, the corners of his mouth whitening with the strain of the memory. "The police found her car and body in Devil's Punchbowl. Have you ever been there, looked down at the water?"

Lauren nodded. The blue-gray waters of the Pacific crashed into the shore and churned furiously in the natural hollow by the cliffs known appropriately as Devil's Punchbowl. She felt sick at the thought of Rosemary's car plunging into the midnight-dark waters churning frothy white.

"According to the only witness, Rosemary had been driving erratically, continually weaving into the oncoming lane of traffic. And then, blinded by the headlights of an approaching semi, she swerved off the road and down the embankment to the sea.

"I heard the news the next morning. That's the last time I was in the cabin. I didn't have the heart to sell it, so I hired a service to keep it up. But after meeting you, I decided to purge all the ghosts from the past and start over." He turned and faced her, his brown eyes searching her face. "You're a strong woman, Lauren, and I feel stronger just for knowing you."

"Don't give me too much credit," she said, pushing aside a windblown lock of coppery hair.

"You're a very special lady."

"Only when I'm around a special man."

He snorted in disbelief. "I thought I wanted to die, you know. A friend took me back to Portland and I had to confront Wendell. It was hell."

"You can't be serious!" Wendell had cried, horrified when Zachary had told him about Rosemary's death and accused him of being the father of her unborn child. "I've never touched your wife, old boy," he'd declared, nervously tugging on the waxed ends of his blond mustache.

Zachary's dark eyes had accused Tate of the lie. "I should want to kill you, I suppose," Zachary had said, and Wendell had taken immediate refuge behind his desk. "But I don't. All I want is the truth, then we'll see what we can do about dissolving the partnership."

The next two weeks had been torture. Rosemary's funeral, phone calls and interviews from the press, and the scandalous rumors were flying. Finally, Wendell had cracked and admitted that he'd been involved with Rosemary.

"That settles it, then," Zachary had said, intent on dissolving the partnership and moving away from the town that had brought him so much pain. Only it didn't work out that way. Three days later, Wendell Tate was found dead from an apparent overdose of sleeping pills. Though there was no suicide note, Zachary had understood—this was Wendell's method of escape. All of Wendell's assets and liabilities were left to his only son, Joshua.

Lauren placed a comforting hand on Zachary's cold cheek, lovingly stroking the stubble on his chin. "You don't have to talk about this."

"I'm okay. It's just that Wendell denied the affair, until he knew that it was useless, then he went home one night, took more pills than his body could handle and didn't wake up."

"And that's how you inherited Joshua as a partner."

"It took a few years, but yes, essentially that's what happened."

"And you blame yourself for what happened to Rosemary and Wendell."

"And the baby," he finished, his jaw set rigidly. "Whether I meant to or not, I caused the deaths of three people."

"So you took in Joshua Tate and made him a full partner of the firm."

"Once he'd passed the bar."

"I don't think you have anything to feel guilty about, counselor," she said, standing on her toes and kissing his cheek. "I think you're wonderful."

He forced a grin. "It's nice to have at least one fan," he teased, linking his arm with hers and spinning her back in the direction of the cabin.

"I'll race ya back," she challenged, hoping to find some way to help him dispel his tortured thoughts of the past.

"You don't have a prayer—" Before he could finish the sentence she had taken off, her bare feet skimming over the cold, wet sand. Zachary was beside her in an instant, his long strides effortlessly diminishing her small head start.

Lauren gritted her teeth and tried to quicken the pace, but just as she did, Zachary's arms reached out for her. She stumbled and they both fell onto the sand.

"Spoilsport," she laughed, tossing her hair away from her face.

"You can't beat me," he announced loftily. "I run seven miles four times a week."

"Like you're the only one in shape. Chauvinist!"

He shook his head and kissed her. "I think that expression went out in the seventies," he said, smiling.

"Still applies." Her arms encircled his neck, and her green eyes sparkled with good humor. Why did she always feel like smiling whenever she was with him? "You know, I'm falling in love with you, counselor, and I don't know if I should."

"Trust your instincts," he said as he pushed her gently onto the sand and stared into her eyes. "I'm one helluva catch."

"What you are is a cocky, miserable, adorable bastard." She laughed and playfully rumpled his hair.

"And you love it." He pulled her to her feet, placed a possessive arm around her shoulders and pointed to the weathered cabin perched on the cliff. "Let's go inside," he murmured suggestively, "and we'll finish this discussion in bed . . . with a cold bottle of wine. . . ."

The rest of the weekend was perfect. Even the sun peeked through the clouds to brighten the sky and warm the white sand. Lauren knew that she would never be satisfied with another man. She loved Zachary with all her heart. They spent their last few hours alone, before the dying fire, and it was difficult for Lauren to leave the rustic little cabin and return to Portland to face the problems at the bank and the all-consuming task of trying to locate her children.

The clock had just chimed nine when Lauren and Zachary entered her house in Westmoreland. After checking the mail and turning on the coffee maker, Lauren rewound the tape player and listened to her phone messages. The third one made her heart stand still.

"This is Sherry Engles," a feminine voice said nervously. "I know you don't know me, but . . . well, I might be able to help you find your husband. I knew him a couple of years ago . . . and well, my number is—" The woman rattled off a long-distance number, and Lauren went white with shock.

"What is it?" Zachary asked, seeing the stricken look on her face and the way her fingers gripped the back of the desk chair near the phone. "Lauren?"

"The woman," Lauren said, her throat suddenly tight. "Her name was Sherry...."

Zachary nodded, waiting for her to continue.

"That was the name. The name of the woman Doug was seeing when he was at Dickinson Investments.... I mean, he called me Sherry that night.... Oh, God." Her voice faded, and she buried her face in the rough fabric of Zachary's jacket.

Chapter Ten

You're sure this Sherry is the same woman?" Zachary asked as Lauren slowly pulled out of his embrace and reached for the phone.

"Positive."

"But you couldn't remember her name a couple of weeks ago."

Lauren picked up the receiver and leaned against the desk for support. "It's the way she said it, what she said, it jogged my memory."

Zachary wrestled the ivory-colored receiver from her tense fingers. "I think I should make the call."

"Why?" she demanded.

"Because of the disappointments you've already faced. Remember how you reacted to Dave Parker's children?" He touched her softly under the chin.

"You can't protect me, you know," she said with a trace of bitterness. "Someday or another I'm going to have to face that woman; it might as well be now, when she has information on the kids."

After a slight pause, he handed her back the phone. "It's your ball game," he said, and paced restlessly to the fireplace.

Lauren's fingers were shaking when she punched out the number.

"Are you sure you don't want me to do this?" Zachary asked, his eyes intent on the drawn lines of her face.

"No...I can handle it."

"All right. But I'll be right here if you need me." He folded his arms over his chest, leaned a shoulder against the cold bricks and watched. Lauren turned away from him as she waited for someone to answer. From the area code, Zachary guessed that the woman lived in western Washington. Other than that small piece of information, Sherry Engles was a complete mystery.

The phone rang three times, then four. Lauren's fingers tapped nervously on the receiver. "Come on," she whispered urgently just as the phone was answered.

"Hello?" It was the same feminine voice that had been recorded on the answering machine. Lauren felt her pulse begin to quicken.

"Hello. My name is Lauren Regis. I'd like to speak with Sherry Engles."

There was an uncomfortable pause. "I'm Sherry," the woman admitted finally. "I called you yesterday afternoon."

Lauren's heart began to pound so loudly she could barely hear her own voice. This was the woman who had slept with her husband in the past and now might be able to help her find Alicia and Ryan. Sherry Engles was both friend and foe. "You said you might have some information about my children."

"I . . . I'm not sure. My friend in Portland saw you on that program . . . *Eye Witness* or whatever it was called."

"*Eye Contact.*"

"Right. Anyway, she remembered that I . . . uh, had been seeing a man named Doug Regis . . . a couple of years ago. So she gave me your number."

"I see," Lauren replied stiffly.

"Hey, look," Sherry said apologetically. "I'm real sorry about your kids—I had no idea that Doug was the kind of guy who would run off with them. . . ."

Lauren braced herself and forced her voice to remain calm. "Do you know where he is?"

"I'm not sure."

Lauren's heart dropped to the floor. "But you said—"

"I've got a phone number. It's over a year old and I don't even know if it works. Doug and I, we had a fight, and I wasn't interested in moving to Boise. I . . . never called him and I haven't heard from him since."

"Boise?" she repeated, her hopes soaring. Out of the corner of her eye, she saw Zachary stiffen.

"Yeah, that's where he moved."

"With the children?"

"I don't know." Sherry sounded sincere and Lauren believed her. "Like I said, I wanted nothing to do with him. I'm married now, and . . . well, once I met Bill, that's my husband, I wasn't interested in Doug. Anyway, here's the number. . . ."

Lauren's fingers were shaking so badly she could barely take down the information. When she had finished, she glanced at Zachary. His expression was stern and his arms were still folded over his chest.

"Got it?" Obviously, Sherry was interested in ending the strained conversation.

"Yes. Would you mind if I visited you?" Lauren asked on impulse.

Sherry hesitated. Lauren could almost feel the other woman withdrawing. "I don't think that would be such a good idea," Sherry replied. "What happened between me and Doug is all over. Has been for a long time. It's something I'd rather not think about."

Lauren persevered, refusing to let this one vital link vanish into thin air. "But I have to find my children. You may be the only person who can help me."

"I don't know—"

"What about if my attorney came to visit you?"

"*Your attorney!* Oh, God. I should never have called you." Desperation hung on Sherry's words. "Bill will kill me."

"It's nothing like that," Lauren quickly reassured the woman. "What happened between you and Doug is over, and it doesn't really matter. Not now. I'm not emotionally involved with my ex-husband. But my attorney—his name is Zachary Winters—is helping to track down the kids, and we need all the help we can get. We need *your* help."

"I just don't want to dredge it all up again. Bill...well, he never did like me seeing Doug—"

"You have to understand," Lauren interjected. "I don't want to cause any trouble for you; all I want is to find the children. I don't want to disturb your life, and considering the circumstances, I don't like asking you to help me, but I have to. I...just don't have any choice. We're talking about my kids, for God's sake."

Sherry let out a long sigh. "Shoot me for a fool," she said, and then added, "Sure, I'll talk to your lawyer, as long as he isn't looking to make any trouble for me."

"He won't be."

"Okay. I live northeast of Seattle, in Woodinville. If he calls me when he gets into town, I'll give him directions."

"Thank you," Lauren said. "I know this isn't easy for you."

When she hung up, Lauren felt like collapsing, but instead she punched out the telephone number that Doug had given Sherry nearly a year earlier.

Zachary quickly crossed the room, took the receiver from her hand and hung up the phone. He'd heard enough of the conversation to know what Lauren was planning.

"What're you doing?" Lauren demanded angrily.

"Trying to save you from making the worst mistake of your life. You can't call Doug and tip him off. Not now." His hand remained steadfastly over the receiver.

All of the pent-up anger and frustration of the past few weeks surfaced rapidly. "They are *my* children, dammit, and I intend to speak with them."

"And say what? That this is Mommy, and I want Daddy to bring you home right now? Think about it, Lauren. Doug will take off all over again, and we'll be back to square one."

"I...I have to do this," she said, watching as he lifted his hand from the cradle and scowled at her.

"I want to go on record as being against it."

"Okay. You've got permission to say 'I told you so,'" she snapped.

"Just don't blow everything we've tried to accomplish."

Hastily she punched out the number. The phone rang twice before a recorded message stated that the telephone number had been disconnected and there was no new number.

"No!" Lauren nearly screamed, redialing to make sure she hadn't made a mistake. The recorded message repeated its dismal information.

Zachary's frown eased a bit as he saw the disappointment in her eyes. Quickly, she redialed the phone and waited impatiently for the operator to answer.

"I'm sorry, but I have no listing for a Douglas Regis, a Doug Regis or a D. Regis," the operator said in response to Lauren's inquiry.

"I know he's there—maybe not in the city, but somewhere close by, maybe in one of the suburbs."

"I've checked my computers—there is no Douglas Regis."

Tears sprang to Lauren's eyes. "Thank you," she whispered, gently replacing the phone and wiping her eyes with the back of her hand. "Damn!" She pounded the old rolltop desk in frustration.

"Lauren—"

"I don't want to hear it, Zachary," she cried passionately. "We were so close, so damned close...." She sniffed but didn't argue when he wrapped his arms around her and kissed the top of her head.

"We still are."

"If only I'd gone on the air a year earlier. If only I'd known Sherry Engles, remembered her name, instead of trying to forget about her affair with Doug!"

"Shh...." His lips touched her hair, his warm breath ruffling the auburn strands. "We'll find them."

She moved from his tender embrace, and her glistening eyes stared into his. Tears ran down her cheeks as she walked across the room. "Will we? Will we?" she demanded before answering her own question. "God, I don't know. A week ago, I thought we'd be able to do it, but now.... Oh, Lord, what will I do without them?"

Her voice cracked, and she crumpled into a weary heap on the couch. Covering her face with her hands, she sobbed quietly.

Zachary walked over to the couch and sat next to her. When his fingers wrapped around her arms, they were tight, the grip painful. "Cut it out, Lauren," he said, giving her a shake. "We'll find them."

Lauren looked into his eyes. "How can you be so sure? Every time I think we're getting close...everything seems to fall apart." She was sobbing uncontrollably now, her battle with tears completely forgotten.

"We *are* closer. Don't fall apart on me now," he pleaded. "It's probably going to get worse before it gets better, but I can't find your children without you. You've got to help me. You've *got* to." He shook her again, quietly insisting that she remain strong. "We can do this, Lauren. We can."

"I'd do anything to find them," she murmured weakly, forcing the tears aside.

"Good. Because what I want you to do is stay here; be strong. I'll call a private investigator in Boise tonight and get the ball rolling in Idaho, then I'll fly to Seattle tomorrow and talk with Sherry Engles." He was stroking her hair, trying to soothe and reassure her by telling her his plans. "I'll take the first flight I can catch out of Seattle to Boise, and depending upon how long it takes to find out if Doug is still in Boise, was there, or whatever, I'll be back."

"I'll come with you."

"No."

"But—"

"I don't want to hear it. You have a job to consider, and you need to stay here and see if any other messages or clues come in."

"That's bull, Zachary. The recording machine—"

"God, Lauren, just listen to me!" he nearly shouted. "I can't take the chance of your falling apart all over again. Okay? Remember the night you thought the kids were in Gresham with Dave Parker? Remember the disappointment? You can't put yourself through that over and over again."

"I can and I will," she declared.

"Every time we come up against a stumbling block, you take it too hard."

"That's because they're *my* children!" She glanced up at the portrait of Alicia and Ryan and felt the tears gathering again.

"And I'm doing my best to find them." He brushed the lingering tears from her eyes, and his face softened slightly. "This time, let me do it my way, okay? That's why you hired me."

She stared at him for a long moment, trying to consider the problem from all angles. "Okay," she finally agreed, forcing herself to gain control of her emotions. "We'll do it your way... for now."

He offered an encouraging smile. "I'll find them, you know. Come hell or high water."

God, she wanted to believe him. She wrapped her arms around his chest and lowered her head to his shoulder, feeling the strength his arms offered. This one man she could trust with all her heart. If he said he would find the kids, Lauren knew he would do just that... or die trying.

Sherry Engles was a short woman with curly brown hair, about six months pregnant and very nervous. It was obvious that she was uncomfortable with the subject of Douglas Regis—she never quite met Zachary's stare; her eyes shifted from one side of the tidy room to the other, continually drifting to the clock over the couch, as if she were fearful that someone would burst into the house and find her talking to the curt lawyer from Portland.

"I wish I could help you more," she said after a two-hour inquisition by Zachary that divulged no other information on Douglas Regis or the whereabouts of Lauren's children. "But, like I told Doug's ex-wife on the phone the other day, I broke all ties with Doug once I married Bill."

"So Doug never wrote to you—you don't have an address?" Zachary asked for the third time.

Sherry shook her head.

"And he never phoned?"

"Not since he gave me the number."

"Then how can you be sure it was correct?"

Sherry frowned petulantly. "I guess I can't."

"But you kept the number, even though you didn't want to stay in contact with him?" Zachary was clearly dubious, and Sherry swayed uncomfortably in her worn rocker.

"I put the number in the front of the phone book and never bothered to throw last year's book away." She shrugged. "Maybe I should have. Then I wouldn't be involved in the mess."

Zachary left the house not knowing much more than when he went in. For all he knew, Douglas Regis could have given Sherry a phony number, or the woman could have written it down incorrectly. The whole thing could turn out to be just another fiasco. And Lauren would be devastated. Again.

His hands were clenched on the steering wheel of the rented car, and he glowered in frustration at the sluggish traffic as he slowly drove toward Sea-Tac Airport.

Zachary only hoped that the private investigator he'd hired in Boise would come up with something—anything—to help him locate Lauren's children. He honestly didn't know if she could take another disappointment.

"Mind if I join you?"

Lauren looked up in surprise. She'd decided to eat lunch alone and for this reason had taken a vacant back table in the small restaurant on the first floor of the Northwestern Bank Tower. She wasn't thrilled at the prospect of company.

"So how's it going?" Bob Harding asked as he balanced his tray of food and slid into one of the cane-backed chairs opposite Lauren.

"It's going," she said noncommittally as she stirred her soup and watched the steam rise from the bowl.

"Ouch." Bob winced a little.

Suddenly Lauren realized that Bob thought her comment had been meant as a sarcastic remark. Obviously he was still feeling guilty about being put in charge of the Mason trust. "I wasn't talking about bank business," she said, managing a smile for her friend. "Especially not the Mason trust. That's your problem now." She smiled good-naturedly. "Actually, I don't miss the headache at all. So quit being so sensitive."

"You're one lousy liar, you know." He placed his lunch and a cup of coffee in front of him, then stashed the tray on an unused table.

"So I've been told."

"George West ripped your stripes off by taking the account from you, and it still sticks in your craw. Admit it."

"Okay, my perceptive friend. It still bothers me."

"Don't let it."

"A little hard to do when the entire trust department can't seem to talk about anything else," she pointed out.

"Well, let's forget about the Mason trust for a while." Then, apparently forgetting his own advice, he added sourly, "That Joshua Tate is a royal pain in the neck."

"Not to mention Hammond Mason?"

"Amen."

Lauren smiled ruefully and took a long sip of her iced tea. "Maybe I'm lucky to be out of it."

Bob pursed his lips and pushed his glasses on the bridge of his nose. "I never liked the way George West handled all that business, you know. It didn't seem fair. Just because you went on television to find your kids and then hired the best man in town to help you locate them…well, it just didn't seem reason enough to pull you off the account."

"You seem to forget that Joshua Tate is Zachary Winters's partner."

"How could I?" That kid's as tenacious as a bulldog!"

"Like his mentor?" Lauren asked, arching a brow.

"Yeah. I guess so." Satisfied that Lauren held no apparent grudges, Bob took a bite of his salad. "Speaking of Winters, how're you doing? Any progress in finding Alicia and Ryan?"

Lauren shook her head. "Not much," she admitted. "Zachary's out of town, in Boise, I think, tracking down another lead."

"Another?"

She toyed with her soup spoon and looked up to see the anxiety in Bob's gaze. "We've had quite a few, but they've all turned out to be dead ends."

"I'm sorry," Bob said, frowning.

"Nothing that can be done about it...." She pretended interest in her soup again, and the conversation turned to less disturbing subjects. It was comforting to know that despite all the tension at the bank, she still had a friend in Bob Harding. These days, friends were hard to come by.

Zachary returned Thursday night. He drove straight from the airport and through the thickening fog to Lauren's house.

When Lauren opened the door, she read the guarded disappointment on his face and her heart twisted painfully.

"You didn't find them," Lauren guessed as she closed the door. The pain in Zachary's eyes couldn't be disguised. He looked as if he hadn't shaved or slept in the three days he'd been gone, and the white shirt that had been fresh and crisp that morning was now rumpled and soiled.

"Not yet," he said wearily, taking her in his arms and stroking her hair softly. She smelled so clean and fresh, looked as enticing as an oasis in a godforsaken desert. "God, I missed you."

Lauren swallowed the lump in her throat and kissed his stubble-roughened cheek. "I missed you, too." She was amazingly calm, though she felt as if all the hope in her heart had turned to ice. She tried to tell herself that all was not lost. At least Zachary had returned. This last separation from him had been difficult, more trying than any separation before. Slowly, her life was beginning to revolve around Zachary, whether she wanted it to or not.

Her arms wrapped around him, and she held the man she loved desperately, clinging to him as if to life itself. What if she never found the children? Could this man be enough? She shuddered at the thought and felt his arms possessively tightening around her waist. Could she ever be content to forget about Alicia and Ryan and start a new life, a new family with Zachary?

Dear Lord, no! If it took the rest of her life, she would go on searching for her dear, lost children. Love Zachary as she might, she could never forget or give up trying to find Alicia and Ryan.

"Tell me about it," she urged, leading him to the couch and trying to hide the disappointment weighing heavily upon her.

Without protest, Zachary slumped onto the couch and let his head fall back. He stared blankly at the ceiling, one arm draped around Lauren's shoulders.

"Doug was in Boise, but he's gone."

Lauren tried to still her pounding heart. At least that was something! For the first time in over a year, Doug had been located. "And you don't know where he went?"

Zachary let out a weary sigh and shook his head. "No. He pulled the same vanishing act that he did here a year ago—no forwarding address or telephone number... nothing. Just gone without a trace. Work records didn't help, either."

"When did he leave?"

"About four months ago." Zachary rubbed his jaw. "As far as I can tell, he went from Portland to Boise and got a job with a lumber mill as a laborer on the green chain. I checked with the phone company, the Social Security Administration, the county records and the schools. Nothing. No one seems to know where he's gone. I even talked to some of the workers in the mill, but they said he kept pretty much to himself. They didn't know much about him except that he was living with some woman named Becky and they had a couple of kids.''

"They?'' Lauren repeated, her lower lip trembling. Another woman was raising her children? Her heart wrenched painfully, and her eyes burned.

"Right. Seems as if Doug let the people he met think that the kids were Becky's.''

"Oh, God,'' she murmured. She had to look away from him for a second to gather her composure. "But...but what about the private investigator?'' she asked hopefully.

"He's still working on it....'' Zachary closed his eyes, sighing. "Sherry Engles wasn't much help, either. She wasn't even sure that the telephone number she'd given me was correct. So I checked. It was, but Doug had discontinued service when he lost his job about four or five months ago.''

"But still, we're closer than we were last week,'' she said, unwilling to accept defeat.

He smiled sadly and turned to gaze into her eyes. "One step at a time, right?'' Tenderly, he traced her jaw with his thumb. "I'd just hoped to return with more encouraging news. I really thought that I could come back here and tell you that the kids were found.''

"You're not giving up, are you?''

Determination glinted in his dark eyes. "Not on your life, lady.'' He pulled her gently to him. "I made a promise to you, didn't I?''

"And I intend to keep you to it,'' she said more bravely than she felt. Her eyes lifted to the portrait of Ryan and Alicia, and she wondered how much they'd grown in the last fourteen months. Would they still remember her? "Soon it will be Alicia's birthday,'' she thought aloud, swallowing past a painful lump in her throat. "I...I was hoping that I would be with her...."

"Lauren, shh...." He kissed her forehead, watching her face and seeing her anguish. "We'll keep trying, and we'll find them."

He followed her gaze to the mantel and stared at the picture for a while. "When is Alicia's birthday?" he asked thoughtfully.

"A week from Friday, the sixth of November—why?"

He frowned slightly. "Because I've got an idea. It might not work, but at this point, I don't think we have much to lose." His weariness seemed to disappear as an idea began to form. Standing, he paced between the couch and fireplace as he thought the concept over. "And it just might work."

"What kind of an idea?" she asked skeptically.

"It's simple, really. All I want you to do is take out an advertisement in all the major newspapers near Boise— the entire surrounding area. It should be a full-page ad, big enough to catch a person's attention."

"An ad? I don't get it."

"The message should be simple and in large block letters. Something like: 'Happy seventh birthday, Alicia. Your mother loves and misses you and your brother, Ryan, very much. Please call, I need to hear from you and know that you're well.' We'll put your name and number in the paper and see what happens."

"But what if Doug sees it? Won't he pull up stakes again?"

Zachary inclined his head. "Maybe, but at least we'll have a fresh trail to follow. It'll take him a couple of days, maybe over a week to find a new place to live, move, finish with his job and straighten out all the problems of taking Alicia out of school."

"But the last time he walked out in one afternoon."

"True, but the kids weren't in school and he had everything planned out ahead of time. This time we'll force him to be spontaneous. Besides, someone else might read the paper, not Doug. Someone who will be willing to tell us where the kids are."

"I don't know...."

Zachary drew her to her feet, pulled her close to him and hugged her enthusiastically. "As I said, it's a gamble, maybe even a long shot—but it just might pay off!"

"Then, counselor," she said, his optimism affecting her, "let's get to it. You take a shower and change, and I'll put on the coffee. Then we'll figure out our new strategy and the layout for the ad."

His dark eyes glinted, and he placed a kiss on her cheek. "You sure bounce back," he said affectionately.

"Maybe it's because I've got such a good teacher."

His gaze darkened sensually, and one finger touched the hollow of her throat. "There are so many things I'd like to teach you...."

She angled her head seductively, letting her hair fall over one shoulder, and arched an enigmatic brow. "Anytime you're ready, counselor...."

His hands spanned her waist, and he pulled her body against his, letting his lips linger against the nape of her neck. "No time like the present," he murmured against her warm skin. "No time like the present."

The next week was torture for Lauren. When Zachary wasn't catching up on other cases at the office, he was in Boise, working with the private investigator. Lauren found her evenings nearly unbearable. Though she tried to concentrate on reading or watching television, her thoughts strayed constantly to Zachary. What was he doing? Whom was he with? Had he made any progress? He called each night, and she hung on to the phone as tightly as if it were a lifeline, a fragile link to the only person she could trust, her only chance at salvation. During working hours, the tension at the bank was nearly tangible as the day for the Mason trust trial got closer. Lauren was pointedly excluded from closed-door meetings, and she'd suffered from more than one unfriendly stare on the day of the trust board meeting.

Only Patrick Evans had seemed to sympathize with her situation. After the board meeting, he'd offered to take her to a nearby restaurant for a cup of coffee. Lauren had felt compelled to accept. Something in Patrick's wise eyes told her that she should listen to whatever it was he had to say.

"So, are you any closer to finding those kids than you were a few weeks ago?" he'd asked once they were settled in the privacy of a leather booth.

"I hope so." She stirred her coffee idly, watching as the cream swirled around her spoon.

"But nothing concrete?"

She shook her head and stared into her cup. "Not really. We did find out that—"

"We?" Patrick inquired, frowning slightly. "By that you mean yourself and Zachary Winters."

"Yes." She watched as Patrick shifted uncomfortably in his seat. "We know that Doug moved to Boise and stayed there for about six months. Now it seems he's vanished again."

"I'm sorry, Lauren," Patrick said sincerely. "I know this hasn't been easy for you, especially with what's been going on at the bank."

"So you're aware of that," she said stiffly.

Patrick shrugged and pulled at the knot of his expensive silk tie. "I know George West and his slightly narrow-minded view of loyalty when it comes to Northwestern Bank."

Lauren looked up sharply. "So what is this—a warning?"

"No." Patrick managed a fatherly smile. "A word of advice, I guess."

"Which is?"

"Watch your step, Lauren. Keep your nose clean. Don't give George any reason to suspect that your loyalties are placed elsewhere."

Patrick's meaning was clear. Obviously George West still thought she was on some spying mission for Joshua Tate. Her green eyes hardened, glittering like cold emeralds. "All I'm trying to do, Patrick, is find my kids. That's not a crime, nor is it a threat to George West or the bank. As for my loyalty to the bank, it's never faltered."

Patrick nodded but avoided her eyes. "I know that and you know it, but George...well, he tends to look at things from a different perspective. He's heard talk that you've been seeing Zachary Winters personally as well as professionally."

"So what?"

"Zack's the guy responsible for pushing Joshua Tate through law school at Willamette University and making him a partner of the firm. That fact alone makes George nervous. Very nervous." Patrick took a long swallow of his coffee, his eyes never leaving Lauren's.

"So what are you suggesting—that I tell Zachary he's off the case, per my boss's orders?"

"Of course not, Lauren. I'm the guy that referred you to Winters in the first place."

"But that was before Hammond Mason hired Joshua Tate."

"I know. Nonetheless, I'm just asking you to watch your step."

"I'll keep it in mind," she replied, trying to keep her voice level. She realized that Patrick Evans was trying to help her, even if it was a little backhanded. She liked the silver-haired attorney and respected his judgment. If he was warning her—and that's what it sounded like, whether he admitted it or not—she should be careful. Anything she might do or say could be construed as an act of betrayal.

Patrick rose to leave, but Lauren placed a hand on the sleeve of his gray flannel suit. "Are you suggesting that I quit my job?"

Patrick frowned thoughtfully. "I don't know," he admitted honestly. "But if I were you, I'd keep my options open. This lawsuit has George seeing red."

"Even though he knows he'll win?"

"Well, that's the problem, isn't it? Nothing in law is a sure thing. Oh, sure, the laws are written down in black and white, but they're open to a lot of discussion and interpretation. That's why there are so many cases you can quote to argue your point, be it for or against."

Lauren's blood was boiling at the unfair situation. She felt trapped, damned if she did, damned if she didn't. "I've always been a good employee to Northwestern Bank," she said as Patrick paid the check, "and I've never done anything to jeopardize the bank's reputation. I've said as much to George. If he doesn't believe me, there's not much I can do about it." She squared her shoulders. "Either he trusts me or he doesn't."

"It's not that simple, you see. George has been taking a lot of heat. Several members of the board have been suggesting that he resign."

"But his family owns the majority of the stock in the bank."

"I know. But his sister and brother have been applying a little pressure as well."

"Because of me?" Lauren was incredulous.

"Because of the Mason trust lawsuit and all the media attention it's been receiving over the past couple of weeks. Once the press links your name with that of Zachary Winters, this whole thing will blow up into a three-ring circus. Some members of the board have even gone so far as to suggest a quiet out-of-court settlement in order to save face."

"For whom?"

"The investors and the account holders of the bank." The groove between Patrick's brows deepened. "This lawsuit could cost the bank a lot of money in investor and account holder confidence. No one buys a stock in or leaves his money with a bank he can't trust."

"I see," Lauren said, gritting her teeth. The whole damned thing was so unfair—blown out of proportion.

Patrick held the door open for her, and she slipped her arms through the sleeves of her raincoat. Gray clouds threatened the skies over the city, and the first large drops of rain began to pelt the sidewalk and street.

As they walked back to the bank in strained silence, Lauren made the decision she'd been putting off for nearly three weeks.

Two hours later she was in George West's office, offering her resignation to the president of Northwestern

Bank. The old man pursed his lips and shook his head but accepted nonetheless.

"I'm sorry it had to come to this, Lauren." He sounded sincere.

"So am I," she replied, looking him squarely in the eye.

"Do you have another position?"

"Not yet."

"If you need a letter of recommendation..."

"Thank you." She turned and headed for the door, feeling as if a tremendous weight had been lifted from her shoulders.

"Lauren," George called as she reached the door. He stood up as Lauren turned around, and suddenly she realized that he looked tired, and older than his sixty-two years.

"Yes."

"I don't think it will be necessary for you to stay on the usual two weeks; I'll make sure that you're paid an extra month's salary as well as the vacation pay due you."

"Thank you."

"And..." He shrugged wearily. "If it means anything to you, I really do hope that you find your children."

"I know that."

She left his office, cleaned out her desk and walked out the front door of Northwestern Bank determined never to look back.

Friday was difficult. Not only was it Alicia's seventh birthday, and the first day Lauren didn't have to go to work, but it was also the first day that the full-page ads would run in the newspapers surrounding Boise. She stayed home all day, trying to work on her résumé and waiting for the phone to ring. But no one called. Not one person.

In the late afternoon, tired of typing a list of her qualifications, she kicked off her shoes and sank into the cushions of the couch, closing her eyes. What were the chances that Alicia or someone who knew her would see the birthday message? A seven-year-old wouldn't scan the papers, even if Doug hadn't seen the message himself and had carelessly left the paper in the house.

Would someone call? *If* they read that particular section of that particular paper. *If* they knew Alicia. *If* they wanted to get involved. *If* they weren't afraid of Doug.

Too many ifs and not enough answers. She withdrew the pins from her hair and let the thick auburn curls fall free as she remembered Alicia's birth. Seven years ago, Lauren had been draped in the crisp sheets of the maternity ward of St. Mary's Hospital, surrounded by cheerful nurses and holding her new, wrinkled, red-faced, beautiful daughter. She had been on top of the world. And now she didn't even know where that perfect little girl was living, or with whom.

"Someone's got to call," she told herself glumly. She carried her shoes to the bedroom and then made herself a quick cup of hot tea. "Someone will call. They will," she assured herself, glancing at the phone suspiciously as she settled into her favorite chair and picked up the suspense novel she'd started reading long ago. "They've got to."

And if they don't?

She took in a long, shuddering breath and angled her chin defiantly. *Then we'll try something else.* Closing her eyes against the very real possibility that she might not hear anything for a long time, Lauren made a silent promise to herself. *I'll keep trying until I find them, if it takes me until my dying day.*

Her fingers drummed restlessly on the overstuffed arm of the chair. Where was Zachary? Why hadn't he called? If only she could see him, touch him, be reassured by the determination in his soul-searching dark eyes. Then everything would be all right....

Zachary returned on Sunday. He walked into Lauren's house that cool, clear afternoon carrying a thick sheaf of newspapers under his arm. Once in the kitchen, he spread the pages on the table and let her look at the advertisements he had placed in twelve different papers.

"That's going to cost me a fortune," she thought aloud, pleased nonetheless. Surely someone would read the message and call.

"Won't it be worth it?"

She tore her eyes away from the newspapers and lifted them to meet Zachary's inquisitive stare. "Every cent," she said.

"Even if it doesn't work?"

"Even if it doesn't work. At least I'll know that I tried."

"No calls yet?" he asked, already knowing the answer from the look on her face.

"None."

"It's still too soon," he said comfortingly, but Lauren heard the note of anxiety in his voice. He shifted and forced a smile, hoping to cheer her. "What do you say to a pizza?" he asked impulsively. "My treat."

"I'd have to change."

His gaze traveled down her body, taking in the fact that she was wearing an old checkered blouse and worn jeans. "What're you doing?"

"Nothing. I've just finished."

"Doing what?"

"Stacking the wood that I've been neglecting for over a month."

"I would have done that for you."

"You were busy, remember?" She pointed to the newspapers. "That was more important."

"I guess you're right." He leaned against the wall, a smile on his lips. "Come here."

"What?"

"I said, 'Come here.'"

"What're you doing, counselor?" she asked as she crossed the small kitchen and stood before him.

"It's not what I'm doing now," he said, placing both arms over her shoulders and bending his head so that his forehead touched hers. "It's what I'm planning on doing later...." His voice trailed off seductively, and he played with the top button of her blouse.

Lauren's heart began to flutter erratically as his fingers brushed the skin at the base of her throat. "You're wicked," she said. "You haven't even kissed me 'hello.'"

The next button slipped through the hole. "A mistake I intend to rectify immediately," he responded, letting his lips touch her cheek and the corner of her mouth before capturing her willing lips.

"I love you, lady," he whispered against her ear. The fourth button was freed and her blouse parted, allowing more than a glimpse of the full breasts that fell over the lacy edge of her bra. "It seems like years since I've been here," he murmured as one hand slipped up and gently traced the taut, budding nipple.

"I thought you promised me a pizza," she teased as he finished the tantalizing job of undressing her.

"Later," he replied, lifting her off her feet and heading for the bedroom. "Much later."

The next morning, after a short run through East- and Westmoreland, Zachary enjoyed breakfast with Lauren and then decided to check in at his office. With very little effort on his part, and maybe because of the current publicity surrounding the Mason trust, the firm of Winters and Tate had acquired several new clients. Zachary's time was once again in demand, and he was determined to make the law practice work.

For years he had suffered over Rosemary's death. Perhaps he had been at fault, giving too much of himself to his practice and not enough to his wife. Then, when Rosemary had died, he'd neglected the business, let it run itself into the ground. This time, he vowed to himself, he would find a way to balance his work against the time he spent with Lauren. It was a new beginning.

That afternoon, Lauren had just finished placing a roast in the oven and was eyeing the kitchen cabinets, contemplating her next project, when the phone rang. She answered it with a sinking heart, expecting to hear Zachary's voice on the other end of the line telling her that he'd have to work longer than expected.

"Hello?"

"Mrs. Regis?" asked an unfamiliar voice with a slight accent.

"Yes."

"This is Father McDougal with Our Lady of Promise. I'm calling from Twin Falls, Idaho. I saw your message in the Boise paper and…well, I was a little confused by it. You sound as if you don't know where your children are."

"That's right," she said with a short intake of breath.

"Maybe I can help. I might know where they are."

"What?" Lauren gasped, leaning against the wall for support. "Where?" she asked.

"Here, in Twin Falls. There's an Alicia Regis in Sister Angela's first grade class. Alicia has a younger brother by the name of Ryan. He's about three, I'd guess."

"Oh, thank God," Lauren said, her eyes brimming with tears of relief. At that moment Zachary walked into the house, took one look at Lauren's face and knew that the children had been found. A smile softened his rugged features.

"Can you explain what happened?" Father Mc-Dougal asked. "We were told the children's mother was deceased. That's why I called. I didn't think anyone who took out an ad like that would be an impostor."

"Of course not," Lauren replied.

"Then, what exactly happened, Mrs. Regis? Why did your husband lead us to believe that you were dead? Are you willing to tell me about it?"

"Oh, yes, yes." Hurriedly, she told him about the divorce and split custody rights and the painful day Doug had taken the children.

"I see," the priest murmured sympathetically. "You realize that I can't release Alicia to you," he said.

"But she belongs with me," Lauren began to protest.

"Be that as it may, I just can't give her to you without her father's consent. However, if you were to come with a court order, that would be different, I suppose.... I'd have to check with an attorney. Quite frankly, Mrs. Regis, we've never had a case like this."

"Of course," she murmured. "Can you give me a telephone number and address where I can reach Doug?"

"I think I can provide that," he said after a slight hesitation. "It's a matter of public record, so to speak, as he's listed in the phone book." Father McDougal gave her a phone number and street address, which Lauren quickly scribbled on a notepad.

"Thank you, Father," she said gratefully.

"Good luck to you, and come and see me when you get to Twin Falls."

"I will," she promised jubilantly. When she hung up the phone, she nearly collapsed. "You've found them," she said, tears of joy streaming down her face. "Doug had them hidden in a private Catholic school! Oh, Zachary, they're alive and well and waiting for me!"

"We can't be too sure about that," Zachary said, tossing his briefcase onto the couch. His triumphant smile had faded slightly.

"What do you mean?"

"There may be another woman involved, one they consider to be their mother. Remember, Doug was living with some woman named Becky."

"It doesn't matter. She has no right...they're my children."

"Then all we have to do is find a way to get them back," Zachary told her, adding grimly, "and that might not be any easier than finding them."

Chapter Eleven

The drive from Boise to Twin Falls seemed endless. Lauren gazed out the window at the ominous gray sky and the patches of snow on the sparsely needled pines and juniper stretching endlessly over the flat country-side.

Zachary was driving the rented car, and the fingers of his right hand curled possessively over hers, giving her strength to face the ordeal ahead. Conversation lagged, and the Boise radio station began to fade as they closed in on Twin Falls.

Lauren's thoughts centered on Alicia and Ryan and what she would say to them after the long, painful separation. She closed her eyes against the thought that they might not remember her or, even worse, might vaguely remember her but believe Doug's lies. Would they think she'd abandoned them without so much as a goodbye?

Perhaps they'd willingly accepted the unknown Becky as a replacement mother. What then?

Lauren hoped that Doug had no idea she was on her way to see him. She and Zachary had decided that it would be best to surprise him. Though she had longed to dial the phone number given her by Father McDougal, Lauren had forced herself to remain patient. The past two days had been difficult for her, knowing where the children were and not being able to go to them; but Lauren had accepted Zachary's advice and waited, trusting that she would be able to touch and see Alicia and Ryan soon . . . very soon.

By the time they reached Twin Falls, it was nearly four in the afternoon. After taking several wrong turns in the small city, Zachary located the address Father McDougal had given Lauren. The house was similar in design to all of its neighbors' houses and appeared to have been built sometime after the Second World War. The exterior of the house was suffering painfully from neglect. Paint was peeling off the small, screened porch, one of the wooden steps was broken and a rain gutter near one of the corners of the house hung at an awkward angle.

Lauren's stomach knotted in nervous anticipation as Zachary parked the car. "You're sure you want to go in?" he asked, searching her face with dark, omniscient eyes.

Lauren's jaw tightened. "I've spent the last year of my life for just this moment."

Zachary forced an encouraging smile. "Okay. Let's get it over with." He helped her from the car and held her hand as she strode through the creaky front gate, past the slightly overgrown yard, up the three short steps to the front door. She pushed the button for the doorbell, but when she didn't hear the sound of chimes within the small house, she rapped firmly upon the door. As she waited, Lauren's eyes scanned the porch and she noticed a slightly rusted tricycle pushed into the corner. The small three-wheeler had to belong to Ryan!

Two minutes later the door was opened and she was staring into the face of the man who had robbed her of her children, the man she'd once loved. Douglas Regis had aged more than a little in the past year. His curly brown hair, now cut short, was receding from his forehead and beginning to gray near the temples.

"Lauren?" Doug exclaimed, his face growing pale beneath the stubble of his beard. He was wearing only a grimy once-white undershirt and dusty jeans. He opened the screen door for a better look at her. "What're you doing here?"

She didn't smile. "I've come for the kids."

"The kids?" He seemed off balance and glanced from Lauren to Zachary and back again. "They're not here."

"Where are they?" she demanded.

"With friends."

"I want them and I want them now." Lauren's voice was firm, her gaze steady.

"Who're you?" Doug asked, his flinty eyes sliding over to Zachary.

"My lawyer—Zachary Winters," Lauren replied.

"Your *lawyer!*"

Zachary extended his hand and noticed that, though Doug accepted the handshake, his palms were sweating.

Doug turned suspicious eyes back to his ex-wife. "Why did you bring a lawyer?"

"To show you that I mean business."

Doug shrugged. "Big deal." He cocked his head in Zachary's direction. "He's not going to make any difference, you know. Alicia and Ryan are with me now."

"And you intend to keep them?"

"Yep." He crossed his tanned arms over his chest and leaned against the doorjamb, effectively blocking her way into the house.

"I'll fight you, Doug—in court, anywhere; I want my children back." Anger surged through her. "It took me a year to find you, and now that I have, I won't rest until the children are with me again."

"Christ, Lauren, you're serious about this, aren't you?" he said, obviously taken aback.

"Dead serious."

Doug looked disgusted at her strong words. "So fight me, then. See how long it takes—what happens. I really don't give a damn what you do."

Zachary's jaw tightened and he had to force his fists into his pockets to keep from strangling the bastard. "You're going to lose, Regis," he announced calmly. He rubbed his thumb thoughtfully, almost distractedly, along his lower jaw. "And I'll fix it so that this time you'll be allowed no custody, no visitation rights, nothing. It'll be just as if you never had a kid."

Doug fought a rising tide of panic. The smart-assed lawyer in the suede jacket and smooth cords *had* to be bluffing. Doug decided to gamble. "No court in the country would take my rights away from me. You're forgetting that this is the time of women's lib and father's rights."

Zachary smiled. "Are you willing to take that chance?" he asked softly.

The bastard looked so calm, so damned sure of himself. Doug felt his insides quiver.

"Wait a minute," Lauren cut in, noticing the ruthless thrust of Zachary's jaw. "There's no need to threaten each other—this isn't doing anyone any good. Especially not the children."

"The kids are fine," Doug said defiantly. "They've adjusted well."

"I don't believe it," she returned.

"Oh, Lauren don't be so goddamned egocentric. Sure, the kids missed you the first couple of weeks, but after that they were fine. Hell, you know how kids are. They bounce back."

"What did you tell them—about why you took them away?"

"Just the truth, Lauren," Doug said cockily.

"Which was?"

"That I wanted them with me and you wouldn't let me have custody." He managed a smile. "How's that for being straightforward?"

Lauren felt her knees weaken. "Oh, God, Doug, you didn't put them in the middle—make them think that they were the reason we couldn't get along...."

Doug shifted his gaze to the distant horizon. "They think you're dead," he whispered after a slight pause.

"What!" Lauren gasped. "Oh, Doug, no...." Instantly, Zachary put his arm around her shoulders. "No...God, how could you?"

Zachary's arm tightened. "You son of a bitch!" he muttered, his dark eyes blazing.

Doug was scared. The cool attorney from Portland wasn't easily fooled. "It's the only way I could handle them," he said hastily. "They were pretty upset and, well...it seemed like the only logical thing to do."

"Logical?" Lauren repeated, nearly screaming. "Letting them think that I was dead? That's sick, not logical. For God's sake, Doug."

Doug ignored her despair and continued talking. Fast. "So you see, you just can't show up here—prove me wrong." Though the temperature was only a little above freezing, Doug had begun to sweat; perspiration beaded on his forehead. "It took a little while, but Alicia and Ryan have adjusted. They consider Becky their mother."

"Becky?" Lauren nearly stumbled backward. Zachary's arm caught her and pulled her to him. "You had no right—"

"I had every right. They're my kids, dammit! I got tired of picking them up every other weekend or having to ask your permission just to take them out to McDonald's." He threw a hand up in the air dramatically. "They're all the family I had left . . . until I met Becky."

"Who is?" Zachary demanded.

"The woman I live with. She loves the kids and they adore her. She's all the mother they need!"

Lauren felt as if she were withering deep inside. "No!"

"It's over and done, Lauren. If you take the kids back with you now, you'll only screw them up. They're happy now, here with Becky and me. Don't blow it by showing up and putting them through hell."

"You did that, Doug. A year ago. I won't leave until they come with me," she said, fighting the tears in her eyes as her hands balled into fists of frustration.

Doug shook his head. "Then you're not thinking about the children, Lauren, you're only interested in your own selfish motives. As always. Any mother who would risk upsetting her children is no mother at all."

"What about a father who steals them?" she demanded. "And after that hides the kids and tells them that their mother is dead?'' She let out a long, disbelieving breath. ''You're more of a bastard than I would ever have guessed,'' she hissed.

''Why don't you and your...'attorney'—isn't that what you called him?—just leave?'' Doug's insolent gaze encompassed both Lauren and Zachary, silently assessing their relationship as more intimate than that of mere client and attorney. The affection they shared for each other might just come in handy. ''You're not wanted here.''

''I'm not leaving until I see Alicia and Ryan!''

''You're wasting your time. They're not coming home tonight.''

''Go get them.''

''Not on your life, Lauren, and don't even think about going to the school. Alicia won't be there tomorrow.'' He started to reach for the door.

''What're you going to do, Doug?'' Lauren asked as she sprang from Zachary's embrace and grabbed her ex-husband by the arm. He couldn't deny her the chance to see her children again. She wouldn't let him. ''Are you going to run away again?''

Doug poised his hand over the doorknob, and when he faced her, his gray eyes had grown cold. Lauren released his arm.

''I'll do whatever it takes to keep the kids here, with me and Becky.'' With that, he slammed the screen door and disappeared into the house.

''No!'' Lauren screamed after him, beating on the door with her fists. ''Doug...please!''

She felt Zachary's hands on her arms but wouldn't stop her pounding. ''Lauren, come on, he's not going to let you in.''

"But I have to see them," she cried, tears running from her eyes. *"I have to!"*

Zachary cast a worried glance at the door. "It won't do any good. He was too cool and calm. I think he told you the truth when he said that the kids aren't coming home tonight."

"Then where are they? And why aren't they with him? God, Zachary, we came all this way…. Oh, please…we have to find them…." He gathered her close and held her until she quieted.

"We're not finished," he promised, holding her close as they walked back to the car. "Not by a long shot…."

Lauren spent a restless night in the room she shared with Zachary at The River's Edge, an inn on the outskirts of the city. Their room was attractively decorated in knotty pine, crisp Priscilla curtains and antique furniture, and it had a breathtaking view of the silvery Snake River; but Lauren barely noticed. When she wasn't pacing restlessly on the polished pine floor, she was staring out the bay window, letting her gaze rest blankly on the distant horizon and replaying the terrible argument with Doug over and over again in her tortured mind.

Though Zachary's strong arms had held her tightly throughout the long night, she'd been torn apart by nightmares of Alicia and Ryan being swept away from her by a fierce, unyielding storm. In desperation she'd clung to Zachary and tried to sleep with her head resting on his chest, her arms and legs entwined with his, listening to the steady beat of his heart.

After attempting to eat a light breakfast of fruit and toast in the dining room at The River's Edge, Lauren braced herself for the ordeal to follow. Zachary drove to

Our Lady of Promise, the Catholic school located just outside Twin Falls.

Snow had begun to fall from the gray skies and collect on the sloping roof of the school. Zachary parked the car in the school lot, which offered a view of the front entrance to the school. Lauren watched as a small, ungainly parade of cars and trucks deposited students on the front steps of the school. Yellow slickers, brightly colored raincoats with matching umbrellas, hooded ski jackets and boots covered most of the uniforms as well as the faces of the noisy children as they climbed the short flight of brick stairs to the school.

"Did you see Alicia?" Zachary asked once the final bell had sounded and a few trailing students had scurried through the double doors and into the building.

"No." Lauren shook her head, unable to say anything else.

"Neither did I." He let out a frustrated sigh and placed the car keys in his pocket. "There's a chance that Doug made good his threat and Alicia isn't in school today."

"A very good chance, I'd say," Lauren replied listlessly.

"Right. So, let's go talk to your friendly priest."

Father McDougal was sitting at his desk when the office secretary announced Lauren and Zachary.

The priest looked up from the notes scattered on his desk and smiled as he extended his hand. His complexion was ruddy, his smile sincere. "You're Alicia's mother?" he asked, nodding his head before Lauren had a chance to reply. "Yes, I can see the resemblance."

"Then you know that I'm dying to see her," Lauren said.

The priest frowned slightly and fidgeted with his pen. "You haven't seen her yet?"

Lauren shook her head and glanced at Zachary before answering. "We tried to, just last night. The children weren't with Doug and he wouldn't tell me where they were. He . . . well, he told me not to bother coming to the school because it would be a waste of my time. Alicia wouldn't be here."

The priest's blue eyes grew troubled and his busy gray eyebrows drew together. "Miss Swanson?" he called, and the tall secretary reappeared. "Are the attendance reports in?"

"Not yet—lots of absenteeism because of the flu, you know," the lanky woman explained.

"What about Sister Angela's first grade class?"

"No."

Father McDougal frowned, took off the wire-rimmed glasses perched on the end of his nose and wiped a hand over his eyes. "Thank you," he said, dismissing the secretary before he looked at Lauren. "Can you prove that you're Alicia's mother?" he asked. "I have to protect the students in the school, and even though I can see a resemblance to Alicia, I'd like something a little more tangible before I let you see her. The way things are these days, one can never be too careful."

Lauren had been anticipating Father McDougal's request. She withdrew an envelope from her purse that contained copies of Alicia's birth certificate, the court papers awarding Lauren Regis custody of her two children and several photographs of Lauren and Doug with their two children. As the priest was examining the documents, Lauren took out her wallet and handed him her driver's license.

"I am Lauren Regis," she said as Father McDougal nodded to himself.

"May I keep these?" he asked, indicating the documents he had just perused.

"Please."

"Good." He offered Lauren an encouraging smile. "Why don't we walk on down to the first grade and see for ourselves if that daughter of yours is here?"

Zachary held Lauren's arm as they walked down the long corridor. She told herself to remain calm, that Doug had probably done what he'd said and kept Alicia out of school for the day. Lauren was so preoccupied that she barely noticed the displays of Thanksgiving artwork tacked to bulletin boards in the hallway.

Father McDougal paused at a door near the front entrance of the school. "This is Sister Angela's class. If you'll just wait here a minute, I'll go in, speak with Sister Angela and bring Alicia back. That way we can avoid any kind of emotional scene that might embarrass Alicia in front of her classmates."

Lauren leaned against the wall and waited. Father McDougal didn't take long. "Alicia didn't come to school today," he said when he returned, closing the classroom door softly behind him and looking at her compassionately.

Lauren nodded disconsolately. "It's not much of a surprise. Doug will do anything to keep her from me."

"Perhaps she'll be in later."

"I doubt it. Doug was pretty adamant," Lauren said with a trembling smile.

Zachary clenched his fists angrily and couldn't restrain a soft oath, which the priest politely ignored. Brian McDougal had heard far worse in his thirty-odd years as the administrator of several parochial schools.

"If there's anything I can do..." Father McDougal offered.

"There is, Father," Zachary replied, seizing the opportunity. "If you have any contact with the child, if Alicia returns to school, or you talk to Doug, please call me." Zachary wrote the name and the room number of The River's Edge on one of his business cards. "We'll be in Twin Falls a few more days, and after that you can contact me in Portland."

Father McDougal took the card from Zachary's outstretched hand. "I'll do my best," he promised. Zachary took Lauren's elbow and propelled her out of the building, urging her toward the rental car parked near the school.

"Where are we going?" Lauren asked when he maneuvered the car out of the school parking lot and headed back into town. The thought of facing the small room at the inn was unbearable. *So near and yet so far.* When would she ever see Alicia and Ryan again?

"We're going to check on your dear ex-husband," Zachary responded grimly.

"Why?"

"I want a few more answers, that's why. He doesn't seem to appreciate the gravity of the situation, and I think I'll lean on him a little."

"Lean on him?"

"Threaten him with a custody battle that would leave him naked."

"You tried that yesterday," she said, staring at the snow clinging to the parked cars and pine trees near the road.

"Yeah, but now he's had some time to think it over and sweat.... Maybe he'll realize that the gamble isn't worth the price he'll have to pay."

The small tract home seemed deserted. Lauren knew instantly that Doug had taken off with the kids again, and her heart sank.

"He's gone," she whispered when she'd looked at the darkened windows and rapped on the locked door. "He took the kids and left—just like before." She had to hike her coat around her neck to protect her from the wind.

"Maybe."

"Doesn't that concern you?" she asked.

"Not yet," Zachary replied cryptically as he walked around and looked through the windows. "I think he'll be back," he said, a gleam of satisfaction in his eyes as he rubbed his hands together and blew on his fingers.

"How can you be so sure?"

"I can't, but the furniture's still in the house, and I could see clothes in a couple of the closets. No, I don't think your ex has skipped town at all. My guess is that he's just waiting until we leave; then, maybe, he'll make some permanent plans for moving."

"Then I've blown the whole thing by coming here," she said miserably. "Just as you predicted."

"Not necessarily." Something in his tone caught her interest, and she looked at him. His eyes were dark but knowing, as if he were a bold and patient predator, certain of his prey.

"What are you up to, counselor?"

Zachary's smile widened. "You should know me well enough to guess that I wouldn't put all my eggs in one basket."

"What does that mean?"

"That I had my private investigator from Boise come here, to Twin Falls, with express instructions to watch Doug and the kids. If Doug left, I'll bet my man is on his tail."

Lauren managed a small, relieved smile. "That doesn't get the kids back."

"Yet."

"Maybe ever."

Zachary placed a finger under her chin. "But it makes sure we don't lose them again."

"Thank God," Lauren murmured.

Zachary glanced at the threatening sky. Snow was beginning to fall in large, crystalline flakes. "Come on, let's go back to the inn, see if there are any messages, and then I'll buy you a cup of coffee...or whatever else you might want," he offered, winking suggestively.

"That sounds like a proposition."

"Maybe."

Lauren's lips opened invitingly as Zachary kissed her deeply, wrapping his arms around her and warming the chill in her heart. Lauren snuggled against him and tried to ignore the fact that her fingers were numb. If only she had a portion of Zachary's strength and confidence. "You seem to think of everything," she said.

"Not everything." He grinned. "But I try, and I'll keep trying until we end up with Alicia and Ryan."

That night, after spending a long day waiting for a call from the private investigator, a call that never came through, Zachary and Lauren returned to Doug's small house and were surprised to see a light in the window.

"So our boy's returned," Zachary said with a note of satisfaction. "Let's go see if he's reconsidered."

Lauren placed her hand on the sleeve of his jacket. "Please, Zachary, *if* the children are inside, I want to avoid as much of a scene as I can."

His dark eyes searched her worried face. "I would never do or say anything that might alienate your children from either you or me, Lauren. Someday we're all going to be a family," he promised, kissing her gently on the lips. "Count on it."

"I am," she replied.

"Good, then buck up. This isn't going to be easy."

Zachary strode up the snow-covered path and rapped soundly on the front door. Within seconds a porch lamp made false daylight out of the darkness, illuminating the small screened-in area that offered little protection against the frigid air. By the time the door was opened, Lauren was at Zachary's side, staring at the young woman inside the house through the still locked screen door.

"Yes?" the raven-haired woman asked, eyeing Lauren and Zachary suspiciously.

"I'm looking for Douglas Regis," Zachary said.

"He's not here right now," was the evasive reply.

"When will he be back?"

"Who are you?" the woman demanded.

Lauren stepped closer to the closed screen door. "I'm Doug's ex-wife, Lauren Regis. I've come for my children."

The woman paled and leaned against the door. "I'm sorry, lady, whoever you are, but Doug's wife is dead...." Clear blue eyes scanned Lauren's face.

Zachary intervened. "Are you Becky McGrath?"

The woman nodded, eyeing Zachary with distrust and something akin to fear.

"My name is Winters. Zachary Winters. I'm Lauren's attorney and we're prepared to go to court if we have to."

"To take the kids away?"

"To return them to their mother."

"Oh, Lord," Becky mumbled, her chin trembling.

"Look, Becky, I saw Doug yesterday," Lauren told her. "He said the children think I'm dead, but I assumed that you knew the truth."

Becky began to close the door. "I think you'd better go away, both of you."

"I just want to see my children," Lauren cried. "Touch them, see how they've grown. Look!" She reached into her purse and withdrew her wallet, flipping it open to a small picture of the family before she and Doug were divorced. "I'm Lauren Regis, and those children you've been taking care of belong to me!"

"I'm going to call the police if you don't leave," Becky said, her voice trembling.

"Good!" Lauren retorted. "Let's see how Doug talks his way out of this one."

Becky hesitated a moment and then finally unlocked the screen door, allowing Lauren and Zachary to enter. "Doug will probably shoot me for this," she said as she closed the door behind Zachary and turned to face her uninvited guests. "Please sit down."

"Are the children here?" Lauren inquired, sitting on the edge of a slightly faded recliner near the door.

"No...they're with Doug. He...he said that you'd come here and that you'd probably insist you were Alicia and Ryan's mother," the young woman admitted sadly.

"I *am* their mother."

"Doug said that you'd be convincing."

"That's because I've got the truth on my side. I have proof with me, documents of the court order giving me custody of the children as well as their birth certificates."

"I'd like to see them."

"We left them at the school. With Father McDougal. You can call him if you like."

"Thank you. I will." Becky disappeared into the kitchen and through the archway separating the two rooms. Soon small pieces of Becky's side of the conversation could be heard.

As Lauren sat tensely on the edge of her chair, her eyes searched the small house where her children lived. The rooms were small but tidy, in direct contrast to the sorry condition of the exterior of the home. Though the furniture was worn, it was clean and enhanced by the needlework that adorned the rough plaster walls. A colorful afghan was folded neatly over the back of the couch, and a hand-embroidered cloth covered a round table near the picture window. Toys were stacked neatly in a basket near the hallway that led to the back of the house. Barbie dolls and action figures were tossed together with stuffed animals, balls and toy trucks.

Lauren walked over to the basket and pulled out a worn teddy bear that had been Alicia's favorite when the little girl had been a baby. New button eyes had been sewn onto the favorite stuffed animal. Clearly, Becky McGrath loved Alicia and Ryan. Try as she might, Lauren couldn't fight the tears building behind her eyes.

She was still kneeling at the toy basket, clutching the ratty old teddy, when she heard Becky's returning footsteps. The young woman was carrying a tray of filled coffee cups and trying to force a courageous smile to her pinched features.

"I talked to Father McDougal," she said, her voice barely above a whisper.

"And?"

"And he confirmed your story.... Here, please, have a cup of coffee." Becky's hands were shaking as she handed a mug to Zachary.

Lauren returned to the couch and accepted a cup of strong, black coffee.

"I didn't want to believe Father McDougal," Becky continued, running her fingers through her fine black hair. "I...well, I love the kids a lot. I've always thought of them as my own."

"I understand," Lauren said sympathetically. Becky's wounds were not unlike her own.

"But Lauren is their natural mother," Zachary pointed out.

"I...I know." Becky took a long breath, then sipped her coffee as she sat in a rocker near the bookcase. "Yesterday, when I got home, I knew something was wrong. Doug, he was...out of his mind with worry. He said some strangers had come claiming rights to the children, though it wasn't possible, as his wife had died over a year ago. He didn't know what was going on, but insisted that he had to hide the kids, keep Alicia out of school, to see that they, the kids, were safe from danger."

Lauren's throat tightened at the irony of it all. The safest place for her children was with her, where she could protect them. "Where did he take them?"

"I don't know." Tears were running down Becky's face, and she wiped them away with the hem of her sleeve. "I couldn't even guess. He wanted me to come with him, but I couldn't get away from work, and the whole thing...it didn't seem right. I thought he was kidding...or that the situation wasn't as crazy as he'd said." She stared into her cup and swallowed with difficulty. "I'd like to help you," she said, "but I don't know how."

"Do you think he'll return?"

Becky stiffened slightly. "I don't know. I think so. Most of his stuff is still here. God, I hope he comes back. He's...he's been good to me, and to the kids," she added hastily.

"That's hard for me to believe," Lauren said, remembering the bitter, painful scenes during her marriage.

"He loves those kids with all his heart," the woman declared. "He'd never do anything to hurt them."

"Except steal them from me and then lie and tell them that I was dead," Lauren cried.

"He's a good man," Becky insisted, sounding as if she were trying to convince herself. "Last year when Ryan caught a cold that developed into bronchitis, Doug could barely go to work, he was so worried. He took Ryan to the hospital himself, just to make sure that the kid wasn't suffering from pneumonia. Then, for the next three weeks, while Ryan was recovering, Doug held him every night, reading him stories, doing puzzles, anything Ryan wanted to do. I tell you, Doug was worried sick that he might lose him. I . . . I guess that sounds a little selfish to you," Becky added, seeing the look of genuine alarm on Lauren's face.

"I should have been with my child," Lauren murmured, fresh tears stinging her eyes.

Becky was wringing her hands in her lap, her eyes reddened from crying. "I don't know what to do." She shook her head. "There's nothing I can do but talk to Doug—see if he's willing to straighten out this mess between the two of you."

"And if he isn't?"

Becky's eyes widened and she shrugged.

"Then we'll go to court," Zachary announced. "One way or another, I'll see that Alicia and Ryan are back in Portland where they belong. *With their mother!*"

A small cry broke from Becky's throat. "I—I'll try to talk to him," she faltered, her hands moving nervously through her hair. "But I don't know if it'll do any good."

"It had better, Miss McGrath," Zachary responded grimly, determination blazing in his eyes. "If not, I promise you, I'll see Douglas Regis in court, and I'll make sure that he never sets eyes on his kids again!"

"You wouldn't!" Becky cried.

"Don't bet on it." Zachary set his empty cup on the table. "I'm not trying to punish you, Becky, I'm just trying to make Doug see that he's got to let Lauren have the kids, as the courts decided several years ago. And I won't rest until that's accomplished."

Chapter Twelve

Lauren's days seemed to run together in a haze of job interviews and anxious telephone calls to Father McDougal, Sister Angela and Zachary's private investigator, wherever the man happened to be at the time. It had been over two weeks since Zachary and Lauren had returned to Portland, and though Lauren had tried desperately to get on with her life, her thoughts continued to drift back to Twin Falls and Alicia and Ryan. From her telephone calls to Father McDougal, as well as from information provided by the private investigator, Lauren knew that her children were back in Twin Falls with Doug and were as well as could be expected.

For two days after the discussion with Becky McGrath, Lauren and Zachary had waited in Twin Falls, hoping that Doug would return with the children. He hadn't, and Becky had refused to speak with Lauren or Zachary again. Zachary had left his business card with the worried young woman, and then he'd insisted that both he and Lauren should return to Portland.

During the day, while Zachary was at the office, Lauren busied herself with projects around the house and employment interviews. She had several callbacks and was hoping for a job with a bank located in the heart of downtown Portland, only a few blocks away from Old Town and Zachary's office in the Elliott Building.

Her nights had been spent in passionate embrace with Zachary, and each day she loved him more than she'd ever thought possible. He was strong but kind, stubborn but open-minded. She thought she would be able to live with him forever.

"Marry me," he'd whispered two nights earlier, after a particularly erotic lovemaking session. His body was still glistening with sweat, and the fires of passion lurked in his incredible brown eyes.

"I will."

"Tomorrow," he'd insisted, his warm fingers touching the nape of her neck and causing shivers of anticipation to ripple deliciously down her spine.

She'd smiled to herself and cuddled closer to him, letting the soft hairs of his chest press against her cheek. "I can't, not yet." Even his words of love couldn't melt the ice surrounding her heart. She was still numb with the grief of finding her children, only to lose them again without even a chance to see or talk to Alicia or Ryan.

"Why not tomorrow?" Zachary had persisted, lazily stroking the sensitive skin over her collarbone and staring into the brilliant green depths of her eyes.

Her fingers had played in the soft hair matting his chest. "Don't you think it would be better if we waited until the children are home and have adjusted to the change in their lives?" she'd murmured softly.

"You're hedging."

She'd laughed softly. Nothing was further from the truth. Marrying Zachary was what she wanted more than anything in the world—except, of course, finding her children. "And you're pushing," she'd replied teasingly.

Her wavy auburn hair was fanned out over the pillow beside him, and Zachary had twined his fingers in the long, fiery strands. "I love you, lady," he'd declared, his voice husky with emotion, and she'd believed him.

Now, she wasn't so sure. In fact, as Lauren stood in Zachary's office, where he sat behind his battered oak desk, she felt as if he'd literally knocked the breath from her body. She'd meant to surprise him, to take him to lunch and tell him her good news—she'd just been hired as a trust administrator for a bank not five blocks south of the Elliott Building. But she forgot everything with the weight of his announcement.

"What—what did you say?" she stammered, still unable to believe what she thought she'd just heard. Her hands gripped the strap of her purse so tightly that the soft leather dug into her palms.

"I said it was all a bluff." Zachary removed his reading glasses and massaged the bridge of his nose. Suddenly he looked older than his thirty-five years. Angrily, as if in self-condemnation, he jerked at the strangling knot of his tie.

"The court battle for the kids? It was a bluff?" Lauren asked incredulously. "Wait a minute, Zachary, I don't know if I understand, or if I want to. Didn't you tell me not two days ago that Doug's attorney in Twin Falls advised him to return Alicia and Ryan to me? What happened?"

Since Lauren and Zachary had returned to Portland from Twin Falls, things had been progressing nicely in her struggle to regain custody of her children, or so Zachary had claimed. Until now, when all of her trust in him had just shattered as easily as fine crystal against stone.

"Doug refused to heed his lawyer's advice. He's going to fight you, Lauren."

She slumped into a nearby leather chair. "Well, I didn't really expect him to roll over and play dead," she said, holding on to her faltering courage. "If it's a fight he wants, then he's got it."

Zachary tapped his fingers on his desk, and his dark eyes impaled hers. "I don't think so."

"You were the one who threatened him in the first place," she pointed out. "Now you're telling me it's all a bluff?"

"You don't want to drag this through the courts."

"The hell I don't!" she cried, glaring at him. "What's this all about?"

"Your kids."

"The kids that I don't have," she reminded him.

"I don't think you want to put them through the trauma and scandal of a custody suit. Think about what it will do to them."

"What?"

"You saw Doug's house, met Becky. When Doug told you that the children were happy, did you believe him?"

"I . . . I don't know. No, I guess I didn't."

"But you called Sister Angela at the school. What did she report on Alicia?"

Lauren looked away from Zachary's intense stare, the pain in his eyes, and gazed instead through the window at the cars moving slowly across the Broadway Bridge.

"What did Sister Angela say, Lauren?" Zachary repeated.

Lauren glanced back at him and sighed. "That Alicia was a good student, a little shy, but..."

"Happy and well adjusted, right?" His brown eyes dared her to deny what the sister had reported. "That's the bottom line, Lauren," he said, more gently, "that the kids are healthy, well adjusted and happy."

"But they don't even know that I'm alive." Her voice cracked.

"Then we'll have to convince Doug to tell them, force him to see that joint custody is the only answer, *without* a court battle." He stood and raked his fingers through his hair in frustration. "Look, Lauren, the last thing you want to do is screw up the kids or make them resent you. This has to be handled delicately."

"But you promised," she said unsteadily, her hands opening in a supplicating gesture. "You threatened Doug unmercifully. Now you're going to back down?"

"Those threats weren't idle. We could take him to court, but it would only hurt everyone involved—Alicia, Ryan, Becky, you and me."

Her eyes narrowed with sudden understanding. "That's what this is all about," she said. "It has nothing to do with the kids or their well-being."

"Of course it does."

"No, Zachary. It's what you just said, about you and me and how it will affect our relationship. I think that now that we're talking about marriage and a future together, you finally realized that you don't want to raise another man's kids." He seemed to pale and she plunged on desperately, praying he would stop her, deny her words. "You're still wounded, Zachary, because of the fact that Rosemary was pregnant with another man's child. You can't bear the thought of being around children that aren't yours."

"That's ridiculous!"

"Is it?" She felt the sting of tears but refused to break down in front of him.

"You know I'd do anything to get Alicia and Ryan back to you!"

"Short of the one thing that will guarantee it." She fought the urge to scream at him, to pound his chest with her fists. "You're my attorney; I hired you to find the kids, and you have. Now I'm requesting that you file the necessary papers to take Doug to court."

She noticed a muscle working in his jaw, read the agony in his eyes. "I can't do it, Lauren."

"Can't?"

"All right then, I won't."

"Why?"

"Because I don't want to tear those kids apart by putting them on the stand. I don't want them to have to see their mother and father go at each other's throats. I don't want to be a part of anything that might make them hate you, Lauren."

"Hate me?" She looked at him incredulously and thought she saw his eyes grow damp.

"Lauren, think! Just think!" His hands clenched in exasperation. "In all probability, Alicia barely remembers you. Doug told her you were dead, and she's worked her way through her grief over the loss of her mother. And Ryan's too young even to remember anything about you."

"No—"

"You *have* to work this out with Doug," Zachary insisted. "That's the only way to protect the children."

"But he won't—"

"He will! We'll make him!"

"How?" she asked, tears beginning to well in her eyes. Zachary was giving up! The one man she had trusted with her life, her love, her soul and he was giving up! Didn't he understand? This was the man she loved with all of her heart, yet he didn't seem to know just how important the children were to her. She couldn't even think about starting a life with him without Alicia and Ryan.

"It'll take time," Zachary was saying, "but I think we can work with his lawyer and Becky."

"I don't have time, Zachary! Don't you know me well enough to know that I'm dying a little each day that I'm apart from them? Haven't you noticed that these last two weeks have been a torture for me? Dear Lord, if I could, I'd drive to Twin Falls tonight and steal those kids back!"

"And what would that accomplish?"

Tears spilled from her eyes. "I'd have my babies with me again—" Her voice broke on a sob.

"And they'd be more confused, frustrated and guilt-ridden than before. You have to be patient."

"I have been, Zachary. It's been fifteen months. *Fifteen lonely, damned near unbearable months!* In less than four weeks it will be Christmas. I can't bear the thought of the holidays without my children. I won't have it. I just . . . can't. How can you stand there and ask me to be patient?"

Zachary watched as the woman he had grown to love slowly dissolved in tears before his eyes. "Even if we petitioned the court today, the kids wouldn't be home by Christmas."

Lauren lifted her chin defiantly. "And then you wouldn't have to deal with another man's responsibility. Right?"

"How can you even ask me that?" he cried with a look that cut right through her.

"Because that's the way it is, counselor." With all the courage she could muster, she stood before him and fought against the arguments in her mind, the arguments that told her to trust him. "I think, under the circumstances, that it would be best if we didn't see each other for a while."

Zachary tensed, and his face grew rigid, a mask devoid of expression. "Think about what you're doing, Lauren. You're throwing away everything we've shared in the past as well as what we could have in the future." She started to back away, but his hands captured her arms in a punishing grip. His face was only inches from hers, and the discipline over his features fell away. Fresh anger twisted his expression cruelly. His near-black eyes drilled into hers, searching for the darkest reaches of her soul. "This argument is just a handy excuse to get out of a relationship you never really wanted in the first place, isn't it?"

"Maybe it was never meant to be."

"That's ducking the real issue, Lauren; a cop-out. People do things because they want to, not because fate deals them bad cards. It's not fate, or kismet or the luck of the draw that brought you here two months ago. You're in charge of your own life, and either you want me or you don't. It's a simple matter of choice."

"Oh, I want you all right," she said bitterly. "But I want the man I knew two months ago—the recluse in the untidy office who agreed to help *me* because he believed in my cause; the man who took my case because he was the best Portland had to offer; the one attorney in town who would be ruthless enough to do *anything* to find Alicia and Ryan and return them to me."

She looked around the clean office. "This man you've become..." She shook her head and refused to see the compassion in his eyes. All she could think about was his crisp business suit, the new staff of secretaries in the outer reception area, the tidy room that was dust-free. She'd lost the man she'd met only two months earlier.

"I'm still the same man, Lauren," he said, pulling her to him and holding her close. "The only difference is that I fell in love with you—"

"Don't—please, Zachary." Firmly, she pulled out of his embrace. "There may be a time for us," she whispered. "But it's not now...not ever, until I get the kids back." She backed toward the door, and when her hand found the cold metal of the knob, she said, "I think it would be best if I got in touch with another attorney, someone who isn't personally involved."

"Like Tyrone Robbins?" he shot back, his wounded pride taking hold of his tongue.

She felt as if he'd slapped her face. "At least Tyrone didn't play with my emotions," she said, jerking the door open and racing out of the office, past the three secretaries who barely looked up from their word processors, past Amanda Nelson's desk in the outer office, through the doors and nearly into Joshua Tate, returning from lunch. Lauren didn't stop but headed for the elevators, hoping that she could erase Zachary Winters from her life as quickly as possible.

When Joshua Tate entered Zachary's office thirty minutes later, he found his partner standing at the window staring at the stark winter's day. Zachary's tie was loosened and hung around his neck like a noose. In one hand was a stiff shot of bourbon; the half-full bottle sat in the middle of the desk. Just like before.

Joshua swore under his breath. "What happened?" he asked as he settled into one of the chairs near Zack's desk.

Zachary didn't bother to turn around, but his eyes narrowed a bit as he studied the murky waters of the Willamette.

"Trouble in paradise?" Josh pressed.

"What's that supposed to mean?"

"That I nearly ran into Lauren Regis as she stormed out of here."

"Hmmph." Zachary took a long swallow of the bourbon, then drained his glass.

Joshua played with the tip of his mustache. "I thought you might like to know that Northwestern Bank settled for two hundred thousand. Just got the call today. I bet that set badly in old George West's craw."

Zachary leaned against the windowsill and studied the younger man. "Quite a coup for you."

Joshua looked puzzled. "I suppose so."

"But you can't find the satisfaction you thought you'd feel?"

"That's a good way to describe it, I guess. Maybe if we'd gone to trial..."

"Patrick Evans would have eaten you alive."

Joshua let out a bitter laugh. "Such confidence in your partner. It warms the cockles of my heart."

"What heart?" Zachary tossed out bitterly, and noticed the wounded look in his young partner's eyes. The kid still admired him, despite all the troubles they'd been through together. Zachary sighed and looked into his glass. "I've never lied to you, Josh. I don't want to start now. Settling was a good move." He frowned into his empty glass and reached for the bottle, but Josh's hand stopped him.

"Come on, Zack, I'll buy you a drink...a real drink."

Zachary was about to refuse, but Joshua beat him to the punch. "Come on, we owe it to ourselves. At least I do. It's not often we get to knock someone with a reputation like Pat Evans to his knees."

"I don't think you did. George West just panicked."

"Nonetheless, we should celebrate. Really tie one on."

Zachary regarded the eager young man before him. He would have been proud to call Joshua Tate his son. Oh, sure, Josh still had a few rough edges, and the kid was a cocky son of a bitch, but with a few more years under his belt and a couple of defeats in the courtroom, as well as the bedroom, the kid would come out on top. And you couldn't ask for more than that. Even if Joshua Tate didn't have Zachary's blood in his veins, Zachary still considered the young man like a son, or at least a younger brother. They were bound together and had managed to make the most of it.

Lauren's furious accusations still burned in Zachary's mind, but he knew that she was wrong. He wasn't the kind of man who needed a legacy of sons to carry on his name. Hell, he'd adopt a kid without a second thought. All he really wanted in life was a family with one woman, and that woman now wanted no part of him.

"A drink? Why the hell not?" Zachary asked suddenly, to Joshua's surprise. "As long as you're buying."

"Wouldn't have it any other way."

Zachary took off his tie and grabbed his jacket. "Let's go." As the two men passed by Amanda's desk, Zachary called over his shoulder, "Cancel everything this afternoon, Miss Nelson. Mr. Tate and I will be out for the rest of the day."

"But—" Amanda's voice fell on deaf ears as the two men strode out the glass doors of the suite of offices on the eighth floor of the Elliott Building.

Nearly a week had passed since she'd seen Zachary, and Lauren couldn't get him out of her mind. She'd called several attorneys, met with them and found she couldn't ask a stranger to help her fight the custody battle for her children.

Time was running out. Her new job started right after the holidays on the second of January, and after that she wouldn't be able to spend much time with an attorney.

She stared at the gray December sky and wondered why she couldn't shake the feeling of doom that had been with her ever since rushing out of Zachary's office last week. He'd called twice, left messages on the recorder, but Lauren hadn't bothered to return them. She needed time alone to think about her future. It looked so bleak without Zachary or the children.

After spending nearly an hour with a Portland lawyer who was more interested in eyeing the clock than listening to her story, Lauren felt hopelessly defeated. She'd missed Zachary's presence in her house, and she dreaded the thought of returning to the empty cottage alone. Too many memories haunted her there. Memories of Zachary with paint splattered over his shirt while attempting to refinish her cabinets in the kitchen; of Zachary studying his notes and trying to think of ways to locate Alicia and Ryan; of Zachary sleeping in her bed, holding her close, making the most beautiful love in the world. And all these memories caught and held in her mind, mixed with the all-consuming loneliness she felt for her children.

Yesterday had been the worst day of her life. The Christmas package she'd mailed to Alicia and Ryan had been returned unopened with a quick note in Doug's familiar scrawl: "Don't try to contact them again. D." The message was simple but infuriating, and it had driven her to the clock-watching attorney's office.

Frustrated and feeling that justice was truly blind, Lauren walked along the sea wall of the park, located on the west bank of the Willamette River. A cool breeze pushed her hair away from her face, and a fine mist settled on her skin. While studying the gray water and watching the Hawthorne Bridge as it opened to let a barge travel upstream, Lauren felt another person's presence beside her.

When she looked up, her eyes clashed with Zachary's enigmatic gaze, and her heart fluttered at the sight of him. He was wearing the same running shorts and gray sweatshirt that he'd worn on the first day she'd barged into his office only two months earlier. Tall and broad-shouldered, with his damp sable-colored hair falling over his eyes, his complexion slightly reddened from exertion and the winter wind, he was as attractive as ever. Lauren felt a lump in her throat at the sight of him. Would she never stop loving this man?

"Lauren," he said, but the smile that touched his lips faded immediately. "I tried to get hold of you this morning."

"I was out . . . business downtown."

She didn't elaborate, but the tightening of his mouth indicated that he understood she was seeing another attorney. It didn't matter. What he had to say was far more important.

"Becky McGrath called this morning," he said, wiping the sweat from his brow.

Lauren's heart nearly stopped beating. Something had happened to one of the children!

"Doug's been in a serious accident in the lumber mill where he worked."

"Oh, no. Is he..."

"Becky didn't know exactly what the prognosis was, but she was worried sick. She thinks that he might die and thought you should know about it."

"Oh, God," Lauren whispered. "The children. What about the children?"

"They don't know how serious the accident was. Becky's managed to keep that from them, but she's pretty shook up herself. From what I understand, Doug's already been in the hospital for three days."

"I've got to go to them. They need me," Lauren cried, starting to turn away.

"I'm coming with you," he said softly as he reached for her arm. "I think *you* might need *me*."

She looked up at him, her eyes glistening with tears. "More than you could guess," she whispered, and felt his arms slowly wrap around her. "More than you could possibly guess." The wind ruffled her hair as she held him, clinging desperately to the man she loved. If the last year without the children had been hard, this last week without Zachary had been worse.

"I've always loved you, Lauren. No matter what you might think, I'll always love you *and* your children." The warmth of his breath caressed her hair, and she had to blink rapidly to fight the tears of relief in her eyes.

"I've been a fool," she whispered.

"No, lady, what you've been is a concerned parent. Come on, I'll take you home," he said. "I've made plane reservations, and we leave Portland in less than three hours."

"But wait a minute. You were out here jogging. You couldn't have expected to find me."

"I thought I'd give you about another thirty minutes and then I'd camp out on your door. If you didn't show up in time, I'd change the plane reservations until tomorrow, but I was certain that we'd be going to Twin Falls—together."

"How did you know?" she asked softly.

"Because, lady, I wouldn't have it any other way."

Doug's house was nearly snowbound as Lauren and Zachary climbed the steps to the front porch. Zachary rapped loudly on the door, and Lauren's heart beat crazily in anticipation. She could hear the sounds of children within the small home and she swallowed back the fear that Alicia and Ryan would reject her.

Becky opened the door. She was older-looking than she had been just a few weeks earlier. "I'm glad you're here," she said without bothering to greet Lauren or Zachary. "Come in, come in."

Lauren stepped into the room, and the two children, who had been playing loudly on the floor of the living room, looked up at the strangers. Tears filled Lauren's eyes as Alicia dropped the doll she'd been holding and studied her mother carefully.

"Mommy?" she asked, her sober blue eyes rounding in recognition. "Daddy said you were dead."

"I told you that was all a big mistake," Becky interjected as a shy smile tugged at the corners of Alicia's mouth.

Lauren bent down on one knee and opened her arms as wide as possible. After only a moment's hesitation, Alicia ran into her mother's arms and hugged her fiercely. "I'm glad you're not dead," she whispered against Lauren's hair.

"Oh, me, too, baby," Lauren said, unable to hide her sobs of happiness. "I've missed you so much. You're such a big girl now and..." She held Alicia back and grinned. "You even lost a tooth."

"Two!" Alicia pronounced proudly. "And the top ones are wiggly. See?" She moved the upper baby teeth with a smile of satisfaction.

Lauren hugged her daughter and looked up to Ryan, who was watching her intently.

"Who you?" he demanded firmly.

"I'm Mommy," Lauren said, her voice shaking.

Ryan shook his blond curls and scooted over to Becky. "Mommy," he pronounced, holding up his chubby arms to Becky. The young woman picked him up and cleared her throat.

"No honey," she said with difficulty. "I'm not your Mommy. Alicia is with your real Mommy."

"No!" Ryan's face pinched together in confusion, and tears gathered in his eyes. "You Mommy," he said brokenly, his arms encircling Becky's neck and holding on for dear life.

"I'm...your stepmother," Becky said for want of a better name as she tried to placate the confused child. "You can call me—"

"Mommy," Lauren interjected, though her heart was breaking. "He's called you that as long as he can remember.... Let's not worry about relationships, not yet." Her worried eyes held Becky's grateful stare in an instant of understanding.

Becky closed her eyes and clung to Ryan. In a few minutes, when the curly-headed boy felt more at ease, Becky placed him back on the floor and Ryan absorbed himself with his toys, only occasionally glancing worriedly at the couch, where Lauren held Alicia.

Zachary stood near the door, getting more than one questioning look from each child. He tried to remain quiet, allowing Lauren a little privacy while he watched the tender reunion. Never would he have suspected that the reuniting of Lauren with her children would touch such a sensitive part of his soul....

"Why doesn't Ryan remember you?" Alicia asked, refusing to let go of Lauren.

"He's too young."

"And dumb!"

"No, honey, I think it's just a little too much for him. Now, tell me, how's Daddy?"

"He got hurt at work. Mom—Becky's real sad about it. So am I."

"Me, too," Lauren said honestly. The last thing she wanted was any more trouble for Doug. The pain she'd suffered at his hands could be forgiven, if not forgotten.

"Maybe your mother and her friend," Becky indicated Zachary, "would like some of those cookies you baked."

"Oh, yeah!" Alicia exclaimed.

"Would you like to serve them?"

"Sure!" Alicia hopped off Lauren's lap and headed for the kitchen.

Ryan was right behind her. "Me, too."

Alicia looked peeved but allowed her younger brother to help. When the children were out of earshot, Becky turned anxious eyes on Zachary and Lauren.

"How is Doug, really?" Lauren asked.

Becky let out a weary sigh and cast a furtive glance over her shoulder, in the direction of the kitchen. "Not good," she admitted. "His accident was very serious. A sharp, heavy piece of machinery broke off and struck Doug in the face. He was unconscious for over twenty-four hours, and for two days the doctors didn't think he would pull through.

"And now?"

"The worst is over, thank the Lord," Becky said, "but the doctors think he'll be blind."

Lauren gasped. "Permanently?"

Becky shrugged. "They're not certain, but the optic nerve was damaged.... It doesn't look good."

Lauren shook her head in disbelief. "Is there anything I can do?"

Becky nodded and braced herself. "Yes. Doug's been down, and you can understand why. Anyway, he's afraid that you'll try to take the children away from him...take him to court, see that he never has a chance to be with them again. All he wants right now is partial custody, like before."

Lauren's voice nearly failed her. "And how will I know that he won't take them from me again?"

"For God's sake, the man is blind!" Becky whispered hoarsely before managing to calm herself. "He can't very well take them from you now. And...well, you've got my word on it. I...I know how much the children mean to you as well as to Doug, and I hope that you can see your way clear to help him."

"I'll think about it," Lauren said as Alicia walked into the room proudly carrying a tray of chocolate chip cookies.

"I baked them myself," she said.

"I helped," Ryan added.

After Alicia had passed out the cookies, Becky rose. "I'm going to the hospital to visit your Dad. You two stay here with your mom and Mr. Winters."

"No!" Ryan cried firmly, running over to Becky and lifting his arms to her.

"It's all right," Alicia said. "It's Mommy."

"No!" Ryan said, and began to cry. Lauren picked him up as Becky walked out the door, but Ryan would have none of it. He held his little hands toward the door and called "Mommy" over and over again, nearly breaking Lauren's heart. Only after two hours did her young son allow Lauren to read to him, and then he watched the door like a hawk, waiting for Becky's return.

The next morning, Lauren went to visit Doug. Zachary was with her, but he stayed in the waiting room while Lauren walked down the stark, polished floor of the corridor to Doug's private room.

"Are you awake?" she asked the bandaged figure lying rigidly on the hospital bed. The room was small, airless and filled with the odors of dying carnations and antiseptic.

"Lauren?" Doug shifted and turned toward her. The entire upper half of his face was covered with gauze, and IV tubes trailed out of both arms.

Lauren closed her eyes against the pitiful sight. This man was the father of her children, the man with whom she'd shared a large, if painful, part of her life. "I'm here."

Doug smiled slightly. "I'm glad. There's something I've been meaning to say to you."

"I'm listening." She took a seat on the edge of a plastic chair near the bed.

"Oh, Lauren, if you could only know how sorry I am for everything I've done."

"Doug, you don't have to—"

"Yes I do, dammit. All I've done is mess up your life. First when we were married... I really never wanted another woman but you... you were so smart, always had the right answers. I guess... because I was such a failure I resented you. It made me feel bigger somehow to sleep with other women."

"I don't think we should go into this right now." All the pain in her marriage came vividly to mind. She didn't want to remember the hate and resentment she'd felt. It had been over long ago.

"Yes. *Now*. While I've got the courage. Look, I've been seeing... Bad choice of words." He grew silent for a moment and then continued. "I've talked with a psychiatrist. Already had three sessions. Once before the accident and then twice here, in the hospital. Anyway, I've decided that I've been an A-one, first-class bastard to you, the kids, even Becky. And I want to straighten it all out."

"You returned my Christmas gift to the kids."

Doug sighed and shifted uncomfortably on the bed. "That package was the reason I went to a shrink in the first place. It bothered me. A lot. I felt incredibly guilty. And I want to start again, with you and the kids. I think I can deal with partial custody now."

"Oh, Doug, I don't know—"

"Look, Lauren, this is something I've *got* to do. I knew it before the accident, and then, when I found out how mortal I was, everything became clear. Maybe it's because I almost died, or maybe it's because I'll never be able to see again. But I've got to get it together. I'm thirty-two years old and I've run out of excuses for my life. I suddenly realized that I couldn't have everything my way, and instead of being mad about it or blaming someone else..."

"Like me?"

"Yeah, like you." His fingers moved nervously over the metal rails of the bed. "I decided that I had to be responsible, for what happened to you, our marriage and the children. I'm letting you take the kids back to Portland for good. The only thing I ask is that you let them come and visit me for a month in the summer each year. And when I'm in Portland, I'd like to see them, if you'll let me."

He waited, a pathetic figure draped in white. Lauren couldn't deny him such a small request.

"How will I know that you won't steal them from me again?"

"Oh, God, Lauren, I know this must be hard for you, but I'm asking you to trust me. One more time. I'm petrified of the thought that my children may grow up and not even know me. Becky and I are planning to get married, once I master being blind, and we've been talking about children of our own."

"That's . . . that's wonderful, Doug. I'm happy for you."

"And what about you?"

"I hope that once the kids are settled I'll be getting married."

"To that Winters guy?"

"Yes."

Doug frowned. "I hope it works for you."

"It will."

She rose to leave and Doug heard the rustle of her skirt. "Lauren?"

"Yes."

"How're the kids, really? Becky . . . well, she tried to hide things from me, make me think things were better than they are, but I need to know the truth. From you."

"I think the children will be fine. Alicia's worried about you, but she's glad that I'm back. Becky explained that I was never dead." Doug winced at the words. "She said that you'd made a horrible mistake. Of course someday Alicia will be old enough to understand the truth." Doug scowled but didn't say anything, so Lauren continued, "I don't know how Alicia will feel about moving back to Portland, but I think she'll adjust."

"And Ryan?"

"He's more difficult. At first he flat-out rejected me. And it hurt, Doug. It hurt like hell. But now he'll let me hold him. He still thinks Becky is his mother."

"My fault," Doug said, self-condemnation evident in his voice.

"What was it you said—something about kids bouncing back?" Lauren asked. "Ryan will be fine."

"I love the kids, Lauren," he said.

"I know," she replied carefully. "And I won't take them away from you forever. I'll let you see them during the summers—or on holidays...."

He sniffed, and his voice was husky. "Thank you. You don't know how much this means to me, after what I did to you; you don't owe me anything."

"Let's just try to do what's best for our children. Goodbye, Doug. And good luck."

"Thanks."

Lauren walked out of the room and hurried back to the waiting room, where the man she loved was pacing impatiently.

"Well?" Zachary asked, his dark eyes searching her face as he folded her into his arms.

"It's going to be all right. Everything is going to be all right!" She hugged him fiercely and promised herself that this time she would never let go.

For the first time in three years, Portland was blessed with a white Christmas. The evergreen trees in the park were laden with piles of pristine white snow, and throughout the neighborhood children made snowmen and sledded on the steeper streets. Laughter and Christmas carols rang through the night.

The lights of the Christmas tree in Lauren's house winked brightly and reflected off the windowpanes. Four stockings hung over the mantel, just below the portrait of Alicia and Ryan. A yule log burned merrily, and the packages under the tree were as brightly colored as the glittering decorations on the sturdy boughs of the Douglas fir standing near Lauren's favorite rocker.

Lauren was pulling the turkey out of the oven when Zachary came up behind her and slipped his arms around her waist.

"What're you doing?" she asked with a laugh.

"Couldn't resist the view," he replied, nuzzling her ear and holding a ribboned piece of mistletoe over her head. "You're a tantalizing woman, Mrs. Winters."

"I'll take that as a compliment, thank you." She turned and faced him, her arms wrapping lovingly around her husband's neck. Snowflakes still clung to his dark hair. Her own feelings of love were reflected in his eyes, and the smoldering flames of passion sparked as he placed his lips over hers.

"You should," he murmured against her neck once the kiss had ended.

"Should what?"

"Take it as a compliment."

"Consider it done. Oh, by the way, a package arrived from Twin Falls today," Lauren said, watching Zachary's reaction. "Gifts for the kids from Doug and Becky."

"Did you put it under the tree?"

"Of course."

"And how's Doug?"

"Becky wrote a note on the card. He's as well as can be expected, she said. And he got home last week."

"His eyes?"

Lauren shook her head thoughtfully. "It still doesn't sound good."

"This is all going to work out, you know."

"Is that a promise?"

He smiled rakishly. "One you can count on, lady."

She laughed and returned the turkey to the oven. "So where are the kids? Didn't you make some wild promise to take them sledding?"

"Not on Christmas Eve. They're still in the backyard. I think I've had all the fun I can take for one night. Your daughter is deadly with a snowball." His wet sweater attested to his defeat in battle.

"Shame on you for letting a little seven-year-old whip you!"

"Mommy…" Ryan's pitiful wail interrupted the kisses Zachary was placing on Lauren's neck.

"Just a minute," she called back, her heart swelling with pride. In just two weeks, both Ryan and Alicia had adjusted beautifully, and though they were still a little wary of Zachary, they were beginning to accept him. Lauren had never been happier. The small, quiet wedding had been perfect, with her two small children in attendance. And the look of love in Zachary's eyes continued to amaze her.

"'Licia put snow down my back," Ryan cried, his eyes filled with tears of frustration.

"You'll just have to learn to defend yourself, young man," Lauren advised, lifting his wet hat and placing a kiss on his forehead.

"You help me, Mom. You put a snowball down her sweatshirt!"

"Not on your life."

Once changed into dry clothes, Ryan disappeared through the back door. Lauren eyed her son lovingly, and her eyes filled with tears as she looked around the small house that had been her home for over three years.

"It's going to be hard to move," she said wistfully.

"But we'll have more room at my place. Room for a dog for Ryan," Zachary replied, thinking of the fluffy half-breed cocker pup that he'd picked up just the day before. Right now the puppy was hidden away in the garage with a large red ribbon that would be placed around his neck early the next morning. Even Lauren didn't know about his surprise for Ryan or the new bicycle he'd bought for Alicia. "I might even spring for a horse for Alicia."

Lauren smiled and wrapped her arms around Zachary's neck. "You'll spoil them rotten, you know."

"Just like I intend to spoil their mother."

"Do I detect a note of bribery in your voice?"

"Maybe.... I think it's about time Alicia and Ryan had a younger brother or sister to pick on."

"Two kids aren't enough?" she asked with a laugh.

"Sure. For a start. But I was thinking more along the lines of five or six."

"That's because you're not the one who'd have to go through pregnancy. Not in a million years."

His hands spanned her waist possessively. "Okay, I'll settle for just one more. How about it? Ryan's nearly four already. It's time he had a brother."

"Or a sister?"

"I'm not picky."

The thought of carrying another child, Zachary's child, pleased her. "Whatever you say, counselor. Whatever you say."

A smile spread over Zachary's handsome face. "The sooner, the better. Merry Christmas, darling." He pulled her close and gently kissed her forehead. "Thank you for forcing your way into my life."

"My pleasure," she said with a smile, and tipped her chin, gladly accepting the warmth of his kiss.

The Silhouette Cameo Tote Bag Now available for just $6.99

Handsomely designed in blue and bright pink, its stylish good looks make the Cameo Tote Bag an attractive accessory. The Cameo Tote Bag is big and roomy (13″ square), with reinforced handles and a snap-shut top. You can buy the Cameo Tote Bag for $6.99, plus $1.50 for postage and handling.

Send your name and address with check or money order for $6.99 (plus $1.50 postage and handling), a total of $8.49 to:

Silhouette Books
120 Brighton Road
P.O. Box 5084
Clifton, NJ 07015-5084
ATTN: Tote Bag

SIL-T-1

The Silhouette Cameo Tote Bag can be purchased pre-paid only. No charges will be accepted. Please allow 4 to 6 weeks for delivery.

Arizona and N.Y. State Residents Please Add Sales Tax

Offer not available in Canada.

AMERICAN TRIBUTE

Where a man's dreams count for more than his parentage...

Look for these upcoming titles under the Special Edition American Tribute banner.

LOVE'S HAUNTING REFRAIN
Ada Steward #289—February 1986
For thirty years a deep dark secret kept them apart—King Stockton made his millions while his wife, Amelia, held everything together. Now could they tell their secret, could they admit their love?

THIS LONG WINTER PAST
Jeanne Stephens #295—March 1986
Detective Cody Wakefield checked out Assistant District Attorney Liann McDowell, but only in his leisure time. For it was the danger of Cody's job that caused Liann to shy away.

Silhouette Special Edition

AMERICAN TRIBUTE

AMERICAN TRIBUTE

RIGHT BEHIND THE RAIN
Elaine Camp #301—April 1986
The difficulty of coping with her brother's
death brought reporter Raleigh Torrence
to the office of Evan Younger, a police
psychologist. He helped her to deal with
her feelings and emotions, including love.

CHEROKEE FIRE
Gena Dalton #307—May 1986
It was Sabrina Dante's silver spoon that
Cherokee cowboy Jarod Redfeather couldn't
trust. The two lovers came from opposite
worlds, but Jarod's Indian heritage taught
them to overcome their differences.

NOBODY'S FOOL
Renee Roszel #313—June 1986
Everyone bet that Martin Dante and Cara
Torrence would get together. But Martin
wasn't putting any money down, and Cara
was out to prove that she was nobody's fool.

MISTY MORNINGS, MAGIC NIGHTS
Ada Steward #319—July 1986
The last thing Carole Stockton wanted was to
fall in love with another politician, especially
Donnelly Wakefield. But under a blanket of
secrecy, far from the campaign spotlights,
their love became a powerful force.

Silhouette Special Edition

COMING NEXT MONTH

RIGHT BEHIND THE RAIN—Elaine Camp
The difficulty of coping with her brother's death brought reporter Raleigh Torrence to Evan Younger, a police psychologist. He helped her deal with her emotions, including love.

SPECIAL DELIVERY—Monica Barrie
Five years ago, the man Leigh knew only as Jared helped her through childbirth and disappeared as mysteriously as he'd arrived. Now he was back . . . but this time she wanted some answers.

PRISONER OF LOVE—Maranda Catlin
When Alexandra hired Joe to work on her ranch she got more than she bargained for. His qualifications didn't list "ex-con," and the shackles of the past threatened to destroy their new love.

GEORGIA NIGHTS—Kathleen Eagle
When the band Georgia Nights had a gig in Massachusetts, Connor met Sarah Benedict. How could he win the heart of a dark-haired, dark-eyed enchantress who wanted nothing from him?

FOCUS ON LOVE—Maggi Charles
Judith found that when she photographed Alex the camera revealed a truth that only pictures could capture. Could Alex forget the ghosts of the past and zoom in on a new love?

ONE SUMMER—Nora Roberts
Shade and Bryan were working together, traveling across the country, recording two views of one American summer. They were complete opposites, but passion was destined to draw them together.

AVAILABLE THIS MONTH:

THIS LONG WINTER PAST
Jeanne Stephens

ZACHARY'S LAW
Lisa Jackson

JESSE'S GIRL
Billie Green

BITTERSWEET SACRIFICE
Bay Matthews

HEATSTROKE
Jillian Blake

DIAMOND IN THE SKY
Natalie Bishop